JET VIII

Survival

Russell Blake

Published by

Reprobatio Limited

CHAPTER 1

San Cristóbal, Chocó, Colombia

Six black Chevy Suburban SUVs bounced along the muddy road to San Cristóbal, nineteen miles from the northern border in the infamous Darién Gap, a stretch of inhospitable rain forest that separated Panama from Colombia. The lead vehicle swayed as it hit a particularly ugly rut, spraying a shower of brown water into the air, and then straightened as it accelerated down a clear section.

Cotton puffs of clouds drifted from the east, following the course of the Rio Atrato as it wound its way to the Caribbean, the sky robin's egg blue, the surrounding jungle a surreal green. The big vehicles lumbered along the track, almost impassible under the best of circumstances and made worse by the morning cloudburst that had blown through at sunrise.

Steam rose from the moist edges of the trail as the equatorial sun rose above the rainforest, its blistering rays intense even at the early hour. Soon the temperature would climb into the triple digits; but now, on a Tuesday morning, it was bearable, although all of the Suburban's opaque windows, tinted inky black, were rolled up, the occupants unrecognizable behind the covering.

The convoy came around a bend and neared a scattering of shacks, no more than twenty squalid dwellings built along the banks of the winding river, a strip of forgotten misery that was the hamlet bearing the name of a forgotten saint. Smoke rose from the dented tin chimneys of four of the buildings. Fading green and blue paint peeled from their weathered plank walls, a luxury from a more prosperous past now all but forgotten.

1

A congregation of children, their clothes barely more than rags, stood beneath a tree with their fishing lines in the water. At the unfamiliar sound of motors they looked up, eyes luminescent in their dark faces, expressions already the wary and somber cast of adults. The oldest, perhaps eight, sprinted for one of the shacks as the younger ones stood transfixed at the approaching procession.

The SUV doors flew open and two dozen men leapt from the vehicles, brandishing AK-47 assault rifles, a favorite in Central and South America. Durable and cheap, hundreds of thousands of the ugly weapons were left over from the wars that had ravaged El Salvador and Nicaragua decades earlier.

The men fanned out, weapons at the ready, and marched deliberately toward the buildings. Only one of the passengers didn't carry a rifle – a tall man with slicked-back black hair, tiny beads of perspiration on his high forehead and skin the color of freshly dried tobacco. His white silk Armani shirt was out of place in the rustic setting, as were his obviously expensive linen trousers and the platinum Rolex Masterpiece on his wrist, but if he noticed, he gave no indication.

It was the engraved Colt M1911 .45-caliber pistol in his right hand that the lone villager who stepped out of one of the buildings was staring at as the gunmen approached. When the tall man with the handgun was ten yards from the villager, he stopped and looked at his watch, then spit in the muddy red dirt at his feet as the riflemen on either side of him swept the buildings with their barrels, eyes alert.

"Did you really think you could screw me, Alonzo?" the tall man asked in a menacing purr. "You think I'd see product disappear like that and not figure it out?"

Alonzo's eyes were wide, but he squared his shoulders and stepped forward. "You've got it wrong. We were robbed by another group. I told you that."

"Who would dare rob you? Knowing that you work for me?"

"I don't know. I think it's a rogue group that's up in the Darién. They hit us hard. Before we could do anything, they'd disarmed us and made off with the powder."

2

"And nobody was killed? You expect me to believe that?"

A muscle in Alonzo's jaw pulsed as he ground his teeth, and his eyelid twitched. "It's the truth. I swear it."

The man with the pistol chuckled. "I let you get away with this, and I'll be able to hear the laughter all the way from Bogotá."

Alonzo held his hands up in a defensive stance. "Don't do this. I'll make it up. Somehow."

The gunman turned to the nearest man and grunted. "Kill them all."

Alonzo's gaze moved to the children by the tree, who were frozen in place as they watched the altercation. He screamed at the top of his lungs, his voice a tortured rasp. "Run!"

The .45 barked three times and Alonzo's chest exploded. Red blossoms stained his shirt as he flew backward. The riflemen opened up on full auto, firing bursts into the houses with methodical precision. A young man ducked his head out from one of the shacks, pistol in hand, and fired a panicked volley at the approaching shooters. One of his rounds punched into a squat man with a braided ponytail, catching him high in the chest. The wounded man jerked before straightening and continuing to fire; his second burst took the top of the villager's head off.

Three young women ran from a building close to the river and were nearing the bend that would shield them from the killers when more rifle fire rang out and cut them down. Their screams echoed off the rushing water as their bodies tumbled like puppets with their strings cut. The gunman who had shot them ejected his spent magazine and slapped another in place, and then continued his systematic shooting, kicking down doors, sparing no one.

The children were waist deep in the river when the pistol rang out. One of the boys hurtled face forward, the slug having slammed into his back and blown half his chest out. His companions watched him float in the current, his life seeping around him in a red stain, and then another child fell to the handgun's wrath. The remaining children screamed in terror and splashed further into the river as a gunman brought his assault rifle to bear on them and churned the water into a bloody froth.

A shotgun boomed from one of the most distant shacks, once, then again, and two of the attackers dropped to the ground, the closest still firing his rifle as his finger spasmodically squeezed the trigger, spraying bullets indiscriminately. Another gunman cried out as a round hit him in the thigh, shattering his femur, and collapsed as if in slow motion, his leg buckling beneath him even as he fired into the air. Three others ran in a crouch toward the building, firing as they neared. Their slugs sent showers of splinters into the sky as they unloaded their weapons at the hovel.

An old man with a cutoff pump shotgun fell out of the doorway as he fired his final shot, which went wide, sizzling harmlessly into the surrounding jungle. His eyes stared sightlessly as the men approached, already gone to whatever afterlife awaited him.

A terrified scream wailed from the largest building and one of the assailants appeared, dragging an unarmed woman from it. Another man followed carrying a baby by one of its legs. Its hysterical cries pierced the sudden quiet after the shooting, the only other sounds the moans of the wounded and the mother's shrieking.

The man with the pistol ejected his magazine and seated another as he strolled unhurriedly to where the woman was on her knees, a gun held to her head, helpless tears of fear and rage streaming down her face. She could barely breathe, her grief choking her, and she gasped and cried as the man paused in front of her. He brushed flecks of dirt from his trousers and shook his head with disapproval, then turned his eyes to her. When he spoke, his voice was arctic.

"I warned your idiot husband. Do you see what he forced me to do?"

"No, please, I beg you. Don't. Anything. I'll do anything," she cried.

"Yes, oh, yes, you will." He eyed her. "What are you called?"

"Lola," she snuffled, her throat tight.

The man smiled: an ugly grin, without a trace of warmth to soften the expression on his reptilian face. "Well, Lola, Alonso has caused me great trouble, for which your town has paid the price. He understood the stakes, and he went forward with his plan anyway. I wonder whether all the dead think it was worth it. My bet is not."

"I...I don't know what you're talking about."

The man shook his head regretfully. "Perhaps. Although it's with great difficulty that I bring myself to believe that your husband didn't confide his innermost thoughts to you. My experience is that men like to brag, especially to beautiful young women. And you are a beauty, aren't you?" He paused, studying her. "How old are you, Lola?"

"Nineteen."

He glanced over at his gunmen, who were gathering in a semicircle now that the village was still. "Such a tender age, is it not? The world is filled with possibility, with only the good, your whole life ahead of you. Ah, to be nineteen again. What I wouldn't give." His gaze returned to Lola, who was shivering with fear even in the humid swelter. "It's a shame that your husband's actions forced my hand. I do not enjoy this. It pains me to have to eliminate everyone to prove a point, but I am in a business where any signs of mercy are interpreted as weakness – and the strong eat the weak. You understand that, Lola, do you not?"

"Please. No more. Everyone's dead," she pleaded.

"Not everyone. You aren't. And this," he said, gesturing at the crying baby. "This little tyke is still alive. What's his name? This son of the man who screwed me like I was his prison bitch? What name did you choose for the fruit of his loins?"

"Oh, God, no, he's only five months old. He's innocent."

The man nodded. "Yes. The innocence of youth. Like young Moses was innocent." He sighed sadly. "Have you read your Bible, Lola?"

"Please," she sobbed, panicking at the look on his face.

"The Bible is an amazing book. Especially the Old Testament. One of the things it stresses is the importance of punishment. 'An eye for an eye.' Tell me, Lola, do you believe in God? Do you believe that all these newly minted spirits are ascending to heaven, going to a

5

better place, off to their just reward?" He gazed into the distance. "Or perhaps traveling to a warmer climate to pay for their sins?"

"I'll…do…anything…" she gasped.

"We've already established that, Lola, and my men are looking forward to testing your skills. But that didn't answer the question, did it? I'm a forgiving man, Lola, strange as that seems, but the one thing that infuriates me is when someone ignores a direct question, especially if I pose it politely. Are you trying to anger me, Lola? Are you testing me?"

She shook her head, unable to speak.

The man wiped a fatigued hand across his forehead and regarded the sweat on it with disgust. After another glance at Lola, he looked to the man holding the baby. "Throw it into the river."

Lola's scream reverberated off the surrounding rainforest as the man with the baby walked unceremoniously to the bank and slung the infant as far as he could. The infant spun in the air and made a lazy arc, its cry fading just before it hit the water with a splash.

The river swallowed the child without a trace. Lola collapsed to the ground, sobbing and keening, the sound of pure misery and hate. The man watched her for a few moments and scowled at his men. "Enjoy yourselves. You have twenty minutes. Make it fast." He returned his gaze to Lola. "I will leave you, out of everyone, alive, to tell the story of what happens to those who betray me. I have no doubt you'll remember this day for the rest of your life."

He turned from the woman as his men closed in, a fatigued frown on his face, and headed back to the lead Suburban, its engine still running. A blast of cold air blew from the interior when he slipped into the passenger seat, and he sighed in relief. He opened the glove compartment, withdrew a pack of Marlboro reds and tapped one out, and then lit it with a solid-gold lighter fished from the pocket of his slacks. He removed his pistol from its belt holster and tossed the two spent extra magazines onto the floor, exhaling a stream of smoke at the windshield.

Even with the windows rolled up he could hear Lola's screams as the men dragged her into the shade. He reached over and punched the stereo on, and the voice of Mana blared from the speakers, drowning out the unpleasant screeching. After another disinterested glance at the shamble of destroyed shacks and the bodies of the dead already beginning to bloat in the sun, he leaned his head back and closed his eyes, humming along with the familiar song as he waited for his men to return.

A lone gull wheeled in a slow orbit over the river before flapping off, nothing of interest to draw it closer. The inexorably rushing brown water and the swaying palms and mangroves bore mute witness to the atrocity that would receive no coverage, no comment, the forgotten berg to be reclaimed by the silent jungle once the scavengers were done with the corpses.

CHAPTER 2

Valparaíso, Chile, one day ago

A cool fog hung over the waterfront like a frigid blanket in the predawn gloom. Warning bells from buoys near the harbor mouth clanged in the mist, and the distorted sound seemed to come from all directions. Huge cargo ships tugged at their groaning dock lines as the tide receded, the swell shifting their steel hulls against the concrete wharf in an abrasive symphony of scraping and grinding.

Three dark forms, their furry bodies the size of small cats, scuttled down the wooden planks of the waterfront pier. Norwegian wharf rats ran the harbor at night, disappearing once the first faint glimmer of sunlight began burning away the covering fog. As its followers waited, the lead rodent stopped and sniffed the air, the aroma heavy with marine decay and petroleum, and then veered right toward a dumpster where a bounty of garbage awaited.

A burgundy Chevrolet rental sedan coasted to a stop fifty yards from a café. It was already open for early rising seamen in the port, its faded sign depicting a crusty captain with a peg leg and a harpoon, a pelican perched on an ale cask next to him for company. The driver killed the engine and the headlights flickered off. Igor and Fernanda got out, their practiced eyes surreptitiously scanning their surroundings. The glistening asphalt was slick from condensation, reflecting the few streetlights that ringed the harbor, but they were the only car on the street. Igor cocked his head to the left and listened as the buoys lowed their cautionary lament. Somewhere in the fog, a crane motor clamored and whined, the job of offloading and loading cargo never done.

8

Igor leaned toward Fernanda, whose Brazilian heritage was apparent from her exotic beauty and high cheekbones, and murmured, "This better be worth losing sleep over."

"He sounded like it would be," she responded.

Igor and Fernanda had spent more than a fruitless week running down leads on their quarry, the mystery woman they'd been paid to find and eliminate, but were no further along than when they'd arrived in Chile. After false alarms and chasing tips that dead-ended in blind alleys, they'd finally gotten a promising break – a member of the Chilean underworld had responded to the generous offer they'd circulated in Valparaíso and Santiago, and this morning they were to meet the man in a café. They had no reason to be particularly suspicious, but even so were cautious on their approach to the restaurant. Fernanda's gaze scoured the upper stories of the buildings facing the water for any telltales of surveillance – a partially open window, perhaps, or lights on when everyone was still asleep. Igor focused on the street level, and his eyes scanned the wharf and sidewalk as they slowly walked toward the entry.

A tall figure appeared out of the soup like a phantom, white tendrils of fog swirling around his navy blue pea coat, a knit seaman's cap pulled down over his head, three days of scruff darkening his swarthy face. They waited by the entrance as the seaman continued past them unsteadily, the sour tang of stale beer following him like smoke. Igor raised an eyebrow as Fernanda's stare followed the man and eyed the door.

"Shall we?" he asked in perfect Spanish.

"Nobody's getting any younger."

The interior of the dining room was century-old beams overhead and dark driftwood walls. Black-and-white photographs of tall ships hung in cheap frames between paintings of whaling vessels and scowling unnamed seafarers, mutton-chop sideburns and gin blossoms the common feature aside from haunting eyes. Fernanda surveyed the room in a quick glance and settled on an olive-skinned man wearing a black leather zip-up jacket and a chocolate dress shirt.

She smiled as she approached him and he returned the smile, but it never reached his eyes.

"Carlos?" she said in a low voice as she neared the booth.

"You must be Christina," he said, using the alias she'd given him. "A pleasure. Please. Sit. And this is…?" he asked, giving Igor a once-over.

"My friend," Fernanda said, ending that line of inquiry.

"I see."

Fernanda slid across from Carlos. Igor took the seat next to her, the bulge of the Glock he'd bought from a street dealer obvious beneath his windbreaker. Carlos glanced at it in passing but seemed unconcerned that Igor was armed as he waved the tired-looking waitress over.

"What would you like? Coffee's not bad," he suggested.

Fernanda regarded the waitress, noting the discoloration beneath her eyes and the deep frown lines that framed her thin mouth, and held up two fingers. "Two cups."

"Breakfast?" Carlos asked.

She shook her head. "No, thanks. Just the drinks and conversation, for now."

Nobody said anything until the woman returned with a pair of chipped oversized mugs of steaming brew and set them on the hardwood tabletop. A sheet of glass protected the hundreds of whittled names that covered every inch of the wood surface. Both Igor and Fernanda sipped theirs black while they waited for Carlos to open the discussion. He glanced around the café and leaned toward them, his voice barely more than a whisper.

"I have what you requested. Or at least as much as it's possible to get."

"What does that mean?" Fernanda asked, an edge to her words.

"It means that I know that my organization arranged for some people to be smuggled aboard a cargo ship bound for the United States last week. I've got the ship schedule, as well as blueprints of the boat. And a piece of critical information that will be of great interest to you."

Igor put his coffee down. "Really?"

Carlos offered him a crooked grin. "Really."

"Care to elaborate?" Fernanda asked.

"Once we have a deal."

Igor caught Fernanda's eye. "How do we know your information is what we're after?"

"Gee. Let's see. You're looking for a woman, a man, and a kid. I have confirmation that the passengers include a man and a kid."

"What about the woman?"

"I haven't been able to get confirmation on that, but when you hear the final bit of info, you'll understand why I believe this is what you want."

Igor shook his head. "I don't like it."

"Fine. Then you have my number. Think it over. But every hour, the boat moves further north and your options narrow."

Fernanda's eyes narrowed. "Why? It's a long way to the U.S."

Carlos gazed slyly at Fernanda. "That's where the information comes in. They're to be smuggled off during the voyage."

"What? Where?" Igor demanded.

"That's all I can tell you. But wait too long and they'll be out of your reach." He sat back and regarded them calmly. "That's it…until we have a deal."

"Will you excuse us for a moment?" Fernanda asked.

"Of course," Carlos replied. Igor slid out of the booth and Fernanda joined him on a hunt for the bathroom.

On the way she whispered to him, "We have no choice."

"I don't trust him. And his information's incomplete. This could be a red herring."

"True. But if we don't take this, we're dead in the water. And the clock's ticking."

"It's a lot of money."

"Yes, but we'll bill the client."

"They're unlikely to pay if we don't perform."

"Obviously. It's a calculated risk. But at this point, we're out of options."

They each used the restroom, and then Igor followed Fernanda back to the table. When they were seated, she gave Carlos a warm smile.

"Fine. You got us."

"Do you have the money with you?"

"Of course. In my friend's jacket. But we're getting a little ahead of ourselves. Time for you to show us what you have."

"I'll give you everything but the details about the method they'll use to get off the ship. That you'll get once I have the cash in hand."

"Fair enough. Now give."

Carlos removed a flash drive and slid it across the table. "The ship's the *Seylene*, flagged in Liberia. Departed San Antonio bound for Long Beach. Crew of sixteen. The schedule on the drive will tell you where she'll be at any given hour, and there's a GPS locator chip aboard you can track. I also included blueprints of the ship and a crew roster."

"Any guns aboard?"

Carlos shook his head. "No. I mean, not legally. Probably some flare guns."

"Where is the boat right now?" Fernanda asked in a low voice.

Carlos glanced at his watch. "Off the coast of Peru, heading into Ecuadorian waters."

"How many miles offshore will she run?" Igor asked.

"That's part of the plan. The captain's going to call in a mechanical problem as a pretext to veer east rather than continuing along the shipping lane. As they hug the coast, the passengers will disembark."

"What country?"

Carlos's eyes narrowed. "When I have the money."

Igor finished his coffee. "This stuff runs right through you, doesn't it? I'm going to use the bathroom again. Excuse me," he said, and made for the back of the café.

Fernanda pushed her cup around and then looked at Carlos. "You should probably go to the bathroom now. He's probably getting tired of waiting in that stinkhole."

"Ah. I see."

When the two men returned, Carlos looked more relaxed. He tossed a few bills on the table and gave Fernanda a small bow. "It was a pleasure doing business with you. You have my number if you have any questions. It's a burner cell phone, but I'll keep it nearby for the next few days."

"I hope we have no reason to be dissatisfied," Fernanda said, a warning in her tone.

"You won't."

Carlos left, and Fernanda and Igor finished their coffee before leaving themselves. The fog was still thick and the area deserted as they made their way back to the car. Once inside, Igor started the engine and turned to Fernanda. "They're planning to rendezvous with a fishing boat off Panama. The ship will make for Balboa for repairs and then experience a miraculous recovery and continue north to the U.S. By which time the fishing boat will have made it to shore, with no annoying customs or immigration to contend with."

"Where will the boat take them?"

"He doesn't know. It's a local contractor. His organization's arrangement was to get the passengers to Panama, and that's it."

"Damn. The obvious way to do this would be to ambush them when they're off the fishing boat. We can't very well intercept a huge cargo ship in international waters." A thought occurred to her. She tapped her phone to life and went to a web site. After a few minutes studying the coast, she smiled. "Looks like there's a storm moving west from the Caribbean. The forecast is for it to hit hard on the Pacific side after it passes over land. Late tomorrow afternoon and into the night."

"And that's useful how?"

"If we know the course she's on and can track the locator chip, we can arrange something before she gets near Panama."

"Arrange something?"

Fernanda explained what she was thinking. When she finished, Igor frowned. "It could work. But there are a lot of moving parts.

Not the least of which is getting there and setting it all up." He paused. "It'll be expensive."

"Yes, I expect it will be. What do you think we should budget?"

Igor thought about it. "Hundred thousand U.S."

"I'll call the client and get his okay. I'll give him a summary and leave it to him whether he wants us to intercept it or not. If he does, he can execute a wire today while we're in the air. If not, we tried. But my gut says he'll go along with it, because there's no way we'll be able to find them once they're on a small fishing boat headed for some obscure harbor. To dodge immigration, they're going to have to avoid Panama City."

"We could look at the ports along that coast."

"Yes, but remember, the area's a major fishing hub, so every few miles there are going to be moorings and bays where they could disembark. Even our most educated guess is likely to be wrong." Fernanda looked at her phone screen. "I'll call our contact in Panama and see if our cost estimate is about right." She paused, thinking. "I don't see a better way to do it. Ideally we want to take them while they're still in Colombian waters. That stretch is a major narcotics smuggling corridor, so we'll have much better luck taking them in Colombian waters than off Panama, where there are likely to be coast guard and naval patrols to stop traffic north."

Igor eyed her appreciatively and put the car in gear. "Have I told you how arousing you are when you're talking operational details?"

She grinned. "Not nearly enough. I was beginning to think you didn't care anymore."

CHAPTER 3

Madrid, Spain

The plane pulled into the Jetway at the Aeropuerto Adolfo Suárez Madrid-Barajas, and Jet watched as the ground crew scrambled to get everything into place so the passengers could disembark. The five-hour flight from Moscow in business class had been bearable, but not something she planned to ever repeat if she could help it. She stretched and continued to ignore the executive in the seat next to her, who'd thankfully spent the entire flight fiddling with spreadsheets and reports.

On disembarking, Jet followed the signs up a long corridor to the connecting international flights. She had a three-hour layover and then a flight to Mexico City, connecting through Panama City, and with any luck at all she'd be in Panama with hours to spare before Matt and Hannah arrived on the fishing boat.

She stopped at a bank of telephones and tried calling Matt's satellite phone, knowing that the odds of him having it on all the time were slim. She wasn't surprised when it went to voice mail, and she left a brief message.

"Hi. I made the first leg with no problem. Hope you're enjoying your cruise. I'm looking forward to seeing you both tomorrow. Matt, this is for Hannah." Jet paused, envisioning Matt holding the phone to her little girl's ear. "Sweetie, this is Mommy. I love you more than anything and I miss you something fierce. I'll see you tomorrow. Be good."

When she hung up she felt deflated, and her gut twisted into a tight knot. She willed herself to relax, reminding herself that there was no way to accelerate her journey, and so to accept that she'd be flying another fourteen or fifteen hours rather than bemoan it.

Jet moved to an area with wireless and powered on the tablet she'd bought. She searched the news and saw another short piece on the dead Russian attorney – a tragic loss to the community, another casualty of depression. The party line, she thought, still no hint of foul play, so her gambit had worked and she was in the clear. Not that she expected anything different, but you never knew, and it was usually something completely unforeseen that tripped you up.

She'd learned to expect the unexpected as part of her conditioning. She might not be able to control events, but she could certainly control her reactions to them. That was her edge: the ability to remain cool in the face of overwhelming odds, in the midst of entropy and chaos.

Next she went to a satellite map of the Central American coast and checked the weather. The tickle of anxiety she experienced when she called Matt returned. A big storm was moving directly into the path the ship would be taking. Although there were no hurricanes that close to the equator, there were still big blows that could make the seas ugly. A vision of Hannah pitching to and fro as the ship plowed through big waves made her cringe, and she focused on calmer thoughts. Those boats went through storms all the time. A nine-hundred-foot ship would barely slow for twenty-foot swells. There was nothing to worry about.

And yet the image of the ship in jeopardy stayed with her even as she moved on from the storm site to more pleasant fare, researching places to live in Panama and Costa Rica and taking in the breathtaking beaches and swaying palms of the Caribbean coast and the steel and glass skyscrapers in Panama City.

After buying a snack at one of the numerous small restaurants in the departure area, she moved back to the phones and tried Matt again, with the same result – voice mail. This time she didn't leave a message, knowing that Matt would see she'd called twice. There was no need to explain why.

He knew her well enough.

The hours stretched like years, and when her flight to Mexico City was finally called, she felt like she'd aged a decade. The plane was only half full, and before the plane was at cruising altitude she'd closed her eyes and reclined her seat into a bed, the cumulative effects of her adventure in Moscow slamming home with the force of an avalanche.

Chapter 4

Pacific Ocean, 45 miles west of Colombia

Black waves hissed out of the darkness as the *Seylene* plowed northeast through the confused seas topped with white froth. Violent gusts of wind blew trails of spray from the swells. The storm had gathered strength in the warm water off the coast, and the big vessel had been forced to slow to eighteen knots as it ran in beam seas.

A 965-foot Panamax container ship and a seasoned veteran of the run from South America to the U.S., she was accustomed to ugly weather, and this storm, while uncomfortable, was nothing compared to the hurricanes she had weathered. This was a Force 8 gale, with twenty-five-foot waves, and she'd been through as high as Force 12 without incident. It took much more than a patch of rough equatorial weather to alarm the crew of a ship the size of a hundred-story building laid on its side

The captain and the helmsman stood on the bridge, watching as the massive bow pushed through the water. Spotlights illuminated the oncoming seas so they could make out any rogue waves on approach. Rogue waves were a threat for any oceangoing vessel, particularly along the coasts of Africa and in the North Atlantic, where moving walls of water fifteen stories tall, their faces as sheer as cliffs, could appear out of nowhere and imperil even the largest ships. While it was unlikely that they had to worry about any this close to the Colombian coast, the captain was conservative and preferred to err on the side of caution.

Sheets of rain blew across the deck outside the bridge windows. The captain, his skin the texture of saddle leather and his eyes ringed by deep wrinkles, turned to the helmsman, a steaming cup of coffee in his hand. At four a.m. he was up earlier than usual, but during a storm it was the captain's responsibility to see the ship through without incident, and he took his job seriously. A thirty-year career in the merchant marines had accustomed him to odd hours, and he took the demand in stride.

"Well, Jorge, looks like the worst of it's past us, eh?" he said, making conversation.

"Yes. I radioed in the alert about our course change, so that's taken care of."

The storm provided a convenient pretext for a course change, and he'd instructed Jorge to signal a mechanical problem. They were now well off the shipping lane, steaming toward the Panama Canal port of Balboa, where they would delay for a few hours before announcing that the problem had been fixed and that they intended to continue north to Long Beach.

The captain tapped a cigarette out of a wrinkled packet, one of only ten he allowed himself in any twenty-four-hour period, and lit it with a cheap butane lighter. He drew the smoke deep into his lungs and exhaled noisily before taking a long pull on his coffee, eyes locked on the bow.

The radio crackled and a tense voice filled the bridge.

"Mayday. Mayday. Fishing boat *Tres Gatos*. Mayday."

Jorge and the captain exchanged glances. The captain stood and moved to the radio. He raised the microphone to his lips and depressed the transmit button.

"Fishing boat *Tres Gatos*. This is container ship *Seylene*. What is your emergency, and what are your coordinates?"

"*Seylene*, we lost power and we are taking on water. Repeat, we have no power and we are taking on water. Latitude 4°51'6.88"N by 79° 2'29.40"W."

Jorge studied the chart plotter and looked up at the captain. "Only two miles away."

The captain gave an exhausted sigh. He couldn't ignore a mayday on the open sea when he was the nearest ship – especially in a storm, even if it was almost past. A sinking vessel over a hundred miles from

RUSSELL BLAKE

the coast was a death sentence if the crew didn't have safety equipment, which many of the boats in these waters didn't. He exchanged a dark glance with Jorge and pressed the transmit button again.

"*Tres Gatos*. This is *Seylene*. Do you have lights or flares? We're two miles southwest of your position and can be there in ten to fifteen minutes. Will your vessel hold that long?"

A long pause, and then the radio crackled again. "Affirmative, *Seylene*. I believe so. But in these seas…"

"We are changing course to intercept. Do you have lights or flares? Over," the captain repeated.

"Yes. Our running lights are operating. I'll see if we have a flare gun. We should. Over."

"Stay on the radio. When we're close, I'll ask you to fire a flare if we can't see your lights. Over."

"Roger, *Seylene*. Thank you. And please. Hurry. Over."

"We're on our way. Over."

Jorge moved back to the helm, punched in the coordinates, and the ship shifted to starboard a few degrees, putting the seas squarely on its beam.

The captain shook his head. "Notify the crew. I want all hands on deck in five minutes." He moved to the radar and changed the range, then gestured at it. "There they are. Small. So not commercial. Idiots to be out in this. What the hell were they thinking?"

"They probably weren't. I'll call it in." Jorge got on the intercom and blared an emergency alert to the sleeping crewmen. The ship listed as the seas rolled past it, the wind still gusting to fifty miles per hour. Both men watched as the storm pounded the ship with everything it had, water coursing across the decks, the wipers working to clear the helm windows so they could see.

Ten minutes later the engines had slowed and the crew was assembled on the bridge in rough weather gear – yellow slickers and boots. The crewmen looked sleepy, unshaved and groggy, faces faintly lined from pillows and hair askew. Most were in their twenties or early thirties, except for the mechanical engineer, who was a portly forty-something.

The captain had explained the situation and issued instructions, and the men were ready to comply. The ship was equipped with long lines and an emergency gangplank that could be deployed for these types of rescue scenarios, and the crew stood at the windows, eyeing the sea while they awaited his orders.

The captain scanned the darkness with his binoculars and called out to Jorge. "There they are. See the lights? To starboard."

Jorge grunted. "I see them." He made a small adjustment of the wheel, inching the bow closer, and eased further back on the throttle. A ship of the *Seylene*'s displacement could take a mile or more to slow, and executing this sort of rescue was akin to an elephant dancing with a mouse. Everyone was keenly aware that the larger ship could crush the smaller like an empty soda can, so care was the order of the day rather than haste. The big vessel was now only making five knots, nearly stationary, and was rocking more with each sidelong roller that struck its hull.

The captain lit another cigarette, rationalizing that this was an emergency so arbitrary rules could be discarded, and radioed the fishing boat again. "*Tres Gatos*. We are a quarter mile from you. You should be able to see us now. Over."

"Roger that. What do you want us to do? Over."

"We'll maneuver alongside your craft and throw you lines. Tie them off securely on your bow and stern, and we'll lower a gangplank. Or if that doesn't work, we'll drop webbing you can climb. Is anyone injured? Over."

"Negative. But the boat's a goner. It's sinking. Over."

"How many are there of you? Over."

"Four of us. Over."

"Okay. Here we come. Watch for the lines. Over."

The process took five minutes, both vessels pitching in the seas, the huge cargo vessel blocking the worst of the wind. Once the lines were tied off, the crew lowered the gangplank and the crew of the *Tres Gatos* scrabbled up seven stories to the main deck, the driving rain and wind lashing them as they struggled against gravity on the rolling seas. The smaller vessel, an old forty-something-foot sports fisher, banged against the side of the *Seylene*'s hull, and two crewmen untied the lines and set it adrift, there being no point in trying to tow a sinking boat. They watched as it drifted away, blown by the wind, destined for the watery deep as the storm had its way with the unlucky craft.

Five stories below the bridge a solitary figure watched the rescue from a watertight porthole, backlit by the dim glow of night lighting. When the last of the drenched fishermen had made it onto the *Seylene*, the figure withdrew to the depths of the superstructure as the rescued seamen followed the crew to the dining room and galley, their clothes soaked, blankets around their shoulders shielding them from the worst of the gale's fury.

CHAPTER 5

Frontino, Colombia

A pall of gray smoke hung over the hills, the ugly byproduct of local farmers burning their fields in preparation for planting new crops. A split-axle bobtail truck groaned up a winding mountain road, sandwiched between two SUVs. Black fumes belched from its exhaust as its motor strained on the steep slope towards its eventual destination: the hacienda perched high on one of the peaks, overlooking the picturesque valley below – a secluded valley with incurious residents who worked the land owned by the occupant of the ranch home that crowned the mountain.

Situated on a coffee plantation that spanned eighty hectares, the compound was guarded by a group of tough-looking men carrying assault rifles. The only road onto the grounds was barred by a heavy iron gate affixed to a high concrete arch with ten-foot walls running the perimeter of the residential area. A guard in a tower inside the wall watched the approaching trucks through binoculars, an ex-military .50-caliber machine gun on a tripod for companionship beside him.

The security team heard the vehicles before they saw them, when the still of the tranquil valley was broken by the laboring of the engines negotiating the serpentine route on the final leg of the private road. The watchman raised a radio to his ear and barked into it. He cocked his head as he waited for a response and then called out to the guards manning the gate. A stocky man with the build of a brick strode to the barricade and raised it as the lead SUV neared, an M16 assault rifle slung across his back as he watched the vehicles close on his position.

The driver of the SUV gave him a wave that he returned, and then the vehicles were past him, headed for the main house, which was surrounded by smaller buildings – a casita for guests should the nine-bedroom sprawl prove inadequate, a six-car garage, a barn. The truck's gears ground as its tires crunched on the gravel of the circular drive. A fountain bubbled in the middle of the centerpiece atop an elevated mound with stone steps leading to two curved stone benches that rested on the impeccably groomed landscaping.

The truck rolled to a stop in front of the house. A dark-skinned man wearing white slacks and a white short-sleeved button up shirt came through the front door and moved down the stairs to where the vehicles waited. He pointed toward the barn at the edge of the complex and growled instructions.

The convoy inched along the drive toward the barn, where three men stood deep in conversation next to a chestnut mare. The tallest, an older man with ramrod posture and hair the color of brushed steel, looked over at the new arrivals before returning to his discussion. His companions, their jeans and flannel shirts a marked contrast to the older man's cream slacks and burgundy silk shirt, bobbed their heads in agreement, and one led the horse to an adjacent pasture enclosed with rustic wooden fencing while the other disappeared into the barn.

The older man watched the mare's gait as she pranced alongside her jogging escort, and his tanned face cracked with the beginning of a smile. He fished a pair of sunglasses from his breast pocket and slid them on, and then turned from the pasture to regard the newcomers.

Four men descended from the two SUVs, shoulder holsters over their obviously expensive shirts. The truck driver killed the engine as they approached the older man and the area grew still, the only sounds the songs of birds in the tall trees that surrounded the clearing and the hum of a distant tractor somewhere in the valley.

"*Don* Mosises. We have taken care of the problem and brought the others, as you requested," one of the four said.

"Good. Any complications?" Mosises asked, his rough voice the result of a lifelong addiction to Cuban cigars.

"No. Everything went as planned, other than losing a few soldiers," the man reported with a shrug. "Nobody you knew."

"So the cockroaches put up a fight, eh? Well, they're gone now. Time to finish this so I can return to more pleasant pursuits." Mosises motioned to the truck.

The driver hopped down from the cab and moved to the rear cargo door as Mosises and the four gunmen approached. With a grunt, the driver pulled up the rolling door, revealing a dark interior with five figures lying on the wooden truck bed, their hands tied behind their backs.

Mosises glanced at his men. "Get them out."

The five captives were dragged from the truck and dumped unceremoniously on the gravel. Mosises paced nearby as he studied them with a scowl.

"So. You set up a deal to cut me out, eh? How did that work out for you? Your friends in San Cristóbal are now a stain in the mud, and any profit you made cost them their lives." Mosises shook his head. "And soon, your lives as well."

One of them spit at Mosises with a sneer, but didn't speak. Mosises turned to his men.

"I see the farmers are burning their fields. It always makes me sad for some reason, but it's regeneration. The cycle of life." He regarded the captives a final time. "Take them away and light them up. I'm sick of looking at their ugly faces. When you're done, bury them in a ditch down by the dump. I'll be along shortly."

The men dragged the captives behind the barn, where tires would be slid over the victims, doused with gasoline, and then lit. It would take several minutes for the tougher of them to die in excruciating pain.

The technique was infamous in Colombia and was referred to by the cartels as 'lighting the torch.' Of all the horrors perpetrated in the constant turf wars and rivalries, it was considered the worst way to go, and for good reason. One of Mosises men would film the spectacle with his phone: the footage would make it onto social media sites that featured such atrocities, where his enemies could see what they had to look forward to if he got his hands on them.

Mosises was a survivor who had gone through the ups and the downs of the Colombian cocaine business, from the giddy years when the Medellín and Cali cartels ruled the country to the current era, when the Colombians were largely only on the production end, relying on the Mexican cartels to transport the drugs north. He had carved out a niche where he commanded respect, with his own trafficking network that could get the powdered gold into Central America. There he supplied an eager affluent class in Panama and Costa Rica who consumed his product with an appetite he hadn't seen since the Escobar heyday of the eighties.

He strode over to the wooden fence and leaned one arm on it, watching his mare run unbridled around the perimeter of the clearing, happy in her youth and momentary freedom. He smiled at her obvious enjoyment and was only pulled out of his reverie by a tortured scream from nearby as the first of the five brothers who had conspired to double-cross him discovered the purifying agony of the fire.

Mosises took a final look at his pride and joy, and then turned slowly and made his way to where inhuman shrieks rent the air as flesh sizzled off bone — a lesson to his adversaries and those who questioned his authority. He'd learned the hard way in countless fights that you never showed mercy — it would correctly be interpreted as weakness.

The only thing people respected was raw power, and Mosises understood that it was a good idea to demonstrate it from time to time. As he advanced in years, younger bucks — like the five Rolerno brothers who were now soaking in gasoline — sought to test him. It was inevitable, but they had underestimated his vitality in his winter years, and now were paying the ultimate price.

Another howl greeted him as a second victim ignited, and he withdrew a cigar from a case in his breast pocket and snipped the end off. He took his time lighting it, pausing as he did to eye the coil of oily black smoke rising from behind the barn.

The one thing he could never get used to was the smell. It stayed with you for days, he knew from experience. One of the negatives of being the dispenser of justice in a kingdom of his making.

CHAPTER 6

The *Seylene*'s powerful engines thrummed underfoot as the four rescued fishermen took seats in the large galley area while one of the crew made them coffee. The ship had resumed steaming toward Panama, still rocking slightly from the larger than normal beam seas.

The captain entered the galley and offered the fishermen a grim smile.

"Sorry about your boat. What happened?"

"Long-range trip. The storm caught us by surprise. We thought we could outrun it, but we had engine problems, and then one of our through-hulls gave in the big waves. We did the best we could, but the boat was too old, and with no power…" The fisherman didn't need to finish the thought.

"You're lucky we were in the neighborhood." The captain looked around. "Let's see if we can get you some dry clothes, at least." He looked at his crew. "Gentlemen? Do I have any donations?" Several of the seamen bobbed their heads and moved to the galley door. The captain looked back to the fishermen. "If you'll wait here, we'll get you outfitted shortly."

The fisherman watched the captain return to the bridge and gave the seaman across from him a wan smile.

"Thanks for helping us. That was pretty hairy," Igor said.

"No problem," the man replied.

"Where are you headed?" Igor asked, drying his hair with the corner of his blanket.

"California. But we detoured for Panama. Something about mechanical problems."

"Well, that's lucky. We're based out of Panama."

"Then it's not a complete loss. You got a free ride to Balboa out of the deal."

Igor offered another smile. He found smiling put people at ease, so he did so often, even when he was about to execute someone. It was a hard habit to break, but he saw no reason to. Sometimes it drove Fernanda crazy, but he figured that if you had to have annoying habits, smiling too much wasn't a terrible one.

"Thanks for that." Igor paused. "How many crew on the ship?"

"Sixteen."

"Wow. That's all for a ship this size? What is she? Eight hundred feet?"

"Almost a thousand."

"No wonder we can hardly feel the storm," Igor said. He accepted a cup of coffee and took a cautious sip. "Do you carry passengers or just cargo?"

"Depends. Sometimes we do. We've got a few on this trip."

"Really? I always wondered why people would want to travel by container ship. I read about it somewhere a long time ago. Never got it."

"It's a different experience. Some people want to have a special trip they can tell their friends about. Something uncommon. How many people go from South America to North America on a cargo vessel? Not many," the seaman explained.

"Where do they stay?"

"We have some nicer staterooms for paying passengers. Same level as the crew, but better digs," the seaman said.

Igor yawned and glanced at his companions, who were watching him, waiting for his signal. Igor was about to give it when the two crewmen who had gone for clothes returned and handed out sweatpants and T-shirts. Igor's men looked to him for guidance, and he stood and asked his new friend where he could change out of his wet clothes. The seaman pointed to a door.

"Head's in there."

"Be right back," Igor said, and walked on squishing running shoes to the bathroom and went inside. He wasted no time changing, instead retrieving the Glock 19 he'd brought aboard and chambering a round. He caught a blur of reflection in the mirror and stopped to look at himself, smiling automatically.

The same smile was on his face when he came out of the head holding the gun. His men took his cue and retrieved weapons from beneath their blankets, and the eight seamen found themselves staring down the ugly muzzles of pistols.

"What the hell is this?" demanded one of the seamen. Igor punched him in the throat and the man collapsed, fighting for breath.

"I'm only going to ask this once. Where's the rest of the crew?"

Nobody answered, the seamen preferring to stare at him in stony silence. Igor tilted his head at one of his men. "Leon? Get a knife. We'll start cutting off fingers and see how long this bunch wants to play hardball."

Leon gave the crewmen a malevolent grin and moved around the galley as he foraged in drawers. "Ah," he said, holding up the gleaming blade of a serrated bread knife. "This should do the trick." He slashed at the air with it a few times and then returned to where the men were sitting.

Igor motioned with his pistol at the youngest captive. "You. Time to lose your fingers. Are you right- or left-handed?"

The seaman, no more than early twenties, swallowed hard. "No."

Igor shook his head. "You aren't very smart, are you? It wasn't a yes or no question. Last time. Are you right- or left-handed?"

The young man looked at his mates and shivered involuntarily. When his eyes returned to Igor's, the hit man smiled.

"Please," the seaman begged, his lip quivering. "There are four down in the engine room, the captain and the helmsman on the bridge, and two more in the staterooms. They're sick. The flu."

"And the passengers?" Igor asked.

"Asleep, I'd expect."

"How many?"

"Two."

"Describe them."

"A guy. About forty. His hand's in a cast. And a little girl. Maybe two, two and a half? I don't know. I'm not good with kids."

"What about the woman?"

The seaman's eyes registered confusion. "Woman? There's no woman."

Igor's voice quieted to a whisper, his tone silky smooth. "You're telling me that the only passengers aboard this rust bucket are this man and his kid?"

"Yes. Two passengers. That's all."

"Which stateroom are they in?"

"Port side. First one before the crew quarters."

Igor's eyes narrowed. "You wouldn't lie to me, would you? Because if you're lying or haven't told me something important, when I come back I'll carve you like a Christmas turkey."

The seaman's eyes widened. "No. I swear I told you everything."

"Do the doors lock? On the staterooms."

"I…yes."

"Who's got the master key?"

The seaman looked to his companions, who wouldn't meet his gaze. "The captain has it."

Igor stared at the floor for a moment and shook his head. "Leon, get some line and tie them up. You," he barked at the seaman. "Line. Now."

The young man walked unsteadily to the galley and opened a cabinet, reached in, and extracted a bundle of yellow nylon rope. Leon moved to him, his weapon steady as he neared, and took the rope from him.

Three minutes later the crewmen were bound, rags stuffed in their mouths. Igor paced in front of them, as though thinking, and then stopped and checked the time on his Panerai dive watch.

"Rafael, keep an eye on them. Leon, Carlos, you come with me to pay the captain a visit."

"What about the crew in the engine room?" Leon asked.

"We'll deal with them once we have the man and his daughter."

"But if the woman isn't there…"

"We'll get to the bottom of that. We've got nothing but time. But first let's find them." Igor slid his gun from his belt and motioned to the stairs that led to the bridge. "But, Leon? Carlos? I do all the talking. Understood?"

Leon and Carlos nodded as Rafael took a seat, his pistol pointed at the bound men. Igor moved through the door and onto the stairs, his running shoes silent on the antiskid coating. They paused outside the bridge. Igor peered around the corner and then signaled to his companions before moving through the bridge door.

The captain's expression changed from surprise to shock when he saw the guns in the fishermen's hands. The helmsman sat frozen as the captain stood, an outraged look on his face.

"What the hell…"

Igor fixed him with a cold stare. "Shut up. I need the key for the staterooms. Now."

"We rescued you…"

"I already thanked you. Now give me the key, or I'll blow your man's head off."

The captain's eyes remained locked on Igor's. "What did you do to my crew?"

"They're fine. Safe. One of my men is watching them. Now, last chance. Do you give me the key, or do I shoot your mate to prove I'm serious?"

The helmsman gave the captain a frightened glance. The captain dropped his gaze and crossed to a locked cabinet at the far side of the bridge.

Igor took a step forward, his Glock steady in his hand. "Easy. You pull anything out of that locker besides a key and you're dead. You understand?"

The captain nodded and slowly slid his hand into his button-up jersey. He retrieved a chain with a key attached to it from around his neck and fiddled with the lock. After unlocking the cabinet, he retrieved a ring with six keys on it and handed them to Igor. "There's no master. These are the keys to the six staterooms. But there are only two passengers, and they don't have much besides what they're

32

wearing. A container ship is a bad bet for piracy. We're only carrying olives and wine, that sort of thing. No electronics or anything valuable on the manifest."

Igor ignored him and glanced at Carlos. "Stay here and keep the good captain company. If he makes a move, shoot him. Same goes for the helmsman. We'll be back in a few minutes." Igor looked through the windshields at the storm raging outside. "Looks pretty ugly," he commented, and then turned, the ring of keys in hand.

The captain called out after him. "It's just a man and a little girl. They don't have anything of value."

Igor couldn't help the automatic smile. "You're wrong about that, Captain."

He and Leon crept down the stairs to the stateroom level. Igor pointed at the door at the far end of the corridor. They took cautious steps until they were standing in front of the steel door, listening for any sounds of movement inside.

Nothing.

Igor tried the first key, and it didn't turn. Second one, same thing. The third was the charm. The lock turned and Igor tilted his head at Leon, who gripped his pistol with both hands and pointed it at the door. Igor took a measured breath and twisted the lever, shielding his body with the heavy door as he pushed it open.

And found himself in darkness. He swept the room with the Glock while he fumbled for the light switch. When his fingers found it, he flipped it on. The room was empty. Leon looked to Igor and whispered, his words a hiss, "Wrong stateroom?"

"The little bastard must have lied to me. He'll pay for that."

They moved to the next stateroom and repeated the procedure, only to be greeted by another empty bed. The third room was clearly crew quarters, as were the other three. The two sleeping crewmen awoke with a start to find themselves staring down a pistol barrel, and Igor had Leon take them to the galley with the rest of the crew. He stood in the doorway, watching Leon herd the seamen down the hall, his mind churning as he thought through what could have gone wrong.

Because something had. The man and the girl were nowhere to be seen. He'd memorized the ship blueprint, and aside from the captain's quarters one floor down from the bridge, there was nowhere else they could be.

Igor tilted his head back and envisioned the ship blueprint in his mind's eye. They had to be either in the captain's quarters or one of the common areas the crew shared. Other than the engine room and the associated mechanical rooms, there was nowhere else.

Of course, there was the question of why they weren't in their room in the dead of night. Could someone have sounded an alarm? How? And to what end?

Igor stalked back to the bridge, huffing for breath after the rapid climb, and wasted no time with niceties. He approached the captain and slammed the butt of his Glock against his head, knocking him out of his seat.

"Where are they?"

The captain felt the side of his head, and his hand came away with blood on it. He tried to get up, failed, tried again, and then managed to pull himself back into his chair.

"How would I know? In their stateroom. Where else would they be at this hour?"

Igor's nostril's flared and his eyes narrowed. "I'm only going to ask you one more time."

"You can ask as many or as few times as you like. The answer's the same. I have no idea. I don't have them on a leash."

Igor turned to the windows and watched as the storm raged, the waves still easily twenty feet with breaking white tops. A feeling of dread spread through his gut.

"Where else could they be?" he demanded.

"What do you mean, where else? There is nowhere else."

Igor turned to Carlos, who was training his pistol on the pair. "Keep watching them."

He stopped at the captain's quarters and did a quick search of the rooms, not expecting to find anything. His expectations weren't disappointed. When he reached the galley, he barked at Leon, "Come

34

with me. We're going to search every room on this thing. They have to be in one of them."

They worked each floor, starting below decks, and after forty minutes it was obvious their quarry was nowhere to be found. When they made it back to the bridge, the storm was fading, the waves flattening, the winds and rain having blown by, leaving only an overcast night sky.

"Could they be in one of the cargo holds?" Igor demanded of the captain, his patience now gone.

"I suppose anything's possible. But why?"

Igor's eyes drifted to the helm, where a red LED was blinking on the console. He stood and moved to the light, staring at it as though hypnotized.

"What's this? Why is it blinking?" he demanded, his voice low.

The captain peered at it, and the trace of a smile played across his face in spite of his obvious best effort to contain it. "It's a warning light."

"What's it warning about?"

"It's the lifeboat alarm."

The blood drained out of Igor's face. "Lifeboat..."

The bridge was silent for several moments. Igor glanced at Carlos. "How long has it been on?"

"I...I don't know. I was watching them, like you told me to."

Igor closed his eyes, barely containing his rage, and then opened them and glared at the captain. "Where's the lifeboat kept?"

Igor and Leon ran to the watertight door and swung it open, then made their way to the sling where the enclosed lifeboat had been stored. Igor wasn't surprised to see it empty, the deployment system dragging along the black surface of the ocean. Leon looked at him with a fearful expression, but Igor ignored him and stormed back to the bridge.

"What kind of lifeboat was it?" he shouted at the captain.

"A twenty-man job. Enclosed, diesel engine, the works."

"What kind of range?"

"I...well over a hundred miles, I'd think."

Igor cursed silently. "How fast is it? What kind of speed can it do in these conditions?"

The captain thought for a moment. "I don't know. Not that fast. Six, seven knots?"

Igor did a quick mental calculation. Depending on when the lifeboat had been deployed, it could have been in the water for an hour or more. The ship was moving at eighteen knots, so it could be anywhere by now.

"Can we see it on radar?"

"Depends on how close we are. In these seas, it'll probably be difficult. It's not very big, and the wave crests are higher than its roof. If we're more than a few miles from it, I doubt we'd pick it up."

Igor pointed his gun at the captain's head. "Try."

The captain stood shakily, dried blood caked down one side of his face from Igor's blow, and moved to the radar display. He stabbed at some buttons and narrowed the range to two nautical miles, then increased it to four, then to eight, then to sixteen. He stopped at forty-eight and pointed at some blips on the screen. "Those are other cargo ships and tankers. I don't see anything else."

Igor debated his options – he could turn the ship around, but then what? That would attract attention and invite the navy to board the vessel and inspect it. And the area that the ship would have to cover to search for the lifeboat would be vast, nearly impossible in the sea conditions. Moving at seven knots in any direction, assuming at least a half hour, possibly up to an hour and a half...it was an impossibility.

He moved to the windows and gripped the rail that ran below them, his face a mask of fury, and gazed out at the remnants of the storm as his mind raced.

Somehow they'd been alerted, and the man had proved resourceful. He'd managed to figure out how to get off a thousand feet of moving ship in a storm without being discovered, leaving Igor holding an empty bag, all his effort for nothing.

CHAPTER 7

22 miles north of the San Blas Islands, Panama

Juan Diego cocked his head as his fishing boat putted along in the predawn gloom that hung over the Caribbean. He knew the sun wouldn't be up for a few more hours, but his eyes still instinctively searched along the horizon for any faint trace of light. Off to the south, dry lightning flashed from over the Panamanian mainland, the thunderheads the last remnants of the storm that had battered the area for the last fourteen hours, and the plum-colored clouds illuminated for a brief second as they brooded over the jungle.

He heard it again. The unmistakable sound of rotors beating the air, a fast-approaching helicopter from the west. He wiped a trickle of sweat from his forehead with the back of his knotted, callused hand, evidence of a hard life of manual labor, and squinted into the darkness.

A high-wattage spotlight flashed to life from the helicopter and fixed on his boat. Now the sound of its turbine was clearer, moving at high speed before stopping and hovering in a position a hundred yards off his bow. He stood transfixed in the beam, a white glare that turned night into day, and shielded his eyes with one hand as he glared up at the intruder.

A male voice boomed over the water from the helo's hailing system.

"Come to a full stop. Now. Prepare to be boarded for inspection."

Juan Diego barked orders to his two crewmen, and they disappeared below as he moved to the wheel and eased the throttle back. When he'd slowed to a crawl, he put the transmission into neutral. The ancient diesel engine rumbled beneath his feet, and he stepped away from the helm, keeping his hands where the snipers in the helicopter could see them at all times.

His crewmen joined him moments later, also with their hands visible. They were longtime veterans of these waters and were used to the nocturnal stops by the Panamanian coast guard, usually working in conjunction with the American navy. As expected, he soon heard the roar of massive motors from offshore, and then the lights of a fast-moving American Oliver Hazard-Perry-class frigate came into view as he stood rocking in the swell, waiting for the inevitable hassling that went with working the waters of coastal Panama.

Juan Diego had long ago determined that the pittance he made as a fisherman wouldn't keep him in the lifestyle he aspired to, and certainly wouldn't support his wife, three children, and two mistresses. So he'd broadened his horizons and become a smuggler, which paid far better, and, like fishing, also involved spending much of his time at sea, which he'd always enjoyed – but carrying more valuable cargo than the haul of fish that served as his cover.

The frigate was moving at better than thirty knots, and Juan Diego and his men watched as it neared, the helicopter maintaining its distance as it did. They knew that a .50-caliber machine gun was trained on them from the aircraft the entire time, and they made no unexpected moves. The Caribbean coast from Colombia to Costa Rica was a primary drug-smuggling corridor, and it was an almost weekly occurrence for the inhabitants of the inhospitable jungle coastline to come across bundled kilos of pure cocaine washed up on the beaches, jettisoned by the triple-engine speedboats that ran the gauntlet north to Mexico. So common was it for locals to find drugs that there were even enterprising middlemen who would buy the discarded packages and sell them back to the Colombian producers. It was a thriving sideline that was little discussed, but had become an important source of windfall income for enterprising beachcombers.

When the big ship was several hundred yards from Juan Diego's boat, a tender lowered into the water, and a dozen heavily armed marines accompanied by a Panamanian customs inspector and a Panamanian coast guard ensign trooped aboard. The craft cut across the water to Juan Diego, and the grim-faced men boarded his craft. Last on were the Panamanian authorities, who shook hands with Juan Diego as the marines performed a methodical search of the boat.

Panama was a relatively small country, where everyone knew each other if they traveled in the same circles, and Juan Diego had been plying the Caribbean waters for two decades. He was used to the searches and recognized both men, who stood apologetically by as the U.S. authorities went over the boat with a fine-toothed comb, inspecting every cabinet and cranny, even the waste, fuel, and water tanks, as well as the small engine compartment.

"When are you guys going to stop harassing me and focus on real criminals?" Juan Diego asked good-naturedly. He was well known to be engaged in more than harvesting the sea's ample bounty, but nobody begrudged him his business – as long as he didn't get caught. The U.S.'s desire to use all of Central America and Mexico as its extended border in order to keep drugs out of the hands of its population – the largest consumer of illegal drugs in the world – wasn't Panama's problem, even though politicians had made it the country's by agreeing to cooperate with the U.S. The tiny country's attitude of live and let live extended to most things, but everyone had to do their job. And just as the Panamanian authorities didn't hold it against Juan Diego, neither did he hold a grudge against his official counterparts. It was all part of the absurd game of life.

"A good question. Nice to see you again, Juan Diego," Humberto Gomez, the customs inspector, allowed.

"I wish I could say it was a pleasure, but I'm losing valuable fishing time with this nonsense," Juan Diego chided.

"We all have our crosses to bear, don't we?" the coast guard ensign said. Everyone knew Juan Diego was guilty as sin, but they could never catch him, so he'd earned a grudging respect, even to the point where he'd buy them a drink if he saw them in one of the seedy waterfront bars he frequented in Colón, Portobelo, and the improbably monikered Nombre de Dios.

The inspection took almost an hour, and Juan Diego chatted with his uninvited guests while the marines completed their task. When they'd finished, with nothing found, he waved as they disembarked and headed back to the mother ship, the men obviously disappointed but not surprised. Once they'd cast off, he put the boat back in gear and resumed his slow journey north as the frigate hoisted the tender in place and the helicopter continued on its way in search of easier prey.

Juan Diego grinned at the two crewmen and looked at his watch. "You'd think they would have learned by now that I'm an innocent man," he said, which drew a laugh from them both. Juan Diego joined in, life's ironies not lost on him.

Twenty feet below the surface, the small submersible he was towing with a steel cable attached to a steel eyelet glided through the deep. Its payload of two hundred kilos of cocaine was relatively small, but enough to make the trip a lucrative one once he met up with a Costa Rican sports fisher thirty miles from Bocas del Toro and handed off his cargo.

CHAPTER 8

Pacific Ocean, 45 miles west of Colombia

Igor's eyes blazed with anger as he faced the captain, for whom fatigue was settling in now that the adrenaline from the search had drained from his system.

"You will tell me everything you know about these two, or I'll systematically cut your mate here to pieces in front of you, then start with your fingers. Do you understand?"

The captain shifted nervously in his seat. "There's nothing to tell. We took them aboard in San Antonio, and we're supposed to transport them to Panama."

"Who are they?"

"They kept to themselves. A gringo and a toddler. What's to know?"

"What names did they use?"

The captain's eyes flitted sideways. "It wasn't that kind of a trip. I didn't ask."

"Ah. Now we're getting somewhere." Igor paced in front of the windows as streaks of pink and purple streaked the sky, the sun finally rising over the jungle almost a hundred miles away. "I know about the fishing boat," he said quietly, as though discussing the weather. He slowly turned to face the captain. "The rendezvous."

The captain's look was defiant. "Then why are you asking me? I'm just providing taxi service. I get paid to take cargo from point A to point B. That's all I'm doing. Like with those containers – I don't care what's in them. It's none of my business."

"It's your business today. What time do you meet the fishing boat, and how is this supposed to happen?"

"At two o'clock this afternoon. We're to rendezvous en route to Balboa, thirty miles south of Punta Coco. The boat takes the passengers aboard and that's it – I'm out of it from that point."

"Does the fishing boat know who to expect?"

"How would I know? They're probably like me. Someone gives them money, they pick up whoever, and the whoever walks off once they're docked. It's a simple transaction."

"Where were they taking the passengers?"

"I have no idea. I get them on that boat, collect a paycheck, move on."

Igor exhaled in frustration. "It sounds straightforward."

"Why do you care?"

"None of your business." Igor didn't share with him that the supposedly sinking boat they'd left was in fine shape, or that its captain was tailing them at a safe distance with instructions to pick them up once they'd accomplished their mission. But now that their quarry had thrown a monkey wrench into the works, a different plan was forming in his mind.

He reached into the side pocket of his pants and withdrew a small sat phone ensconced in a plastic ziplock bag to prevent it from getting damaged during the storm. He powered it on and then went outside on the small bridge side deck. The service indicator showed several bars, and he dialed Fernanda's number.

When she answered, she sounded tired. "How did it go?"

"We had a problem." Igor told her about the lifeboat, and that the woman they were after hadn't been on the ship in the first place.

"Damn. So they escaped," she said.

"Yes. But an idea occurred to me."

"Which is?"

"Those two were obviously the two we heard about when we were looking for her, right?"

"Looks that way."

"Then what are the odds that she was going to meet them when they arrived in Panama?"

"I don't know."

"Probably pretty good, I'd say."

"That's a guess," Fernanda cautioned.

"It's an educated one. If the little girl is, as I think, her daughter, of course she will."

"We don't know that for sure."

"Again, it fits."

Fernanda's voice sounded frayed from lack of sleep. "What do you want to do?"

He explained his thinking. When he was done, she exhaled loudly, as she did when she was mulling over new information. "So you're going to take the fishing boat in?"

"There's a good chance they don't know who they're picking up. Just two people."

"Okay. But what does that buy us?"

"I'll find out where they're headed, and then I was hoping you could arrange with our Panamanian friend to have a welcoming committee waiting when we arrive."

"I see." If the woman was going to meet the boat, they could spot her and take her out when she appeared. "I'll come up to Panama and supervise."

"If you like, but there's also the lifeboat. We lost it off Colombia. I think we should pursue that angle, too, just in case I'm wrong."

"We don't have anyone in Colombia."

"No, but our contact in Panama probably does."

"Good thinking. I'll ask."

Igor gave her the rough coordinates of the *Seylene*'s location around the time he estimated the lifeboat had launched. He heard her fingers flying over computer keys and then another long exhalation. "That's a pretty barren stretch of coast. There's nothing there after Buenaventura, which is a long way south."

"Which would mean that wherever they land, they'll have a hard time getting to civilization. And I'd think a white man and a little girl would be pretty easy to spot in rural Colombia, no?"

"Okay. I'll work this side, you work the Panama side. Hopefully you get lucky."

"It hasn't played that way so far, but today's a new day. Just make sure whoever they send to meet us is good. Remember this woman's MO. She's pro, so she'll spot them if they aren't careful." Igor paused. "The guy probably is too. Who would launch a lifeboat from a moving ship in the middle of a storm?"

"What's done is done. The only reason we care about them is to get to her. I'm beginning to warm up to the idea that she might meet the fishing boat wherever its port is. That feels right."

"It won't be in Balboa, I don't think. It'll be somewhere relatively remote. Somewhere nobody will ask any questions about who gets on or off."

"Call me once you know."

"I will."

"Oh, and Igor? What about the ship? The crew? They've seen your faces."

"I know. I'll leave a couple of guys to handle it. The boat's expecting two passengers, so that will work well."

Fernanda paused. "I miss you already. It was a long night."

Igor watched as traces of gold flickered off the surface of the water, the sun rising to starboard. A pelican flapped in the sky to his right, sleek in the air but ungainly on land. His gaze followed it as it rose and banked in a slow circle, and then folded its wings and dove at high speed at the water, having spotted its breakfast from an impossible height.

"Tell me about it."

CHAPTER 9

Panama City, Panama

The flight from Madrid dropped through scattered clouds on approach to Tocumen International Airport, passing over the tall skyscrapers that jutted into the late-morning sky like steel and glass teeth surrounding Panama Bay. Jet peered out the window at the city in the near distance, surprised by how developed it was – she could have been landing in Hong Kong, if she hadn't known better.

The plane jolted as it hit an air pocket, a warm updraft meeting the cooler thermal layer above the city, and then the landing gear groaned from beneath the wings and their descent steepened. She took a final look around her area and handed the flight attendant her empty coffee cup as the crew prepared for landing, and resumed watching through the window as the plane made a steep bank on final approach.

Jet bounced as the wheels hit the tarmac and pressed forward against her seat belt as the engines reversed thrust, slowing the plane from several hundred miles per hour to thirty in a matter of seconds. Then they were taxiing for the terminal, the pilot's sonorous voice thanking them over the public address system and cautioning them to remain in their seats till the aircraft came to a full stop.

There was a line at immigration due to another flight landing at the same time, and only three officers were working to process hundreds of passengers. When it was finally her turn, she presented her Belgian passport, one of several she cycled through. It was clean, never having been used operationally. Better still, it was a genuine document and would show up as such in the computers – tribute to the Mossad's ingenuity and pull.

The immigration official glanced at her photograph and then gave her a hard look, comparing the snapshot to Jet in the flesh. The passport was four and a half years old, only used twice before in her recent travels, and Jet willed her heartbeat to remain slow and steady as he scrutinized her.

"What is the purpose of your trip to Panama?" he asked curtly.

"Vacation," she answered.

"All the way from Belgium?"

"Why not? I've heard good things."

"Do you have a return ticket?"

She shook her head. "I'm on no firm schedule. I figure if I don't like it, I can get the next flight out, and if I do, I might want to stay a while."

"Occupation?"

"Freelance journalist."

He set the passport down and regarded her again. "You realize that a tourist visa prevents you from accepting any employment while in Panama?"

"Of course. I wasn't planning on working here."

He held her passport below a scanner. The system beeped, and his phone rang. He lifted the handset to his ear and listened, his eyes never leaving her face. She controlled her breathing, as she'd been trained, emitting calm. She saw movement out of the corner of her eye on the far side of the large room and tried not to stare at three soldiers toting machine guns who had materialized from a side entrance. Even as she took in the new development, she smiled at the official, hoping this was just the usual officious bureaucracy, a low-level functionary relishing his ability to make her wait.

After what seemed like hours, he stamped the passport and handed it back to her. "Enjoy your vacation," he said in a disinterested voice, already eyeing the next victim. She took the passport and shouldered her carry-on, to anyone watching a relaxed young woman without a care in the world, arriving in an equatorial wonderland for a tropical vacation.

Jet slipped on her sunglasses and watched the soldiers from behind the dark lenses. All three were staring at her, but she continued through the room to the baggage claim area – she recognized the expressions on their faces, and it wasn't anything unusual or alarming. Just young men bursting with testosterone, eyeing a striking example of the opposite sex.

She pushed past a throng of her fellow travelers and stepped outside. Stifling humidity settled over her, and she peeled off her jacket as she removed her phone from her carry-on and waited for it to acquire a signal. After a minute she dialed Matt's sat phone, only to hear it go directly to voice mail.

"I'm here. See you in a few hours. Hope everything's going well on your end," she said. "Call me when you get this. My cell's on."

Jet hung up and checked the time. Matt was scheduled to arrive on the fishing boat in six hours – more than enough time to get to the tiny port of Vacamonte, west of Balboa, on a remote spit of land twelve miles from Panama City. She'd go into the city center and get a sense of the town, and then meet Matt and Hannah.

The thought of seeing her daughter again sent a thrill of happiness through her. It seemed like forever since she'd hugged her and brushed her hair – for that matter, since she'd been in Matt's arms. Finally, they were safe and could start a new life somewhere nobody could find them. She was exhausted from having to run, enemies from the past constantly chasing them, and wanted nothing more than a boring life as a homebody somewhere modest and quiet.

The thought of herself standing in front of a small house, an apron tied around her waist, waiting for Hannah to run toward her and tell her all about her day at school, tugged at her heart, and a wave of melancholy washed over her. Was that too much to ask? Peace, a good man, a happy kid, the world left to its own devices as she lived out her time in tranquility?

She waited in the taxi line for a bit and then changed her mind and returned to the terminal. A row of rental car agencies vied for her attention, and she chose the farthest from the arrivals salon, where a bored woman sat texting behind a chipped counter, her red uniform wrinkled from the humidity.

Jet exchanged pleasantries with her and ten minutes later had rented a nondescript economy sedan. A shuttle took her to a lot off the airport grounds and dropped her at the car, and after glancing at a map helpfully supplied by the rental company, she cranked over the engine and negotiated her way out of the lot.

The highway into town was clearly marked, and she marveled again at how modern everything seemed. As she neared the city, the high-rises astounded her, like something from photographs of Dubai or Singapore. One building in particular was arresting in a sea of new developments: forty or fifty stories of green-tinted glass that looked like a giant screw sticking straight into the sky.

She took an off-ramp and found herself on Avenue Israel, which was gridlocked, and she resigned herself to finding that quiet spot inside herself where her patience came from. After twenty minutes and having moved three blocks, that pursuit of serenity gave way to restlessness, and she exhaled a sigh of relief when she was able to get out of the worst of the traffic and pull onto a wide boulevard.

A colorful building advertising toys caught her eye, and she found a parking place a block away, locked her bag in the trunk, and ambled down the sidewalk in no particular hurry. When she pushed her way through the doors, she discovered a huge inventory of games and playthings – most made in China, of course. After twenty minutes agonizing over her choices, she bought a doll and a plush bear that she hoped would melt Hannah's heart.

With the toys safely stashed in the trunk next to her bag, Jet decided to walk the downtown area and get a sense of the town's style. Every place she'd spent any time in had its unique mood and vibe, and Panama City proved no different – an eclectic combination of high tech and big money juxtaposed against a laid-back tropical rhythm.

A friendly waitress at a café she stopped at gushed about the new canal and the prosperity it was going to bring, clearly excited at the idea of even more development for the otherwise unremarkable slice of earth. To Jet, after the wine-based economy of Mendoza, Panama City seemed like a schizophrenic stepchild of New York set down in the jungle, all rush and bustle but lacking the sophistication a more mature city would have.

The word that best defined the city for her as she gazed at the impressive skyline was "new." Everything was recently built, barely out of the box, which was both exciting and disturbing. She wondered what the city must have been like twenty years earlier, and decided that she might have liked it better as a backwater than a busy metropolis. But for her current purposes of finding a reasonably civilized place where she could effectively disappear, Panama City was probably as good as any other. The infrastructure seemed decent, the cars mostly new, the natives all dressed as in any commercial on U.S. or European television, regional distinctions long ago lost in a wave of corporate globalization that ensured everyone wore Nike and No Fear, whether in Tel Aviv, Moscow, Buenos Aires…or Panama.

Jet finished her coffee and checked her watch. It was early, but she had nothing else to do but wait for the love of her life and her daughter to arrive. She returned to the car and sat with the AC blasting the perspiration off her face, and caught a glimpse of her emerald eyes in the rearview mirror. She tilted it down and studied her features – after everything she'd been through in the last few months, she was surprised her hair hadn't turned white, like a witch in a Japanese monster movie.

But that was all behind her now. She was here, safe, and her family would arrive in only a few hours.

Life had never been better, she thought as she put the car into gear. Maybe she'd finally caught the break she was hoping for.

It had to happen sometime.

CHAPTER 10

80 miles south of Panama City, Panama

Igor watched the massive hull of the *Seylene* fade into the horizon as the fishing boat that had rendezvoused with the cargo ship motored toward Panama, still out of sight somewhere beyond the endless blue of the Pacific Ocean. Leon stood by his side, their weapons hidden in the bags they'd filched from the ship's crew.

The fishing boat captain had been surprised when Igor and Leon had boarded.

"I thought it was supposed to be a guy and a kid," he'd remarked.

"There was a change of plans. Why, do you charge by the pound?" Igor had asked.

They'd laughed, the captain somewhat uneasily, and then pushed off, anxious not to draw the scrutiny of one of the naval vessels patrolling the waters.

The boat was rancid, a working fishing scow with dried scales stuck to her gunwales and a film of noxious ooze crusted on her decks, and Igor was surprised when the captain pushed the throttle forward and the boat surged ahead. He'd figured that they would be lucky to do ten knots, but the GPS read fourteen, which was unbelievable.

"What have you got in this thing?" Igor asked, impressed.

"Twin Caterpillar 3208 TAs," the captain beamed.

"I would have made this for a single screw."

"That's the whole point. But if I need to outrun a storm…or anything else…better to have some power, you know?"

"Few more knots and you'd get up on plane," Igor teased. The fishing boat may have been supercharged, but there were physical

50

limits to the speed a displacement hull could achieve, given a certain length and width.

"Make yourselves at home. It'll be a while," the captain said.

"Where are we headed?"

"Puerto Vacamonte."

"Near Balboa?"

The captain gave him the beginning of a smile. "But far enough so there are no prying eyes."

"Good."

"How long will it take to get there?"

"Six hours, at this speed."

That would put them into the port at roughly eight o'clock, so dark by the time they arrived.

Igor called Fernanda and gave her the details.

"I'll get on it and have a welcoming committee waiting when you dock. If the woman shows up, she's history," Fernanda promised.

"Where are you now?" Igor asked.

"I'm in Medellín," she said. "Our Panamanian friend has a contact here. I'm supposed to meet him soon, so we'll see what he can do for us."

"Every minute counts."

"As well I know."

"But no pressure."

"Of course not."

He hung up, and Leon joined him as they watched the ocean blow past, the water sapphire blue and crystal clear, the breeze refreshing in the heat. The Panamanian gunman, one of their contact's top enforcers, leaned into him after glancing around to ensure that neither the captain nor the three fishermen that served as crew were nearby.

"So how are we going to do this? If the woman's going to meet the boat, she's going to figure out pretty quickly that neither one of us is a child or a gringo."

"We stay onboard. Your boss is arranging for reinforcements. They'll have the same photo you do. If she shows, they'll take her out."

"But we still get paid the same, right?" Leon asked.

Igor smiled. Of course. The man was worried about his fee, as would Igor in the same circumstances. "Sure. It doesn't really matter whose bullet kills her. She just needs to die."

"How are Carlos and Raphael going to get off the cargo ship?"

"Same trick the gringo played. Lifeboat. When they're only twenty or so miles off Los Santos point, they'll make their way to shore."

"And the ship?"

"They won't be able to do much in another few hours about our hitching a ride. It'll be too late." Igor paused. "And anyway, I got the feeling that the captain wasn't the type to call the cops – he'd have a lot of explaining to do himself. No, they'll continue on their way as though nothing happened."

"Minus their lifeboats."

"It's an imperfect world."

~ ~ ~

As the afternoon drew to a close, the *Seylene*'s captain was growing more nervous. He'd smoked his last cigarette, but Carlos, the gunman, wouldn't let him go below to get more. He hadn't seen any of his crew for hours, not since the ringleader had disembarked onto the fishing boat, nor had he heard from his mechanical engineer or any of the crew in the engine room, and he was getting a sinking feeling in his gut.

When he'd demanded to know what Carlos intended to do with them, the gunman had smiled a psychotic grin and assured him that he'd be out of their hair soon. Carlos had questioned the captain at length about launching the remaining lifeboat, and it became quickly apparent that he and the other thug planned to take it, leaving the crew to keep going without looking back.

Which was a safe bet. The captain didn't need anyone asking difficult questions. Of course, no matter how it played out, there would likely be some kind of inquiry – for instance, the shipping company would want to know what had happened to two expensive lifeboats. And the mobster who'd paid a small fortune to get the man and his daughter to safety would want to know how it went.

It was going to be a difficult week.

The hair on the back of the captain's neck stood on edge when he sensed Carlos walking behind him, and he was about to turn around when the .40-caliber soft-nose slug blew his brains all over the console. The helmsman froze in shock at the sight of his captain executed without warning, and when Carlos spoke, he could barely hear him through the ringing in his ears.

"Set the autopilot so the boat will drive itself," Carlos ordered.

"Why? What are you going to do?" the helmsman stammered.

"I'm taking you downstairs where you can't get into any trouble and locking you in with the crew."

"Why did you kill the captain?"

"Orders. He was into more than you want to know about. The less you know, the longer you live. Now set the autopilot." He gestured with his pistol.

The helmsman didn't need to be told twice. He entered the coordinates that would take the ship back into the shipping lanes, programmed the device, and then sat back. "There. But it's not safe to have a ship flying blind. The shipping lanes are crowded, even though they look empty."

"That's okay," Carlos said, and shot him in the temple at point-blank range.

He studied the two dead men for a few moments and then gazed out through the windows at the calm sea. Hard to believe that earlier the ocean had been a living nightmare. Now it was smooth as glass, a pleasure to be on.

He used the bathroom and then went below, where he'd execute the crew before launching the lifeboats. Igor's instructions had been clear – nobody to be left alive who could identify them. It was bad business to leave survivors, and Carlos hadn't thrived for years in the brutal drug trade as an enforcer, and then a hired killer, by being squeamish about doing what was required.

He and Rafael made short work of the rest of the crew, and then they made their way to the lifeboat and sealed themselves in, ready to launch into the water at the pull of a lever.

Carlos' last thought as the little craft slid down the tracks and then dropped toward the surface of the sea was that it was a nice evening for a boat ride.

CHAPTER 11

Frontino, Colombia

Fernanda felt the car slow after what she estimated was ten minutes of winding road that climbed at probably a ten percent grade. So they had to be in the mountains. She cocked her head, listening to the sound of the tires change from running on pavement to hard-packed dirt. The blindfold over her eyes effectively obstructed her vision but not her ability to commit the route to memory. Something creaked outside as they rolled to a stop – a gate, she supposed – and then the tires crunched on gravel for thirty seconds before the vehicle rolled to a stop.

A sour, unpleasant smell hit her nostrils as the thug in the seat next to her reached over and untied the blindfold. She forced herself to keep her hands folded in her lap as he fumbled with the black fabric, battling the urge to incapacitate him with one well-delivered strike.

Fernanda had been unimpressed by the security precautions the two men who'd picked her up had taken – consisting of a cursory search, where the driver's hands lingered just a hair too long on her curves, and the blindfold. If she'd been so predisposed, she could have killed them both in seconds, but that wasn't why she was here.

Her contact in Panama had given her the introduction to a man who, he assured her, ran much of northern Colombia, with strong ties to the rebels up in the Darién Gap who controlled that swatch of jungle as much as anyone could – it was dangerous beyond belief, infested with every sort of predator and miscreant, completely removed from any laws or government's jurisdiction, a no-man's land where those who went in never came out. She'd read up on the area,

55

which was populated by small Indian villages that rarely had contact with the outside world, and by little hamlets with hapless Colombian natives who'd lived there for generations, eking out a sustenance existence from the sea, rivers, or land.

The stretch of coast that she needed help with ran from the Gap south to Buenaventura, a river town that also served as a Pacific port notorious as a cocaine smuggling hotspot where more of the white gold embarked on its journey north to Mexico than from any other place in Colombia. There were two primary corridors – the Pacific Ocean along the Central American coast, and the Caribbean route, each requiring different techniques due to the disparity in patrols. Buenaventura had become infamous due to the cottage industry of submarine manufacture, where the locals crafted fiberglass subs in the hundred foot and up range in jungle factories, some replete with air-conditioning and other creature comforts. These were single-use craft that would be scuttled once they'd delivered their payloads in Mexican waters. Designed with the ability to haul many tons of cocaine, their production cost was a rounding error.

Grimly poor, the port town was one of the most dangerous on the planet outside of an active war zone, although whether that qualification was appropriate was debatable. Colombia was in its fifth decade of civil war, with rebel forces controlling much of the south, parts of the coast, and the north, including the Darién. Originally driven by communist ideology, the rebels had long ago transitioned from freedom fighters to capitalists engaged in protecting the thriving cocaine production that was the primary industry of southern Colombia and northern Peru, Ecuador, and Brazil.

Fernanda's Panamanian contact had told her that the going rate for a submarine captain was two million dollars, cash. Most only made one trip, preferring to retire once they collected their windfall. Those that were apprehended en route died in prison – the cartels didn't suffer failure gladly, and it didn't matter to them what the circumstances were behind a botched voyage. Someone would pay for their loss, and that was inevitably the captain and crew.

Fernanda blinked in the bright sunlight and slipped on a pair of designer sunglasses. The thug next to her opened his door and slid out, and the driver swung hers wide so she could do the same. She stepped onto the gravel and eyed the large ranch-style house before her. It was perched on top of a bluff, a valley stretching into the distance before it, with distinctive tiers of coffee plants spilling down the slope.

She didn't blink when the sound of gunshots cracked from her left, beyond several satellite buildings that ringed the drive. Pistols, she thought from the timbre of the reports. The thug looked her up and down and grunted.

"This way."

Fernanda followed the man along the drive until he veered off onto a dirt path that led to a grove of trees. More shots echoed from beyond the trees, as well as the sound of laughing male voices.

On the other side of the grove stood four men, pistols in hand. A bottle of Ballantine's sat on a card table, which was ringed by lawn chairs set on the trimmed grass of a small clearing. The men turned and watched as she neared, and then one of the men – older, impeccably attired in linen pants, a Robert Graham shirt, and black suede Gucci loafers – tilted his head in greeting.

"Welcome. We have a mutual friend who explained that you have a pressing problem you'd like some assistance with?" The man's eyes took in every inch of her. "I'm Mosises. Make yourself at home."

He approached and shook her hand. She noted that in spite of his full head of silver hair, he had a youthful demeanor and an alert gaze.

"I'm Fernanda. And yes, I need some help." She recounted an abridged version of her predicament, leaving out why she was looking for the man and little girl. When she was done, he turned back to his companions.

"Have they set up the new targets?" he asked.

One of the men, younger than the rest, nodded. "As you instructed."

"Good." Mosises glanced at Fernanda. "We're having a little contest here. I got some new Berettas in, and there's some question as to who's a better shot."

Mosises raised his weapon and fired off six rounds at a paint can sitting down the slope about thirty yards away. Four of the shots struck it left of center. The last two missed it entirely. Yellow paint streamed from the holes, and Mosises frowned. Fernanda looked at the can and shook her head.

"Are those hand loads or factory?" she asked.

Mosises raised one eyebrow. "Factory."

"Then either you pull to the left, or the sight's off."

He reappraised her. "Sounds like you know your weapons."

"I've had time on my hands," she allowed.

"How's your shooting?"

She shrugged. "Better than some."

Mosises called to the nearest man. "Oscar, give her your gun."

The stocky Oscar waddled over to her and offered her the Beretta. She tested the weight in her hand and smiled. "Feels like you've still got, what, nine shots left?"

Oscar's eyes widened. "That's right."

Mosises pointed with his gun at the paint can next to the one he'd hit. "Do your worst."

Fernanda flipped the safety off and carefully squeezed off six shots using a two-handed grip. All six placed within a three-inch grouping. She engaged the safety and handed the gun back to Oscar.

"That one's fine."

Mosises gave her his pistol. "Try this one."

She repeated the performance, and six shots consistently punctured the far left of the can. Fernanda smiled as she handed him back the gun. "Told you. Pulls to the left."

Mosises returned her smile with a laugh and tossed the gun onto one of the chairs. "Very nice. Come. Let's discuss how I can help you." He paused for a moment, considering. "What exactly do you require?"

"I need men to scour the coast where these two could be. If that's not feasible, then to put the word out that you are to be informed when they're spotted. Our friend told me that you run this area."

Mosises gave a last look at the cans. "It's true that I have considerable influence, but that's a huge stretch of coastline. Based on what you're describing, at least 200 kilometers. And most of it's uninhabited. Jungle. So I'm not sure there will be much chance of scouring."

"Then you can't help me?"

"I didn't say that, did I? I can put a helicopter in the air and have it run up the coast, as a start. And as you suggested, I can circulate that I'm looking for these two. But it's not going to be easy…or cheap."

"Name a price," Fernanda said evenly.

Mosises grinned. "You have an interesting way of putting things. But you did confirm that my gun needs adjustment, which saved me a lot of money in lost bets over the course of the day." He named a figure.

Fernanda's face was a blank. "I'll have to make some calls to confirm, but that seems doable."

"It sounds like the clock's ticking for you, so I'll take that as a yes and will deploy some men. If you can't make good on it, let me know as soon as possible. How long will it take you to get a definitive?"

She glanced at her watch. "One hour, at most."

His grin widened. "Is there anything else you'd like me to arrange?"

"Just find them."

"If they're anywhere on that coast, I'm your best shot, but there's no guarantee. I hope that's acceptable."

"Of course."

He studied her and grinned. "Then we have a deal."

CHAPTER 12

SW of Nuquí, Chocó, Colombia

Matt eyed the lifeboat's fuel gauge as he studied the shore, his face set with grim determination. Hannah was slumbering nearby; the excitement of making an escape in the middle of the night via freefall lifeboat during a huge storm had kept her awake until daybreak. The sturdy little diesel engine purred along as it had for the last twelve hours, but it was a good thing that land was in sight because it was running on fumes and would likely die at any moment.

He estimated they'd averaged six knots, or roughly seven miles per hour, although that had increased as the seas flattened. The first three hours in the water had been hellish, and it had been all he could do to maintain a course east as the mammoth swells pushed them along like a leaf on a river.

He'd taken the precaution of packing their bags when he'd watched the sinking fishing boat drift off in the night and thought he'd seen someone on board as it faded into the gloom. There was no way that the saved men would have left one of their own on a sinking ship, so that meant that, if his eyes hadn't played tricks on him, the boat was fine and the mayday was a ruse.

Taking no chances, he'd moved Hannah to the upper deck where the two freefall lifeboats were stored, bows facing downward. He'd secured the little girl and their things inside and readied the starboard one for launching. The boat was fully enclosed, so he had no fears about them drowning or being capsized in the storm – which had turned out to be a good thing, because when he'd crept down to where the newcomers were drying off in the galley, he'd spotted the crew tied up and a gunman guarding them. Matt had considered overpowering the man, but with a broken hand he lacked complete confidence, and he had no idea how competent the other assailants were. He had to assume the worst.

Any question in his mind that the boarding might have been an act of piracy was put to rest when he'd peeked around the corner on the stateroom level and seen two men go straight to his door. He hadn't waited for any more confirmation and moved stealthily back to the lifeboats on the upper deck and warned Hannah to hold on tight.

The launch had been rough, but the shock of dropping into the ocean had quickly worn off as he started the motor and set a course for land. The moving walls of water pushed them along with a mind of their own.

He gazed through the small windows at the approaching shore and was startled when a geyser of water shot into the air no more than twenty yards to starboard, followed by the mottled gray-brown of a leviathan body. A second whale joined its partner, spraying spume at the sky, and Hannah awoke at the loud noise.

"Look, honey. It's a whale! Come here and I'll hold you up so you can see."

Nothing happened for thirty seconds, and then one of the whales breached again. Hannah's eyes widened at the sight of such a large creature only a short distance away, and she gasped. Matt smiled at the sound. Everything was new and fresh when you were two and a half, but even at forty-something, a whale coming up for air within spitting distance was an impressive sight.

"That's called a whale. It's like a big fish, but it breathes air like we do." He thought about what else he knew about whales. Years of being a clandestine operative with the CIA hadn't prepared him for being a nature guide, so he winged it, figuring his audience wasn't that discriminating. "It's the biggest animal in the world."

They watched the whales for a few minutes, and then he set Hannah back down. "We should be on land soon. Our boat ride is almost over."

Hannah nodded solemnly, as though her permission were required, and then stretched her arms out and yawned. Matt turned his attention back to the coast, looking for a hospitable spot to land the boat. The entire shore was jungle with a black sand beach stretching into the sea, not a creature to be seen other than a few pelicans floating just outside the surf line.

"Hang on, sweetheart. We're going to beach the boat."

"Beach?"

"We're going to pull it up onto the sand."

She smiled. Even though she hadn't complained, Matt could tell that the novelty of boat rides had worn thin on the little girl. He didn't blame her. He'd had enough of the seafaring life to last a long time.

The motor sputtered once with a hoarse cough, and a breaking wave lifted them and pushed them towards the beach. Another came in behind it, and then they were surfing toward the shoreline. Matt gave the dying engine full throttle to try to maintain any control over their direction and keep them from being pushed sideways and rolling.

Sand scraped on the bow as they were pushed onto the beach, the rear of the boat twisting as another incoming wave pushed it onto the sand. The little craft listed to the side, and Hannah's mouth made a small O as her world tilted and they found themselves standing on what had been the side of the boat.

Matt opened the access hatch and climbed out. After looking around to ensure there were no threats, he leaned down and held out his good hand. "Hannah? Come on. I'll pull you up."

He didn't have to ask twice. She grabbed his arm with all her strength, and he gripped her under an arm and unceremoniously hoisted her from the hatch, twisted, and slid down the hull until his feet were on the sand. He put her down and pointed to a spot about five feet away. "Stand right there. I need to get our stuff. I'll be back in a second. Don't go near the water, or anywhere, until I'm back, okay?"

Another nod.

Matt returned to the boat and grabbed their bags. He pushed them through the hatch and grabbed one of the emergency survival kits. He'd rummaged through it; it was heavy, but had some useful items that might come in handy: dry rations, water sanitizer, a first aid kit, a flare gun, collapsible bottles and bowls, a lighter, a knockoff Super Tool, a small flashlight, batteries, a flimsy four-man tent, toilet paper, antiseptic, hand sanitizer, vitamins and electrolyte replacement tablets, a cheap compass, and other odds and ends.

He was back on the beach in sixty seconds with the bags. Hannah was frozen in place, waiting with an expectant look on her face. Matt gazed up at the sun and wiped away the sweat, cursing his broken hand – if he'd ever needed both mitts, now was the time.

The jungle looked dense and forbidding, a vibrant green that quickly faded to darkness, seemingly impenetrable. Matt gathered the bags and, with at least seventy-five pounds of weight, wondered how far he would make it before they had to rest. He hadn't slept in almost forty hours, and his body was sending him unmistakable signals that it wouldn't go forever.

He spotted a break in the vegetation and motioned to it. "Looks like there's a trail. Come on, Hannah. Stay right behind me. Don't stop to look around. I don't want to lose you."

The trail turned out to be a winding path overgrown with vines and plants, probably used by game, although not heavily, by the looks of it. Once they were in the jungle, where the offshore breeze was blocked by the trees, the heat became stifling. The only positive was the overhead canopy, so thick that it blocked the sun; but even so, within fifteen minutes of trudging along Matt was soaked through with sweat.

They came to a clearing, and he set the bags down. "We're going to rest for a few minutes, okay?"

Hannah smiled sadly and, after inspecting the ground, sat down. Matt rooted in his bag until he found the satellite phone. He inspected the screen and powered it on, but the light and signal indicator remained dark. He'd hoped that the trace moisture inside the screen wouldn't pose a problem, but the phone had obviously gotten wet enough in the torrential downpour of the storm that it was dead.

He removed the battery, wiped the contacts off, and replaced it, but got the same nonresponse when he depressed the power button. He stared at it for a few seconds, silently cycling through the many curses he knew in three different languages, and then shrugged and put it back in the bag. It would do no good to rail at the universe. They were both physically fine, they had supplies and a compass, and because it was jungle, it was just a matter of time until it rained or they came across a stream. Matt had spent months in Laos living in worse conditions, so this was nothing new. His only concern was for Hannah, who might not prove as resilient as he was.

"All right. Let's keep moving and see if we can find some water, okay?" The emergency kit had two one-liter bottles, but he'd prefer not to have to drain them until he knew he could replenish their stores. He opened the bag and removed one, took three cautious swallows from it, and then sat next to Hannah and held it for her while she drank greedily.

He pulled the bottle away before she was ready to quit, and she gave him an annoyed look, but he ignored it and screwed the plastic cap back on. "Only a little, then we walk."

The afternoon gradually darkened, and as dusk approached Matt stopped near a mangrove forest where there was a relatively clear area. Working quickly, he removed the flimsy tent from the orange emergency bag and erected the aluminum frame, driving stakes into the spongy ground as Hannah watched. When he was done, he stood back and studied his handiwork – it would do for the night. Not that they had any other options.

The mosquitoes found them shortly after he was finished, and he got Hannah into the tent before following her in, and spent the next fifteen minutes killing bugs that had made it inside. The last thing he needed to add to their problems was to contract malaria or dengue fever, both of which he suspected were prevalent.

The flashlight provided sufficient glow for them to munch on the tasteless dry rations, and Matt sacrificed the rest of the water bottle to wash it down. By the time they were done, it was dark as pitch out, and the mosquito swarm had abated. He held the light while Hannah went potty near the tent, and after she scampered back inside, he did the same.

When he returned to the tent, Hannah was sitting waiting. The interior was mildly cooler from a tiny breeze that managed to flow through the two mesh window openings. He lay down with a grunt and sighed, his stomach rumbling from hunger. The inadequate pickings had been barely enough to keep him going.

Hannah crawled over to him, and they drifted off to sleep with her head on his chest, the sound of her breathing vying with the calls of nocturnal creatures whose feeding time was just beginning. Matt felt by his side to where he'd placed the flare gun, hoping he wouldn't have to use it, and was asleep within two minutes of closing his eyes.

CHAPTER 13

Puerto Vacamonte, Panama

Jet drove across the Centenario Bridge, watching cruise ships and tankers pass beneath in the Panama Canal, guided by tugboats as they made their way between two oceans along the forty-eight-mile stretch that had been dubbed one of the seven wonders of the modern world.

The concrete jungle of Panama City gave way to rainforest as she wended her way west, the heavy traffic in town now a trickle. The freeway had become two lanes in either direction, and it was hard to believe that just a few miles back was a teeming metropolis overrun with humanity.

When she pulled off the highway at the town of Vacamonte, the contrast with Panama City was immediate and stark. Clearly the town was at the opposite end of the economic scale, the road a single lane in either direction and the cars battered and old, corroding from the salt air. She passed a roadside restaurant that was little more than a lean-to, a sheet of corrugated metal suspended over suspect timbers advertising the freshest seafood in Panama on a hand-scrawled slab of plywood.

Jet checked the time – the fishing boat wasn't scheduled to arrive for four more hours, but her natural field caution had her there far in advance so she could take up a safe position from which to watch it dock. She'd bought a pair of small binoculars for that purpose, but as she bumped down the patchy road, she wondered what was at the end of it.

The port was on the tip of a spit of land that thrust into the Pacific Ocean. Only one looping road led out to it, low-end housing projects under construction on either side. The encroachment ultimately gave way again to jungle before she arrived at the waterfront. The entire harbor was only a half mile wide, a good chunk of it devoted to one of the saddest black sand beaches she'd ever seen, next to which was a concrete wharf with a series of piers stretching into the water.

The fishing fleet was almost entirely rusting scows that looked like they might sink at any time, moored side by side fifty yards into the harbor in clumps of ten to twenty boats. A breakwater protected the anchorage from the Pacific's swells, and near the mouth were the larger, long-range commercial net boats, 200 to 300 feet long, built to spend months at sea in any weather harvesting their catch before returning to port.

The rest of the boats were in the sixty- to eighty-foot range, most at least thirty years old, judging by their weathered appearances. Jet drove slowly through the waterfront before passing the shipyard at the far end and looping back around toward the lone entry road. When she was out of sight of the wharf, she made a U-turn and returned to the large parking lot near the industrial buildings that hulked along the entry. She parked and got out, stretching her legs, and then picked up her bag and made her way across the road, away from the harbor, in search of an elevated vantage point from which she could watch the boats arrive.

She found a deserted bunker, covered with graffiti and half-filled with broken beer bottles and detritus, and cleared a small section. With the surrounding brush and vines, her hiding spot was virtually invisible. The binoculars had been a wise purchase, she thought, as she swept the buildings methodically to familiarize herself with the layout and the few vehicles parked nearby. The day was winding down, and it would be dark in two or so hours. From what she could see, the workers in the boatyard were in no pressing hurry to get anything done, and spent as much time chatting and laughing as they did sanding and painting. She watched with absent interest as small clusters of men strolled from the buildings, their day at an end, and moved to their cars, as battered and tired as their passengers.

Time dragged by with little to see. A few boats entered the harbor and moored next to the rest, their crews remaining on board while sheltered from the swell. The vessel Matt and Hannah would be on, the *Paloma*, would put in at the main dock, which she guessed had a higher cost associated with it than tying off in the harbor, judging by the few boats that availed themselves of the cement pier's hospitality.

Light gusts blew off the water, carrying with them the faint odor of decaying sea life and diesel exhaust. In the distance, the sonorous lowing of ship horns from near the canal carried across the water. Jet shifted in her spot, the humid stifle still oppressive even as the sun faded into the sea, and did another sweep of the harbor with her binoculars, there being nothing else to do.

A van rolled down the entry road, attracting Jet's attention. Its brake lights flashed as it slowed to a stop, and the side door opened. Two men got out, and the van continued on its way to the parking lot, where it pulled into a slot near the entrance.

The hair on Jet's arms stood up as she eyeballed the men who stepped down from the van. They looked casual enough, laughing as they walked together to the small restaurant servicing the harbor, but something about them triggered alarms. These weren't fishermen or laborers, in spite of their clothes being the same as the men working the waterfront – they were too clean, their posture too disciplined.

She continued to watch them as they entered the restaurant, while down by the water the first pair split up after shaking hands. Maybe she was being overly paranoid – it had been a rough month by any measure. She followed the first man as he walked unhurriedly along the wharf, smoking a cigarette and gazing out at the water. Jet zoomed in on the second man, who was ambling in the other direction. He stopped by the beach and also lit a cigarette, and then walked into a little shack selling drinks and emerged holding a can of beer.

She ducked down lower, instinct telling her that this wasn't innocent. She picked up the first man again and saw him working his way along the dock, meandering out to the end of the pier, where he stood, watching the sun set.

Jet switched back to the second man, after confirming that the other two hadn't come out of the restaurant. He was nursing his beer, his eyes roaming over the cars and buildings even as he appeared to be completely uninterested in anything but the boats.

That sealed it. Something was wrong. They'd been sold out.

Her mind flitted to Alejandro. She'd thought he was trustworthy, but he was the only other one who knew the details of Matt and Hannah's arrival, and obviously he'd opened his mouth. The thought of him betraying her stabbed through her heart like a blade, but she pushed the emotion away. If he had, she'd find him and pay him back.

Jet froze at her next thought. Matt and Hannah.

If there were pros here waiting for her to show, then it was also possible they'd corrupted the fishing boat in some way and intercepted her daughter and her man.

She told herself she was getting ahead of herself, but the thought did little to comfort her as she studied the drinking man's face. They were good. Very good, for civilians. So good that if she had arrived later – say, only a couple of hours before the boat was scheduled to arrive, instead of four – she wouldn't have picked them out. Jet scanned back to where the first man had been and didn't see him. He'd vanished, either into one of the boats or one of the buildings.

"Probably one of the boats," she whispered to herself. That's what Jet would have done. Found an empty boat on the same dock the *Paloma* was scheduled to arrive at and hunker down, waiting for Jet to arrive, to slip up, to make a mistake.

The two in the restaurant would probably stay put, she thought; their vantage point from the elevated bluff that overlooked the whole harbor was the perfect place from which to spot her.

Twilight transitioned to night, and the beer drinker took a call on his cell phone. It was short, only ten seconds, but it confirmed what she had already suspected. She could imagine the discussion: "Any sign of her?" "Not yet." "Stay put and keep your eyes open."

The harbor was now dark except for the glimmer of stars overhead peeking between the clouds and a few dim lamps outside the restaurant. The little drink-vending shack closed up for the night, and her watcher moved to the sea wall and sat down, looking like a tired laborer who was taking the edge off a harsh day with a few brews.

She slid her cell from her pocket and called Matt's sat phone, praying he would answer. It wasn't her day. The call went directly to voice mail. She checked to confirm that the phone was set to vibrate and slipped it back into her pocket, her anxiety building with each passing minute.

The rumble of an approaching boat drew her attention, and she focused her glasses on the vessel entering the harbor mouth. Its running lights were barely visible, and she couldn't make out the name on the dull green hull. She checked her watch. That was probably her boat. Fifteen minutes late.

She didn't have to speculate for long. The vessel continued to the main dock and tied off alongside another boat. The engines died three minutes later. She watched, her heart in her throat, waiting to see the tiny figure of her Hannah come on deck.

Two deck hands hosed down the transom and then went to work on the exposed surfaces. Ten minutes stretched into thirty, but nobody got off the boat. Jet controlled her breathing, her heart rate slow. It was what it was. This was a game of chess. If Matt and Hannah were on the boat, they were down below. Whoever was gunning for her was trying to draw her out, make her show her hand and come to them.

Because they knew her weakness. They knew she'd have to confirm whether they were on the boat or not.

But they hadn't bargained on Jet being as disciplined as she was, or taking overkill precautions.

Which was her edge.

They'd underestimated her.

And the world was littered with the bodies of others who had done the same.

CHAPTER 14

The harbor was still, save only for the sound of small waves lapping at the wharf and the occasional splash as a seal dropped from a rock into the water for an invigorating dip. The clouds had thickened, blocking out most of the light from the stippling of stars, and in the distance, somewhere near Colombia, veins of lightning streaked through the turbid vault of the night sky.

Two hours after the *Paloma* had moored, a man finally emerged from the cabin, climbed across to the other boat, and made his way down the dock and up to the restaurant. This man was no fisherman. The clothes didn't fit correctly and his hair was too neatly cut. She followed his progress until he went inside and made her decision.

She had to know if her baby was on the boat.

And there was only one way to confirm it.

Jet took a long look around the waterfront, and when she had reassured herself that it would be almost impossible to spot her in dark clothes, unzipped her bag and withdrew a long-sleeved black T-shirt and a pair of knee-length black cargo shorts. She desperately wished that instead of a teddy bear she'd bought a locking survival knife, but it was too late for regrets.

Because the clock was ticking, and if her daughter and Matt were on the boat, it was up to her to get them off.

Ten minutes later, her head bobbed out of the water near the *Paloma*'s stern. She listened, gripping the dock, which she'd swum under for cover. Music played from the boat's cabin area, a cheap radio emitting a bouncing beat as a woman sang about broken hearts and the promise of a new day. She held still while water ran down her face, waiting to hear something that would tip her off about how many were in the boat.

The water was warm, like a bath, for which she was grateful. She had no worries about hypothermia or losing her mental or physical edge from being submerged, which meant there was no real hurry. Any watchers would be waiting for her to come down the pier, not from the sea, which is why she'd chosen that approach. Her hope was that by the time anyone on land realized she'd been on and off the boat, she would be long gone.

She pulled herself onto the transom platform and then crept onto the rear deck. Glancing around, she spotted the gleaming blade of a filleting knife atop a flat plate mounted next to a primitive sink. Her bare feet made no noise as she edged to the knife, and within moments she had it held close to her leg and was cautiously inching toward the metal cabin door.

Leon yawned and shook his head to clear it. He was bone tired, and in spite of Igor's assurances that the woman was likely to come, she hadn't, and it had been hours. He privately thought that the Brazilian had bungled the entire job, but he wasn't going to say anything. Igor was, after all, the customer, and the customer was always right. But as far as Leon could tell, they'd all spent a ton of time and energy only to come up empty-handed.

He glanced with disgust at the captain and his crew, all busy at the galley table playing cards, smoking, and knocking back a bottle of local coconut rum. The boat smelled like a latrine, and the fishermen not much better. He was counting the seconds until the dim Brazilian called it a night and admitted defeat – Leon wanted off the boat now so he could spend his cut of the money at the casino that doubled as a high-end whorehouse, with dozens of gorgeous young professionals from Colombia draped around the tables waiting for high rollers to show up for a little diversion.

Instead he was stuck in a floating cesspool with a bunch of toothless peasants who could barely count. How an adventure hijacking a thousand-foot container ship had degraded into this idiocy was beyond him – it had been a series of stupidities from the word go.

Igor had finally run out of patience and gone to the restaurant to get something to eat after having gone hungry for twenty-four hours, and Leon's stomach was growling a reminder that he hadn't eaten either. He considered asking the captain what sort of food was aboard, but one look at the men's grimy hands and another whiff of the fish stink that permeated everything soured him on the idea.

He pushed himself to his feet and tapped one of his last cigarettes out of a hard pack. Looking around, he withdrew a lighter from his pants pocket and moved to the cabin stairs. "I'm going to get a little fresh air," he announced. Nobody responded. The men were already half drunk on the rum, and if their lingering passenger wanted to dance naked on the back deck, that was his business.

Leon paused at the door. Igor had warned him to stay out of sight.

Then again, Igor wasn't here. He was in the air-conditioned restaurant feasting on seafood while Leon breathed farts and fish guts.

The door opened with a squeal and he mounted the three steps, the fresh air a blessed relief after hours in the confines of the cabin. He lit his cigarette, the flash of the flame blinding him for a split second, and barely registered movement behind him before his world exploded in a starburst of color and his legs went out from under him.

The freshly lit cigarette hissed when it hit the condensation on the deck. Jet caught Leon under his arms and lowered him to the dank metal. The wooden handle of the filleting knife stuck out of the base of his skull where she'd severed his spinal cord with a single practiced thrust. There was almost no blood on the blade when she withdrew it and wiped it clean on his shirt, and after another glance around, she felt along his waist and found the pistol she knew would be there.

She freed it and inspected it, confirmed there was a round chambered, and waited by Leon's body. After five minutes nobody had come to check on him, and all she could hear was the raucous sound of a drunken card game, the insults increasingly colorful. Jet took a deep breath and moved to the cabin entry, anxious to get the inevitable over with.

The captain and crew froze, cards gripped in their hands and cigarettes dangling from slack lips, at the apparition in the doorway – a dripping wet woman holding a gun on them.

"Where are the girl and the man you picked up?" she asked, her voice low and the pistol unwavering.

The captain shook his head. "We never picked them up. There was a change of plans, the man said."

"What man? The one who just came out?"

"No. The other one. He went to get something to eat."

"But there was no girl. You're sure."

"Of course."

Jet debated killing them, but couldn't bring herself to do it. They were innocent, caught in the middle of an ugly situation. She motioned with the gun. "Two ways this can go. If you say anything about having seen me, the guy you picked up on the boat will kill you. Choice B is you chug the rest of that rotgut and I shut the door, and you keep playing cards and never saw anything. So the question really is, how long do you want to live? Is tonight the night you want to die?"

"What about the other one?" the captain asked.

"You don't have to worry about him. This is his gun."

"What about the body?"

"It'll disappear when I leave. In fact, if you know what's good for you, you might want to start the engine in about three minutes and get the hell out of here. Go for a long cruise. Maybe a week somewhere off the coast, and let this all blow over."

The captain put his cards down. "Sounds like we're getting underway."

"Give me three minutes. And not a word, or you're dead men."

The captain held her stare. "I believe you."

The sound of footsteps moving down the pier startled them. Jet shook her head. "Too late. He's coming back. You never saw anything or you're dead. Trust me on that."

Jet turned, any attempt at stealth useless now. Gripping the pistol, she moved to the side of the boat just as the man approaching from the restaurant spotted her. Their eyes locked and he pulled a gun from his belt, and then she was in the air, diving over the side, her splash throwing water onto the deck where Leon's dead form hugged the deck in the darkness.

Igor saw the blur of movement on the boat, and then the woman. He was freeing his gun from his waistband, but it was too late – she was already in the water. He debated shooting at where she'd dived, but it would bring everyone in the harbor down on them. He swore and searched the inky water, but it was no good. She was gone.

He pulled his sat phone from his pocket and dialed Fernanda.

"She came to the boat, but she got away," he said.

"What! How?"

"It doesn't matter. She's still somewhere in the harbor. You said your Panamanian had contacts with the cops?"

"That's right."

"Call him and get them the photo of the woman. And see if you can have them do a roadblock. There's only one way off this peninsula."

"Why do I tell them they should care?"

He glanced down at Leon's body. "She murdered a defenseless man on the boat. She's a killer. Armed and dangerous. If there's such a thing as shoot to kill in Panama, this woman is a prime target."

He could hear the smile in Fernanda's voice. "I'll get right on it."

"Good. I'll have the locals start looking for her." He paused. "These idiots must have tipped her off somehow. She was expecting trouble. She swam all the way to the boat to avoid being seen."

"I told them she was a pro and that they should lie low."

"Obviously not low enough."

"I'll call you back when we have the cops in the bag."

He looked at the water a final time and considered killing the captain and crew, but discarded that option as counterproductive. If they'd seen anything, they were witnesses who could substantiate the identity of the murderer. He tucked his gun back into his waistband and pulled his loose shirt over it to conceal the bulk.

"Perfect. I'll get to work."

CHAPTER 15

SW of Nuquí, Chocó, Colombia

Matt started awake. He listened, senses instantly on alert.

There.

Branches cracking as bodies moved through the brush.

He gently moved Hannah's head and sat up, flare pistol in one hand, flashlight in the other, and peeked through the mesh window.

Someone was coming. He could see the dim glow of lights in the jungle moving down the trail toward the tent.

Now fully awake he checked the time: eleven. He'd got a whopping three hours of sleep. But he was used to worse, and it would have to be enough.

He quickly unzipped the tent entry and slid out. Whoever was nearing would be there in a few more moments. And in rural Colombia, he was under no illusion that they'd necessarily be friendly, especially if they were moving around the jungle in the dead of night.

Three men carrying nets, buckets, and ancient fishing rods appeared, talking in low voices, their clothes shabby and soiled. The lead man, perhaps early thirties and short, with dark skin, ebony hair cropped close to his skull, and a mustache, stopped when he spotted the tent and held his arm out to the side.

Matt studied the intruders from his position behind a mangrove tree. They whispered to each other, and the lead man shined his lamp on the tent, curiosity written across his face. They approached, murmuring among themselves, and Matt stepped from behind the tree and showed himself after slipping the flare gun into his belt.

The men froze at the sight of a disheveled gringo materializing out of nowhere in the middle of the jungle, two days' growth on his face. The lead man's mouth fell open, and when he spoke, he sounded unsure of himself.

"God. You scared us." He hesitated. "What are you doing out here?"

"Ran into some problems with my boat," Matt said, as though that explained everything. "How far are we from civilization?"

The lead man grinned yellow teeth at him, and the others chuckled.

"Civilization? You could argue that for days. But there's a road maybe thirty kilometers inland."

"Thirty kilometers?"

"Yes. But you have to cross a river that's pretty wide right now from the rains. You need a boat to do it if you don't know the shallow spots."

Matt's face darkened. "You going fishing?" he asked, looking at their gear.

"Yes. Better at night."

"Are you from around here?"

The man nodded. "A village near the Arusi River."

"We're in Colombia, right?"

The man laughed good-naturedly. "Of course."

Matt thought for a long moment. "I don't suppose cell phones work out here, do they?"

The fisherman smiled. "There's actually a tower near the road. My phone works, although the signal gets terrible down here near the beach. Too far away."

"Is there any way I can borrow your phone? I have to call my wife and let her know what happened. She's probably going frantic right now."

Hannah's small face poked out of the tent with a rustle, and everyone turned to her. The fisherman eyed her and turned back to Matt. "How old?"

"Two and a half."

"Mine are one and two. Both boys," he said with evident pride. "Strong, like their father."

"We've had a pretty rough day," Matt said, rubbing his face with a tired hand.

The fisherman handed Matt a small, cheap cell phone, the kind sold in convenience stores for next to nothing.

"Thank you." Matt held out his hand. "I'm Tom," he said, using one of the names on the three passports in his bag.

"My name's Luis," the fisherman said.

"Nice to meet you, Luis." He stared at the tiny screen. "What's the nearest town that anyone would have heard of?"

"Oh, maybe Quibdó. But it's not that close. Maybe sixty-five, seventy kilometers northwest, on the Atrato River."

"Quibdó?" Matt repeated, the word unfamiliar to his tongue.

Luis smiled at Matt's attempt. "That's right."

Matt dialed Jet's cell number and listened intently. The line crackled and popped with static, and when the ringing sounded, it was a distorted warble. It went to voice mail, and his mouth tightened into a thin line as he listened to the generic message informing him that the phone was unavailable. He waited for the beep and left his message in English.

"Change of plans. Someone tried to get us. We had to take a lifeboat to shore. Which means they probably know about the fishing boat." He checked his watch. "Be careful. Hannah's fine. We're going to try to make it to the nearest town. It's called Quibdó. On the Atrato River. But it's seventy kilometers from here, and it doesn't sound like there's an easy way to get there, so that plan might change. My sat phone's DOA, but leave a message on the voice mail and I'll call in remotely and check." He paused, thinking about what else to say. "We were double-crossed. Get to Colombia. We'll meet up and decide what to do next."

Matt punched the call off and held it up. "Can I make one more call? I'll pay for them, of course."

Luis's face relaxed. He was clearly worried about the cost of the calls, which made sense. Matt had no idea what a fisherman made in the wilds of Colombia, but he suspected it wasn't much. The irony that everyone now had cell phones, even if they were dirt-poor farmers in the middle of nowhere, wasn't lost on him. The world was a vastly different place than it had been when he was growing up. "Of course."

Matt dialed the sat phone number and entered the code that would allow him to access the voice mail. He listened to the messages, all from Jet, his stomach sinking when he heard her message for Hannah, and then erased them. There was no point in dwelling on how unfair it was that they were again on the run from unknown pursuers. They were, and they would persevere, as they always did.

He handed the phone back to Luis and felt in his pocket for the damp wad of dollars there. He always kept smaller bills on the outside, which made it easy to find a five-dollar bill for the fisherman.

Luis's eyes widened when Matt gave him the money, and an idea occurred to Matt. He looked Luis up and down and then turned to Hannah and smiled before returning his attention to the fisherman.

"Luis, I won't lie to you. My little girl is scared and tired, and we're in real trouble out here. The boat's gone, destroyed in the storm, and we need help. Maybe we can work something out where you help us get to safety and I make it worth your while, instead of you fishing for a few dollars' worth of catch tonight?"

Luis looked at his friends and then turned to Matt. "Anything's possible. What do you have in mind?"

Chapter 16

Puerto de Vacamonte, Panama

Jet watched her adversaries running along the waterfront, any pretensions of subterfuge now abandoned. She counted five including the man on the boat, which was manageable, she thought. The problem was how to get out of the water and to her bag without being seen. She was now by the boatyard ramp, having swum fifty yards into the harbor to a cluster of moored vessels from the fishing boat, instead of returning along the pier as they'd probably expect, and cut over to another group of moored boats.

Three of the five men were walking along the pier, carefully watching the surrounding water, validating her instinct. They weren't that good, or it would have occurred to them that she might have done the unexpected and wasn't trying to make it to shore by the dock at all.

She closed her eyes and saw a map of the harbor in her mind's eye. The only sure way to escape without being a sitting duck involved a tremendous amount of effort on her part, but she could see no alternative. Resigned to having to swim a while, she pushed off from the boats and pulled herself through the warm water toward the surge at the harbor mouth. Nobody would expect her to exit the harbor and swim around the exterior of the long breakwater, which is why that was exactly what she would do.

It took her twenty minutes to swim the quarter mile to the harbor mouth against the incoming tide, and then another fifteen to make it to the point on the other side of the breakwater. She hauled herself out of the water and sat catching her breath, dripping in the muggy heat that had only slightly cooled since the sun had set. She eyed her watch and, aware of the passage of time and that it was working against her, forced herself to her feet.

She jogged down the beach, keeping low, and when she made it to the entry road, she crouched behind a clump of plants, listening for signs of pursuit. The men were all at the waterfront, their attention focused on where she'd try to exit the water, but that wouldn't last forever. She needed to get to her bag and shoes, change into something dry, and vanish before they called in reinforcements or wised up to the possibility that she'd taken the road less traveled.

After several minutes watching for signs of life, she darted across the road. The gravel sent sharp spikes of agony through the bare soles of her feet. She ignored the stinging and powered up the hill until she reached the bunker, and wasted no time changing and donning her shoes. Her feet were bleeding, but there was nothing to be done about it right then. She kept her eyes on the wharf and the men working their way along the shore, refusing to be distracted by physical discomfort.

Done, she field-stripped the pistol she'd taken from the dead man, dried it with a T-shirt, and inspected the bullets. It was a Glock 19, so was no worse for wear in the short term from the sea water, and the bullets appeared fine, so they should fire. Satisfied that she had a viable weapon, she reassembled the gun and stuck it in her waistband.

After another glance at the harbor, she slung her bag over her shoulder and eyed her rental car in the far lot. It would pose a problem for her – the passport and driver's license she'd used to rent it would be compromised if she left it there. It was only a matter of time until it was traced. She hated to lose one of her precious identities, but she could always buy more. She didn't see any alternative and ignored the pang of regret over the gifts that her little girl would never see.

She clamped her eyes shut and sighed. Toys were the least of her problems. Her daughter and Matt were missing, and…possibly…she didn't want to think about it. The idea that whoever was after her had killed them chilled her blood and drained her will to go on. No good could come from that kind of speculation, so she drove the negative thoughts from her mind and focused on the immediate.

Whatever had happened, she first needed to get clear of her pursuers, and then she could formulate a plan. Right now she was still in the lion's den. Objective number one was to escape, and then she'd figure out what to do about Hannah and Matt. She couldn't afford the luxury of speculation or recriminations.

Jet scanned the harbor surroundings through the binoculars, and when she was satisfied that the men were far enough from the main road that she could make a break for it, she bolted from her hiding place and ran down the hill. There was nobody on the road, no lights or movement, and she crossed to the ocean side and set out, paralleling the strip of asphalt that led into the town. She wasn't sure what she would do when she got there, but she'd wing it once she was safely away from the harbor.

Her pace settled into a comfortable jog that she could keep up for hours. Lances of pain shot through her feet, reminding her of the inadvisability of her earlier barefoot slog. She ignored the discomfort and concentrated on getting as far as she could from the waterfront. A glance at her watch told her that it had been an hour since she'd been spotted, but she felt safer with every yard she put between herself and the harbor.

She regretted not being able to extract any information from the man she'd killed, but circumstances had dictated that she dispatch him quickly. It would have been nice to learn who was after her and why, but in the end it changed nothing – whoever it was had learned about Matt and Hannah, and had either done away with them or transferred them to another boat before the *Paloma* had entered the harbor.

Jet passed a cluster of beach homes, some with lights still burning, most dark, and continued to drive herself, keeping her stride fluid as she ran on the sand. Once past the homes the shore veered right, toward Panama City, and she left the beach and continued along the road to town.

Her breathing burned in her lungs as she rounded a gentle bend. She blinked sweat out of her eyes and stopped when she saw the red and blue strobing glow of police roof lights. Up ahead on the road two squad cars were parked across the lanes, creating a roadblock.

She squinted in the darkness, thanking Providence for the overcast that blanketed the shore, making her all but invisible in the gloom, through which she could just make out four officers leaning against the hoods, chatting.

A car approached from the harbor and pulled to a stop as she inched along the shore, not thirty yards from the roadblock. Jet stuck to the clumps of plants growing along the beach, moving from shadow to shadow. When she was past the cars, she heard one of the cops talking to the driver.

"Have you seen this woman on the road or at the harbor?"

A pause. Another voice, presumably the driver, answered. "No. Why? What's she done?"

"Murder. She's considered armed and dangerous. Be careful. If you see anything suspicious, call emergency."

"Murder! Anyone who works at the harbor? I run the restaurant there…"

"No. It's not someone from around here. But that's all I can say. Drive slowly."

Jet cursed her luck. The police asking if anyone had seen her meant they had a photograph. That was bad enough, but that whoever was after her had the juice to get the authorities involved told her that she was in worse trouble than she'd thought. And that they'd linked her to the murder…Panama was a small country. They'd be watching the border to Costa Rica, that being the natural direction to escape. And of course the airports and bus stations. Probably the large ports, too, in case she tried to charter a boat.

She'd seen enough. Jet began moving north again, but stopped when she heard bodies moving through the jungle no more than thirty yards ahead.

She held completely still and heard more twigs snapping. There was definitely someone there. Probably more than just one if it was the cops.

Voices reached her. Male. She couldn't make out what they were saying, but whatever it was probably wasn't good for her. The police had obviously not contented themselves with blocking the road and had put patrols along the jungle perimeter in case she tried to slip by.

Her hand reached for the Glock, her pulse thudding in her ears. Taking out however many cops were in the jungle would pose no challenge, but there was no way she'd be able to outrun a radio. A gun battle would draw a small army to her, seriously complicating her escape.

She'd have to try to evade the patrols. It was the only way.

She just hoped that they hadn't brought dogs. If they had, she was dead meat.

Jet edged along the faint trail she'd been following, ears straining in the near complete darkness for any hint of where the patrol now was. If she'd had night vision gear, it would have been no contest, but without any she was exposed, and it was entirely possible that the police did have NV goggles. In fact, more than possible. Probable.

She glanced around and spied a promising tree behind her. Jet pulled her bag's strap tight across her chest and took in the geometry of the trunk and low branches. Her only hope was that if she couldn't slip past the patrol, she could outwait it and go unnoticed as it moved beyond her.

Jet took a deep breath and ran at the tree. Two steps up the vertical shaft and she pushed off, her body suspended for milliseconds in the air, and then her hands gripped one of the thick lower branches and she used her momentum to swing her legs, once, twice, and then up.

The patrol passed below her ten minutes later. Three policemen toting submachine guns, all wearing night vision gear. She held perfectly still, not daring to breathe as the men moved past her position – none of them looked up, as she'd hoped. She knew that in the dark like this, their instinct would be to keep their eyes on the brush – that was where any threats would come from.

Jet gave the patrol five minutes to continue toward the harbor and then dropped soundlessly in a crouch on the damp ground, the grass cushioning the sound of her landing. After another glance at the time she resumed her push toward town.

Once safely away from the police, she picked up her pace and ran through the brush, ignoring the branches slapping against her as she neared Vacamonte. Fortunately for her, the cops hadn't stationed more men along the road, figuring that she'd never get by the roadblock or the patrols.

Another misjudgment that worked in her favor.

She came to a planned development of cheap row houses, graffiti marring half the exteriors, and slowed, eyeing the sad collection of corroding vehicles lining the dark street. At the second block she spotted what she was after and moved like a phantom between the streetlights to the motorcycle she'd seen.

The lock posed no huge hurdle for her, and within ninety seconds she had the ignition bypassed and was pushing the dirt bike away from the house it had been parked in front of. Three minutes later, she started the engine and cut away toward the highway, reasonably secure that she could rely on the motorcycle not being reported stolen until morning.

She twisted the throttle at the on-ramp and whizzed up onto the highway, the helmet masking her gender and rendering her anonymous to any casual observer. Jet pointed the handlebars south, toward Panama City. Her plan was to lose herself in the crowds, the city large enough that she wouldn't stick out, while she formulated a strategy to evade the manhunt that was sure to follow.

Once over the Panama Canal, she eyed the gas and pulled off at the next filling station – the fuel gauge read empty. A portly attendant filled it for her while she dug in her bag and retrieved her phone. Her breath caught in her throat when she powered it on and saw that she had a message. She paid the attendant and rode to the bathrooms, where she ducked inside and listened to her voice mail.

When she exited the building her face was as placid as a mountain lake at dawn, even as her mind raced furiously at the message from Matt. She glanced around the empty station and pulled up a map on her phone. After a quick calculation she drove back onto the highway, the dirt bike's exhaust buzzing angrily as she gunned the gas. She'd left Matt a confirmation on his voice mail, and now she had a goal: get somewhere safe by daybreak, and ditch the motorcycle where it would never be found so the police would have no idea where she was.

Jet kept her speed down as she drove through Panama City, where traffic was sparse at the late hour, and didn't open the motorcycle up again until she was well out of the city limits, on her way to Colón – the far side of the Panama Canal and the most dangerous place in the country. If she was going to figure out a way to make it to Colombia, she'd need to find someone who regularly crossed the border without bothering with documentation, and in her experience that type of person wasn't to be found in the better neighborhoods. No, she was looking for a cockroach, and cockroaches tended to favor the shadows.

And in Panama it didn't get any more shadowy than Colón.

Her impression as she rode through the city in the dead of night wasn't favorable – the streets exuded menace, the danger palpable. Near the eastern reaches of the city the streets degraded further and the buildings with it, the stink of poverty rising from the dwellings like a gas leak.

She spotted her end point for the night near a market that was selling its wares through a barred window. A garish orange hotel's vacancy sign blinked in the night, the rusting placard in front advertising the cheapest rooms in Colón. After a trip around the block she decided to take a chance. She needed sleep, and she figured the odds that the police had issued a nationwide APB over a waterfront stabbing sixty miles away were virtually nil. Even if they had, this was the kind of place that was off the official map, where nobody asked questions and the police never set foot.

The night clerk appeared to be the proprietor, a sleepy whippet of a man in his seventies, almost completely bald, a huge hearing aid hanging behind his right ear. He showed no interest in anything but her money, and handed her a key on a polystyrene float, in keeping with the place's nautical theme.

The room was exactly what she expected, slightly better than a prison cell but not nearly as secure. Fortunately the window had bars on it, and she was able to prop the lone wooden chair beneath the doorknob, the lock being a bad joke and the safety chain gone, torn from the wooden jamb.

As she lay on the hard mattress in the tiny room, a creaking ceiling fan the only relief from the heat, she thought about her next move. She'd have to alter her appearance and lay low until evening – the sort of men she was interested in meeting wouldn't be early risers and would no doubt be found after dark in the seedy waterfront bars lining the port.

Jet stared at the fan orbiting overhead, the ventilation a joke, and formulated a mental list to complete tomorrow. As she drifted off to sleep, the last image in her mind was of her daughter and Matt, somewhere in the Colombian jungle, a world away.

CHAPTER 17

Colón, Panama

Jet awoke to the sound of a woman screaming at the top of her lungs somewhere in the hall beyond her door. From what Jet could tell, the woman's husband or boyfriend had just now arrived from an all-night binge, and she was expressing her displeasure in an unmistakable way. A man's voice screamed back, and then Jet heard a blow, followed by crying.

She rolled over and pulled the pillow over her head. It was none of her business. The locals could settle their differences however they wanted, hopefully quietly.

She drifted off again, and then a blaring of car horns outside the window ended any further rest. After eyeing her watch through puffy lids, she grudgingly slid her legs off the bed and stood. She'd gotten a total of five and a half hours of sleep, but it felt more like two as she padded to the bathroom, which not unexpectedly looked like a science experiment in the unforgiving light of day.

A tepid shower partially revived her, and she dug new clothes out of her bag. She paused to inspect herself in the hazy mirror and frowned at the abrasions on her face – scratches left by the branches in her mad dash to freedom. A small price to pay, she thought, pulling on a baseball cap and slipping sunglasses on before grabbing her bag and walking out the door.

She pushed through the hotel entrance and took in the bleak neighborhood. Clumps of youths loitered on the front stoops in their best gangsta attire, a testament to the pervasiveness of American rap culture. She ignored the stares and wolf whistles as she moved to where she'd left the motorcycle around the block, and was unsurprised when it was no longer there. One of the positives about predators was they tended to be predictable, and some enterprising thief had solved her motorcycle problem during the night.

She kept moving until she came to a corner market, where she bought a bottle of water and asked about pharmacies in the area. The woman behind the counter scrunched her brow like Jet had asked her the circumference of Jupiter, and pointed off to her right with a vague assurance that she thought there was one a couple of streets away.

It turned out to be three of the most miserable blocks she'd ever had the misfortune to traverse. Every other storefront had been boarded up, and the pungent stench of garbage and urine filled the air as she passed grungy doorways. Faces watched her from upstairs windows framed by bed sheets or towels for curtains, and she was hard-pressed to think of a worse outing – maybe in Africa when she'd been in Sierra Leone for an assassination mission, but Colón was giving it a serious run for its money.

The pharmacy was bare bones, many of the products of the aged inventory past their expiration dates. She found a home hair dye kit that would work, opting for burgundy, which on the box looked like medium brown to her. She also bought a soda and some cheap makeup and asked about breakfast places, but got another blank stare from a teenage boy who looked like he was working that morning because he'd lost a bet.

She found a café further down the street that looked relatively clean and ordered scrambled eggs and coffee, and was surprised when both were delicious. A toothless newspaper vendor entered and waved his wares at the patrons, and Jet signaled him and bought the morning paper.

A photo of the harbor with a close-up of the *Paloma* roped off with crime scene tape was front and center, the coverage long on speculation but sparse on details. A woman was being sought in the murder of Leon Urubia, twenty-nine, of Panama City, unemployed since a dishonorable discharge in the Panamanian army eight years ago. She read the description of the female perpetrator carefully.

Thankfully it could have been any of a quarter of the young females in Panama: slim, dark brown or black hair cropped short, between 5'2" and 5'8", wearing black or gray shorts and a dark top.

The fishermen had obviously taken her advice and seen nothing, so the description was from the man with the gun – one of the bad guys.

The police assured the public that they were tracking down leads and would have more information shortly, which Jet interpreted to mean they had nothing. But that wouldn't last forever, and when they had connected the car with her it would be a matter of hours before they had the passport photo from her Belgian identity – a photo which admittedly appeared so generic it would be hard to recognize her four years later, especially with the help of a little makeup.

Still, it was clear that her time was running short, and this evening she'd need to find someone in the Panamanian underworld who could get her into Colombia with no questions asked.

She ordered a second cup of coffee, and her thoughts turned to Alejandro. If she wasn't afraid he'd sold her out, she would have called him and within minutes had a contact who could provide anything she needed. It still seemed implausible that he was the culprit, but given the circumstances, she had to assume so.

The only reason he would still be breathing this time next month was because Hannah and Matt were alive. If they hadn't made it, there was no corner of the planet safe enough to shield him from her wrath.

Which was all fine, but vows of revenge were no substitute for having a plan. Right now Matt and her daughter were in the middle of a rainforest, doing their best to make it to civilization. Matt was smart and resourceful, and Jet had no doubt he'd lead them to safety. But what then? Where could they go that their pursuers couldn't find them?

Jet turned to more immediate matters. She had money, a gun, and was in the clear, having left no trail for those hunting her to follow. She'd been in far more dire straits at other points in her life and survived, and she had no doubt that she'd live to tell about this one, too. But a part of her was beyond exhausted at constantly having to be on the run, and she promised herself that wherever she and Matt went, this time it would be somewhere safe, beyond the reach of the ghosts of their pasts.

She paid the bill using American dollars, which were interchangeable with Panamanian balboas and accepted everywhere, and began her trek back to the hotel for a makeover. On the way she spotted another hotel, equally suspect, and made a mental note to check into that one for her second night in beautiful Colón.

Jet stopped at a boutique and bought a pair of knockoff fashion jeans and a neon top she'd ordinarily have avoided like the plague, and a pair of kicky heels that would make her taller. She was getting a feel for how the local women dressed, and they didn't appear to be shy about their fashion sensibilities, which seemed to run anywhere from risqué to outright prostitute. If she was going to blend in tonight, like it or not she needed to walk the walk, and if that meant looking like something out of the red light district, so be it. The blouse's only saving grace was that it hung over the waist of her belt, so if she wanted to bring the Glock, she could.

Back in her room she unpacked her purchases and set about dying her hair. An hour later the woman in the mirror had brassy medium-brown locks and looked even less like the passport photo, in which her hair had been long and black. An application of darker base took her skin tone to a light caramel, more like a local, with a racial mix of indeterminate lineage.

She tried on her new outfit and inspected herself, and then shook her head as she grumbled at the mirror. "*Hey, sailor. Twenty dollars makes your dreams come true!*" Her reflection made her laugh, and she sat on the edge of the bed, letting some of the accumulated tension drift away. She was talking to herself and, even worse, cracking herself up. She attributed it to the fatigue and changed back into less attention-getting clothes, preferring not to dote on her little detour from sanity, a pressure relief valve best not examined too closely.

~ ~ ~

Igor paced in his Panama City hotel room, staring through the window at a sliver of Pacific Ocean blue between the skyscrapers on every side. He was on the phone with Fernanda, wearing only his underwear, his body chiseled from countless hours of rigorous training.

"No. They haven't got any leads. She got past everyone somehow," he reported.

"How? I thought you said the police had the road blocked and patrols closing off the jungle."

"They did. I don't understand it either. But she's gone."

"The Panamanian says that they have an APB out on her, and her picture's been circulated with customs. He says with that, the country's locked down. There's no way she can get out."

Igor eyed the buildings and the jungle beyond. "If someone wanted to hide in Panama, it could take decades to find them. It's three-quarters jungle, and Panama City has almost two million people. This is anything but a lock, Fernanda."

"I know. They're doing everything they can."

His tone softened. "How's Colombia? Any progress on that end?"

"I met the gangster who runs the place, and he's got his people looking for the man and girl, but it's kind of the same situation as you're facing. That's a huge slice of jungle, and they could be anywhere."

"You don't sound optimistic."

"Because I'm not," she admitted.

"Did the client okay all this? The expenditures?"

"So far. The instructions were clear: find her and terminate her at all costs. But I get the sense there are limits even to their means." She hesitated. "We'd be better off performing than having to tell them we were unsuccessful."

"You know these are both long shots," Igor said.

"Of course. But what else can we do? We've never failed yet. I don't want this to be the first time. Not with this client. And not with this kind of money involved."

"I'll stay here until I hear otherwise, then," Igor said.

"And I'll remain in Colombia. The gangster has me staying at his compound."

"Well, cross your fingers. So far, everything about this has gone wrong."

"Which means the odds are that it will start to go right from here on out."

"Positive thinking. I like that."

"I don't like the alternative. Think of it as whistling past the graveyard."

"Sure thing. In the meanwhile, I'll keep my eyes open. If she slips up, I'm all over it."

Igor could hear Fernanda sigh.

"Then let's hope she does, and soon."

CHAPTER 18

SW of Nuquí, Chocó, Colombia

Matt and Hannah followed the fishermen down the dirt road. They'd walked for hours after returning at dawn from their fishing expedition, the catch a seven-foot shark and a number of dorado that were schooling close to the beach. They'd agreed to take Matt and Hannah to the nearest rural bus stop fifteen miles away, across two rivers, where a groaning, overloaded 1950s school bus painted every color of the rainbow stopped four times a day.

Bluebottle flies buzzed around them, lured by the fish filets in the burlap sacks, and Hannah busied herself with swatting the air to keep them from landing on her. Matt blotted her face, and then his, with one of his clean T-shirts he was using as a makeshift towel as they took a short break.

"How are you doing, Hannah?" he asked.

"'Kay. When see Momma?"

"Soon, sweetie. Right now we have to keep walking. Can you do that?"

"Feet. Owie."

Matt nodded. "I know. Mine too. But it won't be much longer."

Luis came over and studied the little girl. "She's very good, isn't she?"

"That she is."

"It's a shame about your boat."

Matt looked off into the jungle. "Life can be difficult sometimes. What can you do but keep trying?"

"That's always been my philosophy. No point in complaining."

"No." Matt eyed his almost empty water bottle. "Where can we refill these?"

"There's a stream about another kilometer down the trail. But you'll need to sterilize it before you drink it."

"No problem. I have tablets."

Luis smiled. "My wife boils it. Everyone in my village does. In big vats. Safer that way."

"How big is your town?"

"About a thousand people. Everybody knows each other. It's a simple life, but a good one."

"Sounds pretty appealing to me right about now."

"There is much to be said for it. I moved away, took a job in Medellín, in construction, for five years, but I didn't like living around all those people. I guess I'm not a city kind of guy."

"They have schools here?"

Luis looked at him strangely. "Of course. There's one that serves five villages. It's the law. Everyone can read and write. It's not that primitive. I mean, we have cell phones, and a few even have satellite TV. There's power from the main road. We aren't savages."

"I meant nothing by it, Luis. You've been very kind to show us to the road." Matt held his gaze. "Although I wonder. If I wanted to lie low for a while, with my daughter, someplace remote…would your village be a good spot?"

Luis's eyes narrowed. "Lie low? That depends on what you're lying low from."

"I'd rather not go into it. Let's just say there are some dangerous folks who might be looking for me."

"Cartel?"

Matt shook his head. "No, nothing like that."

"Police?"

"We haven't broken any laws. No, it's more about our not having passports," Matt lied. "We're not in the country legally."

"Ah. Immigration. Yes, that can be a problem." Luis thought about it. "We may be able to put you up for a few days at my house.

We have an extra room. But it's very rustic. Very. You may not like it."

"I'm not picky." Matt lowered his voice. "I would be extremely grateful. I could pay whatever you thought was fair."

"I'd have to discuss it with my wife."

"Of course."

Luis studied Matt's face. "Shipwrecked off the coast, and problems with immigration. You haven't had an easy time of it, have you?"

"No. But as you said. What can you do, other than waking up every day and putting one foot in front of the other?"

Luis laughed. "Very well, then. We'll go to my town. It's about ten kilometers from the main road and called Antonio Salguero. There's no reason you'd have ever heard of it. Most haven't. All that's there are homes, a small market or two, and a few bars. But I like it."

"Sounds like just what the doctor ordered."

Luis considered him. "You may think it's time to get a new doctor once you see it, my friend."

"Well, let me be the judge of that. We're low maintenance. Just need a place to sleep and a bathroom."

"It will ultimately be up to my wife. I hope you understand. She runs the house."

"Of course."

They set off again, the going easier on the wider trail, until a rumble from the sky gave them pause. Luis squinted at the sky through the overhead canopy and sniffed the air. He turned to the others.

"Probably going to get wet."

As if in response, a deafening boom shook the area and the clouds opened up in a deluge. There was nowhere to take shelter, so they kept marching forward. The trail turned to muddy slop as rain collected in dips and ruts, sucking at their shoes with each step. Hannah struggled to keep up, her wobbly legs inadequate for the new challenge; seeing her difficulty, Matt lifted her into his arms and carried her.

The cloudburst lasted half an hour, and when it was over, steam rose from the wet leaves around them. The muggy swelter was almost unbearable, but Luis and the other fishermen trudged on, seemingly impervious to the heat.

At the next rest break, Matt filled the water bottles from a swollen stream and dropped a tablet into each. He shook the bottles until the milky cloud dissipated, and then took a cautious sniff before swallowing a big gulp. He held the bottle for Hannah and she swallowed, then pulled away and made a face. Matt smiled sadly.

"I know. Tastes like poop. But it's medicine so we don't get sick."

Hannah kept drinking, her expression unsure, and Matt's heart skipped a beat. She was trying so hard to be good and to not complain, but she had to be every bit as uncomfortable as the rest of them – maybe worse, because her little tennis shoes weren't made for long treks in the Colombian hinterlands.

When she was done, he carefully removed her shoes and socks and confirmed what he'd been afraid he'd find – angry red blisters. He retrieved antiseptic ointment from the first aid kit and spread the soothing salve on her feet while she put on a brave face, and then dug out a pair of clean socks and pulled them onto her feet as she winced in pain.

Once he'd gotten her shoes back on, Matt repacked the kit and closed it up, and then approached Luis. "I hate to ask you guys for any more help, but I can't carry her as well as all the bags for another ten kilometers. I'd like to buy one of your sacks of fish filets and we'll leave it here, and then maybe you can help with the bags? How much would the fish be worth if you sold it?"

Luis frowned. "That's not the point. It's not about selling it. We're going to eat that for the next week."

Matt had anticipated the objection. "How much does it cost to buy a week's worth of food?"

Luis calculated. "Maybe...twenty dollars?"

Matt fished a twenty from his pocket and handed it to the fisherman. "Done."

Luis slipped the bill into his pants and eyed Matt's bags. "Which one would you like me to take?"

"This one," he said, patting the emergency survival kit.

Luis shouldered it, tested the weight, and grunted. "Okay. Let's get going."

Matt lifted Hannah and seated her on his shoulders, which he knew she loved, and then hoisted their bags. The going was still going to be hard, but the burden was now manageable, and with any luck they'd be able to reach the town before Matt's back or muscles gave out.

Though luck was far too scarce a commodity in the Colombian jungle for his liking.

CHAPTER 19

Frontino, Colombia

Fernanda strolled from her guest room in Mosises' hacienda to the kitchen, where an old woman was chopping vegetables, her breakfast chores completed an hour ago.

"Can I get you anything?" the woman asked upon seeing Fernanda.

"No, I can get it myself," she said, sniffing at the rich smell of fresh brewed coffee. "Just point me to the cups."

"Over here, ma'am," the woman said, gesturing to a cupboard. Fernanda swung the heavy mahogany door open, pulled out an oversized ceramic mug, and then moved to the coffee pot.

She carried her drink out to the veranda, where Mosises and another, younger man, tall and handsome in a swarthy way, were sitting together at a round wooden table. The familial resemblance was immediately apparent as the young man got to his feet along with Mosises.

"Ah, our guest is up and about. Please. Sit. Fernanda, this is my son, Jaime. He is my right-hand man," Mosises said. "I trust you slept well?"

"Yes, thank you," Fernanda said as she shook hands with Jaime. "Pleased to meet you, Jaime."

"The pleasure is all mine," Jaime said with a small inclination of his head.

"Have a seat. We were just discussing your situation," Mosises said, lowering himself into one of the wooden chairs gathered around the rough-hewn table.

Fernanda could almost feel Jaime's eyes roaming over her figure as she took a seat. Her face gave nothing away, but she noted the interest. It was nothing unusual – being Brazilian she was used to the frank admiration of men, ever since she'd blossomed at thirteen, and she didn't hold his reaction against him. Looking was free; but the most beautiful flowers usually had thorns to protect them, and Fernanda was no exception.

She sipped her coffee, the brew rich and strong, no doubt made from the plants lining the hill. Jaime did the same as Mosises – snipped the end from one of his ubiquitous cigars and sniffed it appreciatively before lighting it, puffed to ensure it was fully lit, and then placed it carefully into a clay ash tray in the center of the table.

Jaime cleared his throat and continued from where they'd been interrupted by her appearance. "We've deployed several dozen men and have put the word out to all the local police departments, offering a generous reward for any information leading to the capture of your targets," he said. "Now it's a matter of waiting for something to come back to us. It can take time for news to percolate through to the more remote locations, but they're our best bet."

"How did the search go? With the helicopter?" Fernanda asked.

"It's underway as we speak. But it's well over two hundred kilometers of coastline, most of it covered with jungle, so it will take time," Jaime said, offering what Fernanda guessed he thought was a winning smile.

"My problem is that I have pressing issues that make finding them urgent," Fernanda said.

"Which I fully appreciate, my dear, but we can only do so much," Mosises said, his tone patronizing.

"That wasn't why I hired you," she fired back, annoyed.

Mosises eyes hardened and he took a long, contemplative pull on his cigar before answering, his voice soft but the menace unmistakable. "I'd remind you that it wasn't me who came looking for help. I certainly wasn't in the market to be hired. I did this because you were compelling in your request, and out of respect to my colleague in Panama. But hired?" He shook his head. "I don't think so."

Fernanda sat forward, a small smile playing at the corners of her lips. "I'm sorry, Mosises. Perhaps a poor choice of words. What I meant is that I came to you because I was assured that you controlled the Chocó and Darién regions, and that if anyone could help, it was you."

Jaime cut in. "Which is correct. What my father was trying to convey was that it's a huge area, and there are many scavengers who survive from fishing and by living off whatever drifts up on the beaches. If this lifeboat landed on these shores, it may have already been dismantled or towed away by one of these groups. It's not as straightforward as patrolling the beach and reporting back. Would that it were."

"I can appreciate that," she acceded.

"Our best bet is that we get a tip," Jaime explained. "By letting the right people know that we're willing to pay for information, we've broadened our reach to thousands of villagers and fishermen, not only our handful of men. It's the approach that's most likely to bear fruit, because these little outposts are dirt poor, and a few hundred dollars is a small fortune to many of the police in the area."

"Then all we can do is wait?"

"The helicopter won't be done until this afternoon. I'm hopeful that it will spot something. If not, our insurance is the greed of the villagers." Jaime sipped his coffee and sighed. "Betting on greed is always a safe approach."

They sat in silence for several moments. Clouds of pungent smoke drifted from Mosises as he drew on his cigar. Eventually Jaime finished his coffee and pushed back from the table. "It was a pleasure meeting you, Fernanda. If you need anything while you're a guest in my father's house, don't hesitate to ask," he said, his gaze locking on hers.

She took in his strong jaw and obviously athletic physique and gave him a beaming smile. "I appreciate that, Jaime. It was nice meeting you, too."

He slipped a card from his back pocket and handed it to her. "My cell is always on. Anything you need, I can take care of," he reiterated. "Anything."

Jaime bent down and gave his father a kiss on the cheek, retrieved his cigar from the ashtray, and then turned and strode into the house. Fernanda's eyes followed him, noting the assurance in his step as well as the impeccable tailoring of his clothes. The rumors that the Colombian cocaine business was losing its financial appeal as consumption in the U.S. dropped had obviously not reached Mosises or Jaime.

Mosises regarded her with a wary expression and then sat back in his chair, smoking thoughtfully. "Don't worry. If it can be done, he'll do it. You just need to be patient. His network is second to none, and it would be almost impossible for anyone to hide for any length of time. Even though the jungle can seem like a place where anything goes, it's actually fairly well traveled by the locals, and they'll know if a gringo and a little girl appear in their midst." Mosises glanced up at the sky, where a hawk was soaring above the valley, studying the land far below for unwary prey. He watched its deliberate glide and economical motion, only an occasional flap of wings to maintain or change its elevation, and smiled. "Have faith."

Fernanda didn't push it. She sat back, masking her impatience, and returned the smile. "I have tons of it. But I'm a big believer in being one of those who help themselves. I've found it's bad business to wait and hope."

He nodded. "I understand. The young are always in a hurry. It's only when the years have seasoned you that you realize the virtues of biding one's time."

"I hope to get the chance to discover that for myself. But right now I'd settle for the helicopter radioing in that it's found the boat."

Mosises laughed. "Yes, I believe you would. But it's out of my hands now. The game has been put into motion, and all we can do is watch and wait...and be prepared to strike when our opportunity presents itself."

"I specialize in the striking part."

Mosises appraised her, his laugh dying on his lips. "I have no doubt that you do." He took another puff on his cigar and regarded the glowing ash thoughtfully. "No doubt at all."

CHAPTER 20

Colón, Panama

Jet's heels snicked on the tile floor of the seedy bar as she pushed her way through the double entry doors and made a slow beeline to where a lone bartender stood polishing glasses. This was the second watering hole she'd been to this evening, and she'd already had enough of Colón's waterfront entertainment possibilities to last a lifetime. Rough-looking men with scruff on their faces, their skin burnished dark by constant exposure to the sun, sat drinking at small circular tables, talking among themselves. A few working girls leaned against the bar, giving the patrons the eye, open for business before the night rush got underway.

Jet surveyed the tawdry interior, with its peeling paint, grungy tabletops, and ceramic tile floor so old and stained it was impossible to guess the original color, and her gaze settled on a pair of younger men sitting at the bar – hard-looking, but dressed better than the seamen and laborers at the tables.

She sat on an empty stool next to the men and ordered a beer, which she'd nurse for two hours if necessary while she trolled for the right kind of predator – the sort who either ran the border himself or knew someone who did. The aging bartender at the last bar had told her that she'd have better luck in some of the waterfront towns down the coast from Colón, but she was here now and would give Colón her best effort. Traveling increased her risk of being stopped by the police, even if it was fairly remote, and while her newly dyed hair and more provocative outfit would probably exclude her from serious scrutiny, it was foolish to take unnecessary chances.

The two men looked her up and down, making no effort to contain their leers as she waited for her drink to arrive. The bartender, a middle-aged man with a bulldog face that looked like it had taken more punches than Ali, set a bottle of Panama beer in front of her. She handed him a twenty-dollar bill, drawing raised eyebrows from her new admirers, the closest of whom elbowed his companion.

A bulky television sat on a ledge behind the bar, showing a martial arts movie on an endless loop in the background, the sound off. A has-been B movie actor now more in the C category waddled toward the camera, his bad hairpiece dyed black in defiance of his fifty-something paunch and deeply lined face, the wardrobe department's efforts to conceal his girth by keeping him in a buttoned dinner jacket for most of the movie having the opposite effect, and sneered his lines at another actor. The actor mugged, making it clear he was the villain, and then ten toughs with lengths of pipe, two-by-fours, hatchets, and axe handles appeared from the shadows.

Jet sighed, wondering why nobody had a gun, and watched as the portly star took on the lot of them, barely able to lift his arms in his getup, while his adversaries never landed a blow or mussed his rug. She shook her head and rolled her eyes, then studied the beer bottle label as though it contained ancient wisdom.

"Haven't seen you around before," the man next to her said.

Jet turned and looked at him. A lean build, three days of stubble dusting his jaw, and dark circles under his eyes even though he looked younger than she was. He was wearing a hoodie in spite of the heat. She raised the sweating bottle to her lips and took a swallow, then set it on the wood bar and offered a tentative smile.

"First time for everything," she said in a playful tone.

"What brings you to lovely Colón on a night like this?"

"I want to make new friends."

Another elbow, a snort from the second man, and obvious interest from the nearest one. "Yeah? You don't look like you'd have any problem making friends."

"I'm looking for a special kind of friend."

The man smiled. It had the effect of stretching his skin, making him look like he was in pain. She noted that he didn't waste effort on dental hygiene, his teeth yellow from smoking and neglect. "Is that right?"

"Yes. Someone connected."

The men exchanged a glance. "Connected," the man next to her repeated.

"That's right."

"You a cop?"

She laughed. "Do I look like a cop?"

His eyes were hard and he didn't smile. "It's a yes or no question."

"Then the answer is no, I'm not a cop."

"Because if you were, and you lied to us, nothing we said would be usable."

"Is that right?" she said, her tone bored. The other man hadn't said anything, but when he leaned forward and stared at her, she could see that beneath his beard he had some sort of scar tissue on the right side of his face. If she had to guess, she would have gone with a broken bottle in a bar fight.

When he spoke, his guttural voice matched his looks. "What do you want? Dope? Guns? Somebody taken care of?"

Apparently these boys were a one-stop shop. She took another sip of beer and wondered how likely it was that they weren't full of shit. Probably fifty-fifty, she thought; but she'd come to dance, and these gentlemen were the most likely partners on the floor.

"Nothing like that. I need somebody who can get in and out of Colombia."

"What's the cargo? The customs patrols don't mess around. It's practically impossible to get any serious weight out of Colombia with the number of boats being inspected."

"I don't want to bring anything north. I have a friend who wants to go south."

The man nearest her stared at her in surprise. "South?"

"Yes."

"Why?" he asked suspiciously.

107

"Because he wants to. What does it matter to you?"

The steel in her tone shut them both up. She kept her eyes on the pair, her gaze unblinking, assessing whether they were zeroes or had game. The bottle-faced man cleared his throat and leaned toward her.

"When?"

"Nobody's getting any younger."

"Just one?"

She nodded. If they asked what her imaginary friend had done that he wanted to cross into Colombia without going through formalities like customs or immigration checks, she was walking. Nobody pro would ask that, she knew from experience, and there was no point in wasting her evening on anyone who couldn't deliver.

"I might have a guy."

Bingo.

"A guy?" she echoed.

"A buddy. Has a float plane. Might be interested in doing some low-level night flying if the price was right."

She cocked an eyebrow. "Yeah? What do you think that would cost?"

Bottle-face pulled his friend's sleeve. "Let's go to the bathroom. I need to make a call." He looked at Jet, his expression unreadable. "Don't go anywhere."

"This is as far from anywhere as I can get."

The bartender approached once the two had gone to the back of the bar and pointed to her beer, which was still three-quarters full. He glanced around without seeming to and leaned forward across the bar.

"None of my business, but those two are bad news."

"Really?"

"I didn't say anything."

"Of course not. Listen. I'm looking for someone who can help me with a problem. You know anyone like that?"

"Depends on the problem."

She was about to tell him when the two men reappeared. Jet caught the look of caution in his eyes as he turned away and made a mental note not to underestimate the pair. They returned to their seats and Bottle-face sat next to her this time. He was clearly the brains of the operation, which spoke volumes for whom she was dealing with. Bad news indeed, but perhaps useful.

"My buddy said he's interested, but it'll cost ten grand American."

Jet didn't say anything for several beats. She shook her head.

"Sorry for wasting your time. Have a nice night."

She pushed the beer away and stood. Bottle-face registered surprise and grabbed her arm. "Wait. Sit down."

She looked down at where his hand gripped her, then at the man, and calculated which of the fifty ways she could break his hand or arm she would use if he didn't let go of her. He must have registered the danger because he let go and sat back. She considered possible responses and decided to play out the scenario to see what they came back with.

"He wanted ten, but I told him the going rate's half that," the thug tried. On screen, the chunky action hero was just finishing off the last of the stuntmen, looking like a bear with a beehive stuck on its face as he swung at the villain implausibly. Jet watched the man launch back in a graceful arc as the tubby hero grazed his face with a puffy hand; he landed on the ground, twitched once, and then lay still.

"Still seems pretty steep for, what, a half-hour plane ride?" Jet countered.

"There's a lot of risk."

"Really? The Colombians really patrol the Darién for planes going the wrong way?" she asked in a low voice, with obvious skepticism.

"Five gets him into Colombia, within fifty clicks of the border."

She appeared to think about it, taking her time considering the deal. Reality was she had no other options.

"How much notice does he need?"

"He said he could do it tonight. But payment in advance."

"Oh, yeah? I'll tell my friend. How do I get in touch with you?"

Bottle-face frowned. "Don't you have a cell? Call him. This is a one-time offer."

Jet didn't smile at the hard close attempt, merely nodding instead. "Now it's my turn to head to the bathroom. I'll be back."

The facilities might have been better than a Turkish prison, but not much, starting with the lack of a toilet seat and extending to unmentionable globs of mysterious goop on the floor that gave even Jet pause. She waited long enough to have called someone and then exited, breathing through her mouth until she was back in her seat.

"He says it's a go," she said.

"Cash only," the thinner friend said.

Jet eyed the man. These weren't the brightest, but then again, she wasn't talking to them for their scintillating wit. "I got that. How do we do this?"

"Can you get the money and be back in an hour?" Bottle-face asked.

"Of course."

"Then we'll meet you by the statue of Christopher Columbus in the park near the waterfront, on Paseo del Centenario. You can't miss it. Everyone knows where it is." He held up his cheap, oversized watch – overcompensation for something, she had no doubt. "One hour."

"At the statue. Got it. We'll be there," she assured them.

Bottle-face and his buddy looked her up and down, grinning like fools. They'd probably just made off the finder's fee what they pulled in on a good week. They both gave her the creeps, low-level maggots, but it was a seller's market, and she wanted to see Hannah and Matt before the sun set tomorrow.

She didn't look back as she strode to the door, heels tapping out a tattoo on the tile as half the eyes in the place admired her. She couldn't wait to get the outfit off, but she had to admit she fit in now, whereas with her usual black cargo pants, running shoes, and muted top, she would have looked out of place.

In the end it didn't matter. She had an hour to kill, and then, with any luck, she'd be winging her way toward her daughter.

CHAPTER 21

Santiago, Chile

The lights of the Metropolitan Hospital were dimmed for the night. The wards were empty except for nurses and the sick, the teaching hospital's doctors having gone home earlier. The corridors were redolent with the distinctive aroma of antiseptic and bleach, the odor of hospitals everywhere, a smell that permeated clothes and hair and never completely washed out no matter what the staff did.

An air conditioner hummed overhead, blowing a stream of frigid air into the already cool halls, as if modern medicine could chill infirmities away rather than battling them on a daily basis. The doors to most of the rooms were open on the critical care floor, where death was a regular visitor and few stayed long.

Two nurses sat behind a circular counter, talking in muted tones, occasionally glancing to where a bank of monitors displayed the vital signs of the unfortunates asleep in the ward's occupied beds. Most would leave in body bags, but that was the job, and after enough years it either ate at you to the point where you quit the field, or you hardened and dug in, watching the endless stream of humanity come and go, a constant reminder of the frail hold living things had on this world.

Down the hall, in a room with four beds, one of the reclining patients' eyes flickered open. The prone man blinked several times, as though confused by the darkness, and then slowly worked his fingers into a fist – first one hand, then the other, ignoring the discomfort of the IV line.

Five minutes later he repeated the process with his lower appendages, taking his time, waiting until he was confident that all the circulation and feeling had returned. He had no idea where exactly he was, other than in a hospital. Memories of his last waking moment rushed back to him and he tried to sort through them, to make sense of the jumble of images. After another minute, he turned his head, first in one direction, then the other, testing, ensuring he wasn't paralyzed or injured so severely that he couldn't easily move.

Satisfied that he was intact, his hands roved down his torso, probing. A lance of pain spiked through his ribcage when he reached the lower ribs – broken, no doubt, but he could manage the discomfort. When he was finished with his body, he felt his head and the cool, soft bandage wrapped around it. He repeated the inspection and drew a sharp intake of breath when he reached the back of his skull – it felt like he'd taken a hell of a blow, that was for sure. His fingers slipped beneath the bandage and fumbled with the clips that held the long strip in place.

He got it loose and felt his hair, which was greasy from being under the wrap. A ridge at the back of his head got his attention – a strip of stitches, now removed, but still swollen.

And yet he had no recollection of a head injury, much less getting patched back up. He wondered whether he could have suffered some sort of brain damage that had expunged his memory, but since there was nothing he could do about it if he had, he dismissed it as a distraction.

He studied the IV cannula in his arm and the pulse oximeter on his finger. The monitor behind him beeped softly with each beat of his heart, but instead of reassuring him, it annoyed him.

He needed to get out of the hospital. Now.

Because...

It all came back to him in a rush. Of course. He had a job to do. One that he obviously hadn't finished. But he needed to if he was going to get paid.

Eyeing the IV, he saw that it was only plasma, no antibiotic in the mixture, and was barely dripping, keeping him hydrated. He didn't know how long he'd been out, but judging by the healing scar, it had to have been at least a week.

He drew a deep breath and extracted the cannula, then applied pressure to the vein until the hole in his skin had clotted. He waited an extra minute and wondered whether he had any clothes in the small closet on the other end of the room. Only one way to find out, he figured, and sat up.

His head throbbed a protest, but it was manageable. He'd dealt with worse. The bullet scars and knife wound were more than enough proof of that. He waited, looking at the other beds, all empty, which was a mixed blessing – if he'd had roommates, at least they might have had clothes, increasing the odds of his being able to slip away without attracting attention. A naked man would draw stares.

When he felt stable, he removed the pulse oximeter sensor and cringed involuntarily at the alarm that sounded from both the infernal machine and the nurse's station down the hall. Running footsteps greeted him as he walked unsteadily toward the closet, and he swung the door open, half leaning against it for balance.

Maybe he'd been bedridden for more than a week, he thought sourly as a frumpy nurse with a frizz of curly red hair filled the doorway.

He ignored her and studied his clothes – the pants were ripped at the knees, and his shirt was missing. At least his windbreaker was there, if a little worse for wear.

"You…you need to lie back down. You're in no condition to be up," the nurse said, surprise and caution in her voice.

Drago cleared his throat, and it felt sore. He must have been intubated, judging by the raw swelling. Up until a day or two ago, he knew from prior experience. After two days it wouldn't still hurt.

"I need to go," he said, the four words all he could manage.

"Go? You can't go. You can barely stand."

He looked down at his bare legs and the blue paper gown he was wearing. "How long have…how long have I been here?"

"Nine days. You're lucky to be alive. You suffered a concussion, broken ribs, blood loss, hypothermia…"

"Where?"

The nurse didn't understand the question, so he narrowed it for her. "Where was I found?"

"You don't remember? It was north of Santiago. In the mountains. Near San Felipe."

Right. That rang a bell.

"Where am I?"

"In Santiago. At the specialty hospital. Neurology. You were in a coma. There was subcranial bleeding. They were able to stop it and dissolve the clots, but you didn't regain consciousness…until now."

"Well, I'm leaving. You can stay if you want to watch me dress," he said, and retrieved his clothes from the hangers. At least someone had laundered them, he noted, as he turned toward her.

"I'm calling the doctor. You're endangering yourself."

"I appreciate that, but I'm an adult."

"You're not well."

He tore the robe off and stood, naked, staring her down. "Are we done?"

She turned and practically ran out of the room.

He had his pants on and his windbreaker zipped up in twenty seconds, and then cursed silently when he realized he had no shoes. But he'd be able to deal with these inconveniences once he was out of the hospital. The first vulnerable pedestrian within reach would supply him with sufficient money to buy essentials – and most importantly, would probably have a phone.

Because, Drago thought, he needed to make a few calls and reassure his client that he was on the job.

And then finish it before the client expressed his displeasure in an unmistakable, and permanent, way.

CHAPTER 22

Colón, Panama

Jet walked quietly down the dark winding street to the waterfront, cautiously aware of her surroundings, the area deserted except for the occasional scavenger rooting through the garbage. The heat was still oppressive and the air heavy with moisture, the humidity and temperature a constant at the equator.

She'd changed out of her heels and donned her boots, and the Vibram soles were silent on the pavement in spite of her hurried pace. She'd gone back to her hotel and gotten her bag, slipping out without the night clerk seeing her – not hard given the volume of the television in the office near the front desk.

The clerk had looked up when the brass bell mounted above the door had sounded, but his curiosity had only extended to a glance, and by then she was already over the threshold and on the sidewalk. Jet breezed past a group of teenagers loitering in the doorway of a run-down building, their sneers and bold looks of no consequence to her, and stopped at the corner market to get a bottle of water, partly to ensure they didn't follow her. She wasn't worried about fending for herself, but she didn't have the time to deal with any distractions and so opted for discretion.

When she returned to the street, she was relieved to see that the group hadn't moved, and she continued around the corner to the main street that led to the waterfront. It would take her no more than fifteen minutes to make it to the statue, an iconic centerpiece in a park that ran down the center of the main boulevard just before it dead-ended at the Caribbean Sea.

The streets were empty, the main boulevard lined by structures in serious disrepair, plaster peeling off the façades, doorways boarded up, and trash choking the gutters. As she neared the park, she made a mental note that the Colón waterfront was not the neighborhood in which to take a pleasure stroll at night. She caught movement out of the corner of her eye and glanced over her shoulder – no obvious danger, just a drunk vagrant passing a bottle of cheap rum to a companion in a darkened doorway.

She crossed a side street to another long block where bright yellow, green, pink, red, and blue houses fronted the street. Their porch lights were mostly broken or turned off, leaving only slim illumination from the infrequent streetlamps to light her way. The contrast between Colón and the seemingly boundless prosperity of Panama City, on the opposite end of the canal, was stark, and she wouldn't be sad to see the last of Colón once she'd done her deal with the two miscreants.

As she passed a pink and white church at Calle 5ta, the buildings degraded even further, becoming abandoned husks, windows broken out and doors sealed with discarded wood scavenged from pallets and crates. Now the graffiti was constant, running across every surface –turf marks from street gangs to warn away any would-be interlopers.

She gazed down the length of the remaining park, which was dark as a tomb, and slowed her pace. The location of the meet was troubling, but not overtly so. Criminals tended to favor the shadows, and it didn't surprise her that those engaged in human trafficking might want to do their transactions in a place where the police didn't dare go. Her eyes swept the area as she walked the final two blocks to the statue. The bronze depiction of Columbus was faintly visible against the partially cloudy night sky, standing silent in the boulevard park lined by palm trees, the greenery of its grass marred by garbage.

A loud crack like a sound-suppressed rifle startled her from her right and she spun, ducking. Her eye roamed over the two-story clapboard building from where the sound had come and she relaxed. Laundry hung from a clothesline, and one of the wet sheets had caught in a random gust from the sea and slapped the deteriorating wood siding. She willed her breathing back to normal, and her pulse slowed to its usual moderate pace.

She stopped at the cement base of the statue and looked around. There was nobody about, anyone sane having abandoned the dangerous streets to the nocturnal predators. She waited, watching her surroundings, occasionally checking her watch. The two losers were late, but that hardly surprised her – they hadn't impressed her as being particularly organized or punctual.

Muffled footsteps greeted her from the side street, and she turned to see who was approaching. It was the thinner of the pair, still wearing his hoodie and glancing around nervously, possibly because even a lowlife like him wasn't comfortable in the deserted area.

When he was ten feet away, he stopped. Jet didn't like that he had his hands in his hoodie's pockets, nor how his eyes never stopped roaming around the park.

"You got the money?" he asked in a low voice.

"Of course," she answered.

"Let's see it."

She reached into her bag and pulled out a wad of hundreds secured with a rubber band. "See?"

The thin man offered her a skeletal grin. "Hand it over."

"Not so fast. Where's your pilot buddy?"

"He's waiting for me to call him and confirm you paid."

Jet shook her head and replaced the wad of cash into her bag. "That's not how I play. No pilot, no money."

The thin man took a step toward her, his expression tightening. "Give me the money," he snarled.

Jet heard a scrape from behind her and spun just in time to avoid being brained by Bottle-face swinging a length of heavy chain at her head. The chain struck a glancing blow on her left shoulder, and her whole arm went numb. But she remained in motion, and she followed through on her move by whipping an eighteen-inch length of pipe from her bag and swinging it hard against Bottle-face's ribs.

Her efforts were rewarded by his scream of rage and pain as several of them broke with audible snaps.

Jet didn't have time to congratulate herself – the thin scumbag was rushing her with a knife. She had to keep him far enough away that he couldn't stab her, the pipe and the reach of her legs her only options. She'd trained sufficiently and been in enough hand-to-hand combat situations to know that if he got close enough to use the knife, even if she won the fight, she'd be cut up, the only question being how badly.

Fortunately the thin man wasn't very good with the blade, and when he took a swipe at her she easily avoided it before kicking him full in the center of the chest, knocking the wind out of him. He wavered for a split second, just long enough for her to bring the pipe to bear on him, and when it struck his hip he blanched and went down, hard.

Bottle-face had recovered enough to swing the chain again, but he was too slow, and she jumped back with catlike grace. He glowered as she flexed her left hand, willing the feeling to return, and he swung at her again. This time she didn't jump back, but rather ducked the blow and slammed him in the knee with the pipe. He howled in agony as his leg buckled, his kneecap shattered, the pain obviously excruciating.

She regarded the two downed men, both having apparently lost their appetite for tackling her a third time, replaced the pipe in her bag, and removed the Glock, chambering a round. The two men's eyes widened at the sight of the gun wielded by the completely calm, hardly winded woman who now had it trained on the thin man's head.

"Everyone dies eventually. Tonight could be your turn."

He shook his head and dropped the knife. "No. Please."

"Where's the pilot?" Neither said anything. She pointed the gun at the thin man's knee. "You don't answer, you'll be walking around on sticks the rest of your miserable life. I'm looking for an excuse to shoot you. Please. Please give me one."

The thin man grimaced in pain. "There…is…no…pilot."

"So this was all a setup for your incompetent robbery attempt?" Her face darkened with anger at having wasted valuable time she didn't have.

The distant rumble of engines from the canal drifted over the waterfront as huge ships worked their way through the harbor to begin their trip to the Pacific side.

Jet considered further injuring the men but decided against it. Right now they'd have to go to a hospital for the broken bones and contusions, but they probably wouldn't tell anyone that a woman had beat them up when they were trying to assault her. If she took this any further, they might have second thoughts. Best to leave them to their fate and get going while she could make a clean getaway.

"You two are so lucky my friend hasn't shown up yet. He'd take great pleasure in carving you into dog food with your own knife." She paused and looked them over. "Empty your pockets."

Bottle-face glared at her. "What?"

"Empty them. I want to see your wallets and your money, so I know who he should come after if I hear you're causing us any grief." She motioned with her gun. "Do it, or I'm going to play drums on your skull with the pipe. Want to add a concussion to your night's earnings? Try me. Or maybe I'll just wait for him to get here and leave him to deal with you."

They had their wallets out in seconds.

"Toss them over here," she said. Jet took their driver's licenses and all their money – maybe sixty dollars between them. She stood and slipped the Glock back into her bag and waved the money at them. "Pleasure doing business with you. I ever see either one of you again, you're going to be in wheelchairs. Do you understand me?"

They nodded, and she pocketed their IDs and cash. There was no point in prolonging the exchange, so she pirouetted and sprinted into the darkness, leaving them to find their way to help on their own. By the time they did, she'd be long gone from the area, although her problem hadn't changed – she needed to get to Colombia, and there was no land route through the Darién Gap. Which meant she was right back where she'd started the evening, and had only a few more hours to find someone to help her.

CHAPTER 23

Antonio Salguero, Colombia

Luis led Matt and Hannah through the muddy lane that served as the main drag of the rural hamlet of Antonio Salguero. Most of the homes were little more than shacks built from rough timbers hewn from the native trees, single-story affairs all badly in need of paint. Luis pointed out a bar and the hut next to it that served as one of the town's restaurants, as well as another building, the only cinderblock building in sight – a market, which featured a corroded sign advertising the local beer and a stack of blue plastic five-gallon water bottles in a dusty rack outside the front entrance. A few yards behind it, the brown water of a river swirled and rushed past, the town's principal source of food.

A group of small children ran screaming after a mud-smeared ball in the middle of the road, smiles of delight on their faces that changed to frank curiosity when they saw Matt and Hannah approach, Hannah perched on Matt's shoulders like a princess riding an elephant to her coronation. They stopped their impromptu game and stared at the apparition, as unexpected as if the little Caucasian girl had landed in a flying saucer.

Luis introduced Matt to a few neighbors who were sitting on upended crates in front of their dwellings, whose doors and windows were flung open wide for ventilation as the sky's purple and blue transitioned to burnt orange and red, streaks of high clouds marbling the sunset as night approached.

The other fishermen split off at a junction, Luis and Matt plodding right, they going left. Luis waved to friends of his working on some sort of fish trap next to one of the larger buildings as they lugged the bags to a modest home at the end of the way. Luis eyed them when they arrived at the house, and shrugged apologetically.

"I told you it was a simple place," he said. "But we have electricity, running water provided by the cistern on the roof, and mosquito netting on the windows, so you won't catch dengue or malaria."

"That's fine, Luis. We're not expecting a palace."

Two brindled dogs ran out the front door and loped to Luis, tails wagging at his arrival. He set Matt's bag down and knelt near what passed for his porch and petted them, hugging them both and murmuring in their ears. Expressions of pure adoration beamed from their canine smiles, and then he released them and they moved cautiously to Matt, who lowered Hannah down and set her on her feet. The dogs sniffed them, and the youngest of the pair licked Hannah's face with a wet slurp, causing her to giggle and try to pull his ear. Matt could see they were used to young children, because he suffered the abuse without protest and the second dog joined in the lick fest.

"That's Oscar and Sammy. They're good boys. Very friendly," Luis said, and looked up when a slim woman in her twenties filled the doorway. He stood and gave her a hug and a peck on the cheek, but her eyes never left Matt and Hannah. Matt saw that she was still somewhat of a beauty, high cheekbones and raven black hair pulled back into a tight bun, a light sheen of perspiration on her face shining in what remained of the daylight. "This is my wife, Carlita." He gave her a smile. "Carlita, this is Tom and Hannah."

She stepped forward, a shy look in her eyes, and shook Matt's hand before kneeling down and shaking Hannah's. She looked up at Matt with a smile. "She's gorgeous. You're a very lucky man, Tom," she said.

"Thank you. I am."

"Carlita, I invited them to stay with us for a day or two, in the extra room," Luis said, and after giving her a pointed stare, moved into the house. He looked over his shoulder at Matt. "Will you excuse us for a minute?"

"Sure. We'll just enjoy the evening," Matt said, understanding that he needed to explain the situation to his wife in private. Matt suspected Luis didn't appear from his fishing trips with gringo guests regularly, so it would take some discussion for Carlita to get used to the idea of strangers in the house.

Hannah was fully occupied by the dogs, who had taken an instant liking to her and were lavishing her with attention as she played with them, running a few feet and being chased by the pair before exploding in peals of laughter. Matt was glad to see she wasn't limping too badly, and for a moment, at least, had forgotten about her blistered feet. His, on the other hand, felt like someone had poured liquid fire on them, and his first project after a shower was going to be to coat them with antiseptic so they didn't get infected.

The thought of a shower led his eyes to the black plastic cistern on the roof, which he guessed refilled automatically with the regular rain. He glanced around the dirt street at the few cars, all of them badly rusting, Japanese economy sedans from the sixties and seventies that should have gone into a crusher twenty years ago. He was accustomed to poverty from his time in Thailand and Laos, but even so, this was about as bad as he'd seen outside of the most remote hill tribes in those impoverished lands.

A man in the next house came outside and smiled at Matt in greeting. "*Buenas tardes*," he said, as if he'd known Matt for a decade.

"Nice evening, isn't it?" Matt replied in Spanish, waiting for Luis to return.

"That it is. You a friend of Luis'?"

"Yes," Matt said, not elaborating.

"Cool out tonight. Probably will rain later," the neighbor said.

Matt nodded noncommittally – if this was cool, he didn't want to know what hot nights were like in the Colombian jungle town. "Could be."

Matt was spared more small talk by Carlita and Luis' return. Carlita was all smiles, Luis having no doubt explained the financial windfall their stay meant to the little family. Two small faces peeked around their legs from the interior of the house, and Luis patted the little boys' heads.

"These are my sons. This is Baco, and the little one is Miguel."

Matt smiled, and Hannah eyed the little boys curiously, as they did in return.

Carlita cleared her throat. "Luis tells me you've had a rough couple of days. Come. Let's get your things inside, and I'll show you to your room. I'm sorry it's not more than it is…"

"Lead the way." He turned to Hannah. "Hannah? Come on, sweetheart. Let's go."

She tottered over to him as he hefted the bags, the dogs following like guardians. Carlita led them through the main room, its simple furniture made from the same wood as the house, to a bedroom at the back, ten feet square, with a mattress on the floor. To Matt, after a night in a lifeboat and another swatting at bugs in a tent, it looked like the honeymoon suite at the Ritz.

"I told you it's nothing to brag about," Luis said from behind him.

"And here is the bathroom," Carlita said, swinging a door open. Matt glanced inside and was surprised that it was not only clean but had a shiny linoleum floor.

"I built it myself," Luis said with pride. "All that time in construction taught me a thing or two about plumbing and finishes."

Matt eyed the bathroom and smiled. "It's perfect. In fact, my first action is going to be to wash Hannah and myself off. It's been a long couple of days."

"There's soap in the shower. I'll get you some towels," Carlita said as Luis sniffed the air.

"Mmm," Luis said. "Smells like stew of some kind. Carlita is the best cook in the world. You're in for a treat."

Matt, who hadn't had anything but dry survival rations for two days, was suddenly starving, his mouth watering at the mention of stew. "Great. Give us twenty minutes and we'll be there," he said as Carlita reappeared with two towels.

Once Hannah was scrubbed clean, he fitted her with fresh clothes and did a fast rinse himself. The trickle of water from the showerhead never felt better, and when he emerged from the bedroom carrying Hannah in one arm, her shoes, socks, and a tube of ointment in the other, he felt human again.

Carlita was in the kitchen, moving between pots and pans. The two little boys were playing on the clay tile floor, which mostly consisted of the older one tickling the younger one and making faces while the one-year-old laughed. Matt moved to the sofa, which appeared to be older than he was, and sat down with Hannah on his lap. Carlita watched as he dabbed ointment on her feet and carefully rolled her socks on, assuring her in a soft voice that she was very brave and they'd feel better soon.

"You're really good with her," Carlita said. "That's touching to see."

"She's had a bad time of it. But she'll heal. Kids do."

"What happened to your hand?"

"I broke it in a fall. It was stupid. I should have known better."

Carlita sighed as she stirred something that smelled delectable. "Luis is more traditional. He hunts and fishes and leaves the children to me." She gave him a smile, and he noted again that she had a quiet beauty. Something flashed in her eyes, and he looked away. "It's good to see a man who isn't afraid to be gentle."

Matt wasn't sure, but was Luis' wife flirting with him? If so, he wanted no part of it. He was lucky the fisherman had agreed to give them shelter, and the last thing he wanted to do was rock any boats.

His speculation was interrupted by Luis emerging from his bedroom wearing a colorful shirt and a pair of jeans. He walked into the kitchen, sniffed at the pots, and gave Carlita a kiss on the back of her neck before moving into the living area and sitting on the floor with his boys. The dogs trotted over and nudged him, everyone wanting attention. As Matt watched Luis, he thought that he looked like a truly happy man. Would that someday Matt would have his family gathered around him in a safe place, maybe a dog or two to warm his feet, enjoying the simple pleasures of companionship and love.

Carlita announced that dinner was ready, and everyone took their places at the dinner table, a slab built from planks and held together by heavy iron nails. The meal was extraordinary, a fish stew with a dizzying variety of spices and vegetables, and by the time he was finished, Matt had eaten so much he felt like he could barely walk. Even Hannah, usually finicky, slurped down her whole bowl with some help from Matt, and when dinner was over, the large pot of stew had been drained.

Conversation revolved around the chickens Carlita and Luis raised and sold to a distributor who dealt with restaurants in the larger towns. Apparently it was a competitive business, nothing ever certain, the prices rising and falling as supply and demand waxed and waned.

Once the table was cleared, Luis rose, stretched his arms over his head, and regarded Matt. "I'm going to the bar with some of my friends for a beer. You want to come?"

Matt shook his head. "Thanks, Luis, but no. I'm tired. Maybe some other time."

Carlita glanced at Hannah. "If you want to go, I can watch your daughter."

"No, I'll stay in tonight."

"You sure?" Luis said. "The beer's always really cold."

"That's good to know. Maybe tomorrow?"

Luis shrugged. "Okay." He glanced at his wife. "I'll be back later."

A pot clattered in the sink as she rinsed it. "Not too late, please, Luis."

He waved a hand at her and furrowed his brow. "Don't worry."

When he left, the two dogs trailing him down the muddy way, Matt saw Carlita watching him through the open window, a sad expression on her face. As if sensing his scrutiny, she turned to him and offered a pout. "Another night alone with the boys," she said, and went back to her chores.

Matt didn't require a long explanation to understand the dynamic that was likely the norm in their little household, but it was none of his business. Everyone had to carve what life they could out of their circumstances. He was in no position to pass judgment.

"Good night, Carlita. Thanks for the wonderful hospitality. I'll never forget that dinner," he said, rising and reaching out his hand to Hannah. He thought Carlita looked sad when she glanced over at him.

"Sleep well, Tom. And you too, Hannah."

CHAPTER 24

Colón, Panama

Jet returned to the bar where she'd met the two scumbags and took a seat at the counter. The bartender saw her and came over, a surprised look on his face.

"Nice to see you again," he said.

"Thanks."

"What'll you have?"

"A Panama," she said.

"Coming right up."

He turned back to her with the beer and set it down on the bar. "Anything else?"

She leaned forward after glancing to either side. "I need to find someone who can help a friend of mine get to Colombia."

The bartender's eyes narrowed. "There are plenty of flights. The ferry. Lots of options."

"He wants something more…private."

A loud voice to her right called for a rum and coke, and the bartender looked over and frowned. "Let me think about it."

When he came back a few minutes later, he had a slip of paper in his hand. "That's the name of a bar in Portobelo. It's about twenty miles east of Colón. It's a rough place, but that's where the captains hang out. Ask for Juan Diego. Tell him Paco sent you." He studied her. "Did those two try anything?"

She fought the smile that tugged at the corners of her mouth and took a single sip of beer. "I have no idea what you're talking about."

His eyes flitted to her top and then back to her face. "Glad to see you made it back in one piece."

She slipped a twenty across the bar to him. "You never saw me. Thanks for the tip."

He palmed the bill with the dexterity of a magician, glanced around the bar again, and then fixed her with a playful expression. "I have no idea what you're talking about."

They both smiled at the same time. "See you around."

He watched her walk out of the bar and shook his head as he muttered to himself. "I highly doubt it."

Finding her way to Portobelo was more of a challenge than she had bargained for at the late hour. Two of the taxis she flagged down refused the fare, and the driver that finally agreed looked at her like she was mad. She tossed her bag into the backseat and slid in, checking her watch as she did so: 10:40.

"How long will it take to get there?" she asked.

"An hour, hour and a half."

"I thought it was only twenty miles."

"Maybe as the crow flies. But the road's a two-lane and winds all around the coast." He eyed her in the rearview mirror. "And it's very dangerous at night."

"Bandits?" she asked.

The driver laughed. "No. Cows and goats. They like to sleep in the road."

"Oh."

The drive was harrowing, through jungle, not a star in the sky, no traffic lights, just the old taxi's dim headlights barely cutting through the gloom. The radio played a string of calypso songs the entire way, and by the time they rolled through the grim town's outer reaches, she'd heard enough of steel drums to last a lifetime.

The driver dropped her off a block from the bar, near the old fort that was the centerpiece of the town. She was the only person on the street as she neared the watering hole's entrance, which was about as inviting as an open wound. Within a few feet of the door she could hear inebriated laughter, loud music, and voices raised to be heard over the din. She glanced up at the sign over the entrance, which featured a billfish with its fin around the waist of a stylized woman so

129

pneumatic she looked like a female version of the Michelin man, and shook her head. It was after midnight, she was in a certifiable hellhole, had no place to stay, and was being sought by the police. And her best option was to look for a mysterious captain based on the tip of a bartender she'd known for all of five minutes.

She pushed the door open, stepped inside, and was greeted by a scene that confirmed her worst fears: five or six tables of rough-looking men sat smoking and drinking with obviously paid company, the women harder than the men, used up and running out the clock. She didn't allow her gaze to linger on any of them as she approached the bar, ignoring the stink of tobacco and rot and unwashed bodies, the single overhead fan inadequate to do anything but blow the clouds of smoke from one side of the room to the other.

Jet had changed back into her heels in the taxi and so looked right at home with the other hoochie mamas working the room, although there was no comparison in either age or beauty. She ignored the stares and walked to the bar, where a thick man with a shaved head and skin the color of tree bark eyed her impassively.

"Panama," she said. He gave no indication of having heard her, merely slid a drawer open, pulled a beer out, and set it in front of her. She nodded to him and he gave her a blank stare. Any hope that Portobelo was a friendly place evaporated. If the bartender was any indication, she was in for a rough time of it.

She took a pull of the beer, which was so cold it made her teeth ache, and leaned forward. "Is Juan Diego here?"

The man's eyes flitted to a table in the corner before he turned away, ignoring her. She took a slow sip before twisting and looking where he'd glanced. A scruffy man in his fifties was sitting alone at one of the little tables, a cigar smoldering in the ashtray and a three-quarters empty bottle of Seco Herrerano in front of him, its white label gleaming in the gloom.

Jet rose from the bar and crossed the room. When she reached the table, she gave the man her best disarming smile. "Juan Diego?" she asked.

He looked up at her with bloodshot eyes. "Go away. I don't want any."

She pulled the chair out across from him and sat down. "I was given your name by Paco."

He studied her. "Yeah? What's that thief doing handing my name out?"

"He said you might be able to help me."

Juan Diego appraised her, then refocused his attention to the scarred tabletop. "Help you with what?"

"I have a problem. I have a friend who needs to get to Colombia in a hurry. But he doesn't want to have to deal with immigration."

Juan Diego grinned morosely. "Who'd he kill?"

She forced herself to laugh. "It's nothing like that."

He drained the rest of the tumbler of seco and poured another two fingers. "It never is."

"There's some urgency to it, though."

"I figured that, since you're in this armpit after midnight and you're not selling your ass."

She sat back. "Can you help?"

He tossed back half the glass in a swallow and looked at her hard. "I'm kind of busy right now."

"You don't look busy."

Juan Diego grunted and eyed the bottle. "I am."

"I can pay."

He sighed and took a puff of his cigar, frowned, and then set it back in the ashtray. "You got cash?"

"Yes."

"On you?"

Jet parried. "How much is it going to take?"

"Five grand, no negotiations. Payment in advance."

"How will you get my friend across the border?"

"I have a boat."

She absorbed that. "Can you leave tonight?"

He shook his head. "Too drunk. Tomorrow night. Got to fuel up, change some filters, get my crew onboard and prepare. You don't make that run alone, or without full tanks, or not checking the weather. That's one of the most dangerous stretches of water around. Get too close to shore in the wrong spots and you'll get shot at. Go too far offshore and you'll pick up a patrol. It's not something you do after a bottle of seco with no planning. Sorry."

Jet eyed the inebriated captain's unshaven face, bleary gaze, and sun-damaged skin. She'd done similar deals in the Middle East, in Africa, on every continent. Those whose business it was to skirt the law tended to burn the candle at both ends. Occupational hazard.

"When do I have to pay you?"

"Before the boat sails. Not here. I don't want to get killed on my way home." He looked her up and down. "Assuming you have the money with you."

"Do I look stupid?"

Juan Diego shook his head again, slowly and deliberately. "You look a lot of things, but stupid isn't one of them."

"How do I get in touch with you?"

"I'll sleep this off and reach out to you tomorrow. Where are you staying?"

"I haven't decided."

"There's a bed and breakfast two blocks from here. Let's assume you're going to be there. I'll leave a message at the desk."

"You want to know my name?"

"Sweetheart, there won't be a lot of young women checking in at two in the morning. My guess is the message will find you just fine."

Jet pushed back from the table. "Five grand. Tomorrow night." She eyed the nearly empty bottle. "Don't forget."

He laughed, which turned into a phlegmy cough. His callused hand gripped the smoky cigar and he closed his eyes. "You got it."

Jet couldn't get out of the dump fast enough. She threw her bag over her shoulder, ready to whip out the Glock if any threats appeared. She made her way toward the fort down the narrow cobblestone streets until she came to a gaudy red and yellow two-story building with a sign out front advertising rooms for rent.

The front door was locked, but after a few minutes of pounding, a sleepy-looking young man materialized and peered at her through the glass at the side of the doorframe.

"What?" he growled, clearly not happy about having been awakened.

"I want a room."

He looked at his watch and then regarded her suspiciously. "Just you?"

"That's right."

A bolt slid open on the heavy wooden door and he pulled it open. "Come in. Room's thirty dollars. Check out's at 1:00."

The transaction took less than a minute, no request for a passport or even her name. The room was spartan but clean, with a fan by the window for ventilation, and she hurriedly brushed her teeth and prepared for bed. She turned off the light and lay down, still dressed, the Glock on the bedside table, and slept fitfully until dawn streamed through the cloudy glass, bringing with it a cloudburst replete with thunder and lightning.

CHAPTER 25

Antonio Salguero, Colombia

Voices sounded from outside his window, and Matt rolled over on the lumpy mattress and then came fully awake. Hannah was snoring softly beside him, oblivious to the noise. He slipped on his clothes and shoes, and then moved through the silent house like a ghost.

At the front windows he looked outside. Luis was facing two men, and it sounded like they were arguing about something. Luis backed up when one of them stepped forward, obviously inebriated.

Matt opened the front door and stepped out onto the plank porch. The sound of the door closing caused the two men facing Luis to look over at Matt as he approached.

"Luis, is everything okay?" Matt asked, his eyes never leaving the two men. The one on the right seemed angry; his face was dark, and an ugly expression twisted his lips into a scowl.

"This is none of your business, gringo. Go back inside," the angry man growled.

Matt ignored him. "Luis, come on. Time to hit the sack."

"I told you, stay out of it," the angry man warned, taking another step toward Luis.

Matt shook his head. "I'm afraid I can't do that. Let's resolve whatever this is in the morning after everyone's sobered up."

The man's companion spit at Matt's feet. "You're telling us what to do in our town?" he demanded.

"I'm telling you that this is over, and Luis is coming inside with me."

Moonlight flashed off the blade of a knife that appeared in the angry man's hand. "You want to make this your problem? I'll gut you like a fish."

"I don't want to fight," Matt said, gauging how drunk the man was. Pretty drunk, judging by how he was swaying. Even so, a drunk with a knife was nothing to underestimate. The man's companion stepped back, seeming to have second thoughts.

"Then get out of here. My business is with this shit grub," the knife wielder snarled.

Matt shook his head, waiting for the man to make the move he was telegraphing with his body language. "I told you. That's not going to happen."

Some kernel of reason battled against drunken rage in the belligerent man's brain as he regarded Matt. The gringo hadn't reacted to the threat as expected, so now he had to either attack or back off. After a few moments, anger won out and he lunged forward without warning, trying to stab Matt. Matt easily avoided the thrust and brought his cast down hard on the man's wrist, snapping its bones. The knife dropped into the mud as the man howled in pain and fell to his knees, clutching his hand.

Matt bent down and retrieved the knife, wiped it off, and folded it closed. A cheap switchblade, he noted, probably ten dollars, but deadly. He slipped it into his back pocket and glanced at the moaning man's friend. "Get him out of here. Or do you want to try your luck?"

The friend eyed Matt, obviously trying to assess whether he could take him. Matt returned the favor of spitting at his feet. "Hurry up. I've lost enough sleep as it is. You want the same treatment, or are you going to get him up and move on? It's all the same to me."

Luis came to life behind him. "Go on. This is over." His words were slurred.

The friend hauled his companion to his feet, who held his wrist, grunting with each exhalation. A string of curses trailed the pair as they stumbled off, along with promises to exact revenge on Luis and the gringo coward.

Matt turned to Luis. "What was that all about?"

"It's personal. The one with the knife, Pedro, hates me. Always has. He was trying to date Carlita before I married her, and she rejected him for me. He's never forgotten it. The man's a bully, and a dangerous one. You should have let me handle it."

"If I had, you'd be holding your guts in right now."

"I can take care of myself," Luis insisted.

"You're drunk. Anything can happen when you're drunk, Luis. Besides, what's done is done."

"He's not going to let you get away with breaking his hand."

"That's his problem, not mine. I didn't come at him with a knife. Maybe he'll learn to avoid trying to kill people he's just met." Matt sighed. "Come on. Let's go to bed. Unless you think he'll be back."

"No, not tonight. He knows I have a shotgun in the house. Even he's not that stupid. Although I wish he'd try it, so we could get this over with once and for all."

"Then let's get some sleep." Matt glanced at his watch. "It's really late."

Carlita's voice called from inside the house. "Luis?"

Matt eyed him. "Now you're in real trouble."

Luis smiled ruefully. "I deserve it."

Matt followed him into the house and pulled the door closed behind him, taking care to lock it. He watched Luis move to where Carlita was standing by the bedroom, hands on her hips, Oscar and Sammy wagging their tails sleepily, and left the tipsy fisherman to his fate, hoping to get at least a few more hours of sleep before the new day arrived.

CHAPTER 26

Panama City, Panama

Igor weaved down the hall of the Veneto hotel, the night's cocktails having finally caught up with him. Two Colombian girls, no more than eighteen or nineteen, smiled professionally at him as he got out of the elevator. The hotel was crawling with attractive working girls, so much so that the casino appeared to be less about wagering and more like a sexual amusement park for the almost exclusively male guests. He'd toyed with the idea of an hour of slap and tickle with the young beauty he'd been drinking with, but decided to call it a night rather than invest the hundred dollars in what would probably prove to be an unhappy encounter after as many rum and cokes as he'd had.

The search for the woman had so far proved fruitless; she'd disappeared from the harbor without a trace. The police, for all their reach, had come up dry, and with every hour that passed the likelihood of her being caught dropped significantly.

There was nothing for him to do but wait, and he didn't do well on the sidelines. He was all about action, not hoping something would come up. The waiting was like Chinese water torture, and he'd finally succumbed to the hotel's charms and spent a few hours whiling away the time downstairs at the slot machines; and later, the card tables; and still later, at a quiet booth with Carmella, who was twenty, wanted to be a dentist, and was just in town to make money for three months before returning to school in Cartagena, where she was in college.

He pushed his way into the room and stared at his satellite phone, which he'd left charging. The red message LED was blinking in the darkness. He switched on the lights and lumbered toward it, regretting the last two drinks, which he'd known at the time had been excessive – unlike the four that had preceded them.

He stepped out onto the terrace and dialed his voice mail. A terse missive from their Panamanian contact, an hour and a half ago: two thugs had been taken to the hospital in Colón, injured, they said, by a young woman. Of course they didn't have an explanation for why they were in a deserted area of Colón after dark or why the woman attacked them. Their story was that they were minding their own business, presumably sightseeing in the worst neighborhood in the country, when the woman materialized and assaulted them.

The police had shown them the picture of Igor's quarry, and the men had identified her as their attacker – or at least, they thought she looked like she might have been.

Igor checked the time. It was after two. Nothing would be open until tomorrow. If the woman was in Colón, he'd find her, with the help of the police. But it wouldn't be in the wee hours of the morning.

He shook his head to clear it and drank two glasses of water before stripping off his clothes and lying on the bed, which was spinning by the time he nodded off.

The next morning his headache was monumental, the sugar from the soda and the rum conspiring to create a perfect storm hangover. He sat up and cringed as spikes of pain shot through his head from his eyes. His brain seemed to bump against the inside of his skull with the slightest movement, sending agony through his body.

Igor forced himself to stand and moved to the bathroom, where a ten-minute hot shower rinsed away the worst of it. The three aspirin he'd downed before soaking himself under the spray also blunted the pain somewhat. He eyed himself in the mirror as he toweled off, his customary smile replaced today with a pained scowl.

He called the Panamanian as he dressed, but there was no update to the information relayed the prior night, other than the names and addresses of the two injured men from the police report. Igor's next call was to Fernanda, who listened to his account without comment before cutting straight to the chase.

"What's your plan?"

"I want to find the two she thrashed and confirm it was actually her. And find out what she wanted. They had to be involved in something with her – it sounds like their deal went bad. I'm thinking it might be appropriate to pay them a visit."

"And maybe spread some generosity around with the Colón cops, so they prioritize finding her over whatever else they're working on?"

"You read my mind. Anything happening on your end?"

"Waiting for word to come back from the feelers we put out. But nothing yet."

"Any idea how long it will take before it's either a success…or not?"

"If we haven't been able to locate them in another forty-eight hours, I doubt it will ever happen. I mean, for all we know, they're already dead. That was a bad storm, and there's no guarantee they made it to land. Over a hundred miles in terrible seas…"

"Oh, they made it. I read up on those lifeboats. They can go through anything. That's the entire point of them," Igor said.

"Well, let me know what you learn."

Igor terminated the call and finished his preparations, and then went downstairs to check out. While he paid his bill, he considered whether he'd need any backup from the locals, and decided against it. So far all they'd managed to do was botch everything and get themselves killed. He liked his odds better working on his own. After looking up the first victim's address and memorizing the route from Panama City, he started the engine of his rental car and pulled into traffic, his headache now quieted to a dull roar.

His impression of Colón was that it was a dump. The word that popped into his head as he negotiated the streets was "squalid." The neighborhood he pulled into was so run down that he actually felt some trepidation when he parked his car down the block from the first victim's address – and he was a hired killer.

The apartment block was one step above abandoned – a small step at that. He mounted the stairs to the front security door and found the lock broken. Inside was all gloom, and it stank of rot and human waste.

Igor arrived at the steel door of apartment 1F on the first floor. He checked the victim's name and address, confirmed that it was the right apartment, and knocked officiously.

A man's voice called out from the interior. "What?"

"Emanuel Rojas?" Igor said in his best policeman's tone.

"Who wants to know?"

"Police."

"What do you want?"

"I'm following up on the report you signed yesterday. I've been assigned to the case."

"Great. I already told them everything I know."

"Mr. Rojas, please open the door. I don't want to have this discussion in a hallway." *Charming as it is*, Igor thought silently.

"Wait a minute," Rojas called, and Igor could envision him hiding his drugs and weapons. Two minutes later the door opened a crack, a security chain in place, and a ferret-faced man with pockmarked, jaundiced skin stared out at him. "Do you have any ID?" Rojas asked.

"Sure," Igor said, turning slightly and stepping back from the door as he reached for his wallet.

He put all his weight into the kick that tore the chain out of the wall and knocked Rojas backward. Igor glanced both ways down the corridor and stepped inside as Rojas held his broken nose, blood streaming through his fingers. The Brazilian closed the door behind him and looked at his victim, who'd lost control of his bladder from the pain and shock, to judge from the spreading dark stain on his pants.

Igor knelt next to the man and spoke in a low tone. "We'll make this short and sweet. The woman who beat you to a pulp. What were you doing with her? What did she want?"

Rojas didn't answer, instead glaring at him through bloody hands. Igor stood and kicked him hard in his injured hip, and Rojas blacked out.

When he came to, he was bound to a chair in his kitchen, and Igor was heating something on the stove. It smelled like…burning oil? Igor saw the man stir and moved to where Rojas could see him.

"I need to know what the woman wanted, Emanuel. This isn't a game, and as you've guessed by now, I'm not the police. I have no issue with you, but if you don't tell me the complete truth in the next two minutes, I'm going to fry your skin off. So if you want to be cooked like a chicken leg, lie to me or hold out. But a word of warning – if you make me start, no matter how cooperative you are after I begin, I'll continue to the bitter end. Do you understand?"

Rojas nodded mutely.

"So let's try this again. What were you doing with the woman?"

"We were going to rob her."

Igor smiled. "That didn't go so well, I see. Why were you going to rob her?"

"She had a bunch of money on her."

"How do you know?"

"She wanted us to hook her up with a plane."

Ten minutes later, Igor closed the apartment door behind him and wiped the knob before moving unhurriedly down the hall to the building entrance. There were no security cameras – not that he expected any in a barely habitable tenement – so his passing went unremarked.

In the end, Rojas had told him the complete truth before he'd begun the oil treatment. But Igor had needed to be sure, and the world wouldn't be any poorer for the loss of a fecal speck like him. The fire Igor had started as he left would engulf the cinderblock apartment in a few minutes, helped along by the cleaning fluid he'd liberally doused the corpse and furniture with, which would in turn cause an explosion when the gas line he'd torn loose had spewed enough propane into the place.

A whump from the building as the apartment blew shook the car, and he smiled at himself in the rearview mirror before pulling away from the curb.

Because now he knew the woman was trying to get to Colombia. And as of last night, was in Colón. With a little luck and some smart detective work, he should be able to find her. And finish the job that had taken him from Argentina to Chile and now to Panama.

It wouldn't be long now.

He could feel it.

CHAPTER 27

Frontino, Colombia

Fernanda was hanging up with Igor when a knock sounded at her bedroom door. She glanced up and called out, "Yes?"

"Fernanda, it's Jaime. Mosises' son?"

She moved to the door and opened it. "Of course."

"I hope I'm not interrupting anything."

"Not at all. What's going on?"

"We got a call from the police in the Chocó region. It's good news. They think they've found your gringo."

"Really? That's great. Where?"

"In a small river town deep in the jungle. I advised them not to do anything until we get there. Which is why I'm disturbing your morning. We need to go."

"Of course. Let me get my things." Fernanda stopped, thinking. "How far is it?"

"Four, maybe five hours." His eyes twinkled. "I drive fast."

"I was hoping you'd say you had a plane."

"There's no nearby airstrip. By the time we filed a flight plan and got there, and a car made it in to pick us up, it would be nearly the same amount of time."

She walked over to her bag. "Give me two minutes."

Jaime grinned, and Fernanda could sense him admiring her figure again. "I'll give you as much time as you need."

He turned and left her to pack. She glanced over her shoulder as she calculated how she could use his obvious attraction to her benefit. Fernanda viewed every interaction as a transaction, and part of her profession was reading people and determining what they wanted. In this case, Jaime was a powerful man who apparently had his run of Colombia, and it was clear what he wanted.

That might come in handy at some point.

She resolved to flirt with him on the road. It couldn't hurt, and if he thought his obvious interest was reciprocated, she might be able to turn his desire to her advantage. In her experience most men were narcissists, especially Latin men with their bravado and machismo, preening peacocks intent on displaying their finery to the world. That meant they could be controlled by a deft hand without realizing what was happening.

Fernanda was an expert at manipulation. The only man she'd been unable to bend to her will was Igor, which was part of what accounted for their powerful bond. She'd never met anyone like him – smart, ruthless, confident, utterly fearless…and incredible in bed. A man like Igor had no need to impress the others in the herd. He was his own master and didn't care what anyone thought about him.

Jaime had some of those qualities, from what she could see, but he also had the ego of a drug lord who'd been born to power, who took privilege for granted. Which made him malleable, should Fernanda decide to play him.

He was attractive in a Neanderthal sort of way, she thought, wondering whether he was any good in the sack. Her relationship with Igor was flexible when it came to sex – if either of them had to consummate in the course of an assignment, there were no questions asked. They were beholden only to each other, but they were also pragmatic, and sometimes a little intimacy with others was required in order to achieve an objective. If it happened, it was purely mechanical, strictly business, no emotional attachment possible from either of their perspectives. They were hunters, and everyone else was the kill, to be used and discarded as necessary. Which included meaningless physical connection if required.

She hoped it wouldn't come to that, but if it did, it probably wouldn't be entirely unpleasant. But for now they were just going on a drive, and hopefully would soon have the man and his daughter in their grasp.

From there, it was just a matter of convincing them to tell her where they were planning to rendezvous with the woman, and being there when she showed herself.

Igor had just finished reporting about the woman's search in Colón for someone to get her to Colombia. There could only be one reason.

In the highly unlikely event that Igor didn't finish the job in Panama, Fernanda would be waiting for the woman in Colombia.

Fernanda entered the bathroom and studied her reflection, then moistened her lips and dabbed a hint of perfume on her neck and breasts.

A lot could happen with four hours in a car.

No point in letting the opportunity to solidify a promising relationship with a new ally go to waste.

CHAPTER 28

Portobelo, Panama

When Jet descended the stairs to the lobby of the bed and breakfast, she saw that the breakfast portion of the hospitality consisted of fruit covered with flies, a few crusty pastries that looked as though they'd been saved from the prior week, and a dented thermos of what she hoped was coffee. She was the only guest in evidence. After confirming the contents of the thermos with a cautious sniff, she opted for coffee only, in light of the culinary offerings.

Ten minutes later, a stirring from behind the desk alerted her that the clerk had returned from wherever he'd been. She approached him and asked whether there were any messages for her. After making a production out of looking, he told her there weren't. She wasn't surprised. After drinking a bottle of seventy proof rotgut, her captain was probably passed out in a pool of his own sick, not attending to business.

She decided to kill time by wandering around what passed for the town, centered around an abandoned fort complete with rusting cannons. Sailboats bobbed in the protected anchorage along with a variety of fishing boats, and she wondered absently which was Juan Diego's. Not one looked like it could make it around the point, much less the two hundred miles to Colombia, and she hoped that he kept his vessel elsewhere.

For the first time since she'd touched down, the sky was clear of clouds, an endless vibrant blue that stretched to the turquoise horizon of the Caribbean Sea. It was only ten o'clock, but the heat was already rising, and she found herself following the example of the few locals she saw, darting from shady spot to shady spot in order to spare herself the worst of the sun's blistering rays.

She completed her tour of the fort within a half hour and planted herself below the heavy branches of an ancient tree, where the cool wind from the water blew through her hair and provided a slight relief. An old man pushed a handcart nearby, an ice box on wheels with a hand-painted illustration of a snowcapped mountain, and sporadically rang a bell to alert customers that the Popsicle man had arrived.

Jet waved him over and, after perusing his selection, decided on mango with chili powder as her breakfast flavor. She paid and watched him continue on his route, which he'd probably been doing his entire life, and would continue to do until he died. Unlike more developed countries, Latin America had no social safety net, no nanny state to support the fallen or the aged, and you either worked or starved. When you got too old or too sick, it was the obligation of the family to care for you. It had been like that for centuries, and nobody expected anything different.

The frozen confection was oddly delicious, the combination of fruit and heat from the chili unexpected. She considered getting up and going in search of the vendor for another, but opted to conserve her energy as the sun climbed high in the cobalt sky.

An inflatable tender with a grizzled sailboater accompanied by a golden retriever putted from a vessel that looked like it had circumnavigated the world, and she watched as it made its way to a small dock that floated off to the side of the fort. She more than understood the fantasy of taking a boat to nowhere, spending each day without a care other than what fish could be caught or where to navigate to before nightfall, but that wasn't for her, even if she entertained the vision of herself, Matt, and Hannah, hair tousled by an ocean breeze, standing on the deck of a schooner as they sailed to Polynesia.

A wave of melancholy washed over her as she regarded the boats tugging at their anchor lines like restless dogs on too-short leashes. Somewhere on the other side of the inhospitable jungle that was

Panama's southern border were the man and little girl she loved, who made everything worth doing and validated her continuing struggle. It wasn't like her to wallow in self-pity, but the last months had been the hardest of her life, and occasionally, in quiet moments like this, her introspection turned maudlin and she just wanted to cry.

Jet shook off the unusual emotional turbulence and closed her eyes, still tired after a restless six hours of sleep. A high-pitched squeal sounded from her left, and she opened them and glanced over at the source – a little girl about Hannah's age, wobbly brown legs running as fast as they could carry her, chasing after some unlucky seagulls that had been congregating near an inoperative mineral-encrusted fountain.

Behind her, a young mother, her glowing face full of life, walked in the sun, watching her progeny celebrate freedom as only the young can. Jet felt an envious tug at her heart at the sight. That should have been her. She'd bowed out of the covert life, paid her dues, disappeared. That a seemingly endless stream of miscreants was hell-bent on exterminating her was…so damned unfair.

She took several deep breaths and forced her thoughts back to the present. Railing at the world because it was failing to live up to expectations did no good. If she was ever going to see her daughter again, she needed to get to Colombia, not throw a pity party for herself in some equatorial dung hole.

The hard self-talk always worked, and in a few minutes she was back, focused and ready to deal with the problem at hand. If Juan Diego didn't get in touch with her, she needed to find another smuggler. A place like Portobelo probably had more than one. She'd just have to apply herself, start over, and keep at it until she was successful. Like any other problem, this was solvable.

And she would solve it. Because the rest of her life – and her daughter's – depended on it.

At noon she pushed herself to her feet and retraced her steps to the bed and breakfast, hot and drained by the emotional storm that had blown through her like a whirlwind. When she entered, the clerk glanced up at her like he'd never seen her before, and she wondered to herself what he was on. Probably marijuana, judging by his red eyes and the vague sour stench clinging to his clothes. She approached and, keeping her tone neutral, asked him if there was a message for her.

He repeated the process from earlier and seemed surprised when he held up a small note with a sloppy scrawl on one side.

"Guy came by maybe five minutes ago and left this. Didn't say who it was for, though."

"Do you have a lot of guests today?"

The question stopped him as he processed the ramifications. He turned and looked at the series of cubbyholes, all of which had keys in them except her room number, and turned back to her and sheepishly handed her the note with a mumbled apology.

She read it quickly. Juan Diego had graduated from a school of prose that valued brevity. There were only five words. "Fort dock, nine. Bring cash."

Jet looked at the clerk. "I'll keep the room for another night," she said, digging in her pocket. He took her money, made a note on an empty ledger, and then turned his attention back to her.

"Anything else?"

"Breakfast was delicious."

She left the dullard staring at her as she mounted the stairs to her room, warmed by the puzzled expression on his face more than she should have been. But today was a day of small triumphs, and she resigned herself to taking what pleasure she could.

If she managed to find a lunch spot and not get poisoned, that would be another victory, she thought as she entered her room, which was the temperature of an oven. Jet turned on the fan and lay down on the bed, the stream of air from the window as hot as a hair dryer, and steeled herself for a long day of waiting. She closed her eyes and, as she drifted off, regretted not getting the second Popsicle.

CHAPTER 29

Antonio Salguero, Colombia

By the time Matt and Hannah made it out of their bedroom, morning was long gone and it was coming up on lunchtime. Carlita was in the kitchen, and the dogs dozed by the dining room table, the children on the floor next to them. Hannah joined them in their simple play, and Matt approached Carlita.

"Good morning," he said.

"More like afternoon," Carlita corrected with a smirk. "Would you like some coffee?"

"That would be wonderful."

She poured a mug full to the brim with the steaming brew and handed it to him. He took a sip and nodded appreciatively. "Thanks."

"It's we who should be thanking you. Luis told me what you did last night."

Matt shrugged. "It was no big deal. I'm sure he would have done the same for me."

"Well, you're wrong that it's not a big deal. Pedro is as mean as a snake and twice as treacherous. You're not safe in town now. He has a few friends, all lowlifes, and if they get you alone…"

"I can take care of myself."

"That's obvious. But it's hard to defend against a bullet or a knife in the back."

"You really think he'd go that far now that he's sobered up?"

"I don't trust him. He's a petty, cruel man. He beats up women, too. Everyone in town knows it."

Matt watched Hannah playing with the boys and took another sip of coffee. "Where's Luis?"

"He had to run some errands. He should be back soon for lunch."

"I imagine his head hurts."

She sighed. "Yes, it does. He's a good man, but he likes to drink, and sometimes…well, nobody's perfect, right?"

"Nobody I've met, anyway," Matt agreed.

Twenty minutes later Luis pushed through the door, out of breath. He saw Matt and removed his straw hat. "Oh, good. You're up. I have bad news. Pedro went to the police about you this morning. Said you jumped him."

"He can say anything he wants. I have witnesses, like you, who can vouch for me."

"That's not the problem. If you're trying to lie low and evade immigration, having the police take you into custody probably isn't a good way to do it."

Matt sighed. Without adequate caffeine, his brain wasn't processing as quickly as normal. "You're right, of course."

"Rumor is that they're coming for you later. Everyone is talking about it. Pedro has a big mouth, and he's been telling everyone who will listen that you're going to jail."

Matt eyed Luis with a frown. "Well, this little slice of paradise didn't last long."

"I'm sorry I got you into this."

"You didn't. I put myself into it."

Carlita stood silently, a pensive expression on her face as she stirred something on the stove. She put the wooden spoon down and fixed Matt with a frank gaze. "You need to get out of here."

"And fast," Luis agreed.

Matt eyed them both. "How? If the police are going to be watching for me…" He paused, thinking. "Do you know anyone with a car?"

Luis shook his head. "Nobody I'd trust to keep his mouth shut. This is a small town where nothing ever happens. Most people would know the exact time you left, and half would throw you a parade for putting Pedro in his place."

"Then what? Hannah's in no shape to walk."

Carlita snapped her fingers and looked to Luis. "Armando is coming today to buy some chickens." She leveled a thoughtful stare at Matt. "Maybe for the right amount he'd give you a lift?"

Luis nodded. "That could work, as long as you're gone before the police arrive. They probably won't be stopping cars over a drunken fight."

"How well do you know this Armando?" Matt asked.

"He's been a regular customer for four years. A nice young man. Polite. From a good family," Carlita said. Matt hoped that good manners would be enough to keep the chicken merchant from selling him out.

Matt asked. "Where's he based out of?"

"Santuario, southeast of Medellín a few kilometers. It's a beautiful hill town. He distributes to a bunch of restaurants around there," Carlita explained.

"How far is it from here?"

Luis looked at Carlita. "Maybe…a hundred and sixty kilometers?"

Matt did the math in his head – a hundred miles. That would be more than enough distance to avoid a run-in with the local gendarmes.

"When will he arrive?" Matt asked.

"Should be any time. No more than another half hour."

"Good. That will give me time to pack and get Hannah ready. Do you really think he might do this?"

Carlita blushed and turned away from Luis. "He's always very nice with me. I think I could convince him. For the right amount of money, of course."

"Of course."

"Well, you'll need full stomachs if you're going to travel. I've got lunch ready," Carlita said.

They sat down to eat, and Carlita served large helpings of a chicken dish, like a curry, spicy and thick, ladled over rice and beans, all washed down with a fruit concoction that left a red mustache on Hannah's face. When they finished eating, Luis took up watch out on the front porch while Matt packed. Shortly after he was done with the bags, Luis called to him.

"His truck's coming."

Carlita went out to meet Armando while Luis made himself scarce, rounding up the kids and taking them into the bedroom. The big flatbed truck stopped in front of the house, and after several minutes pulled around to the back where the pens of chickens were kept. Hannah hummed to herself in the bathroom as she tried to brush her own hair, and Matt busied himself with helping her while he waited for the chicken merchant's verdict.

When Carlita came back inside, she spoke in a low voice. Outside, the truck started up and pulled off. "It will cost fifty dollars. He'll wait for you just outside of town so nobody sees him pick you up. Luis?"

Luis stuck his head out of the bedroom. "Yes?"

"You need to take them to the bend in the road outside of town. Show them the trails. Be quick about it – there's no telling when the police will be here."

Luis sighed. "Let me put my boots on."

Carlita moved to Matt and hugged him as they waited for Luis, pressing just a little too close and lingering a few moments too long for a polite goodbye, and then embraced Hannah. "Take care of your daddy, young lady," she whispered, and Hannah nodded agreement, her eyes serious.

The gray sky opened up just before they got underway, drizzling a warm rain as Luis led Matt and Hannah into the jungle. After a half hour slogging along the winding game trails, they arrived at the bend in the road where Armando's truck was parked on the shoulder of the muddy strip. The penned chickens on the back were soaked, as were Matt and Hannah.

Luis made introductions and then turned to Matt and shook his hand. "Thanks for everything. Safe travels. And again, I appreciate what you did for me last night."

"What will you tell the police when they come?"

"That you slipped away after Pedro pulled a knife on you. That you were afraid for your life."

"It's a shame some of your neighbors saw me arrive in town with Hannah. That will make us easier to identify if they put out a bulletin or something."

"I wouldn't worry about it. Our police are lazy. They'll come to the house, ask some questions, and leave, the matter forgotten once I tell them Pedro attacked you and you defended yourself. He's got a reputation as a liar, so they'll take my word over his."

"I hope you're right."

"I am."

Armando stowed their bags behind the bench seat of the thirty-year-old Dodge truck and then helped Hannah aboard. He was handsome in a brooding Colombian way, and Matt couldn't help but wonder whether the chicken merchant's purported attraction to Carlita wasn't reciprocated at least somewhat.

Armando wasn't loquacious, preferring the radio and Latin pop songs over small talk, and soon they were bumping along the road toward the highway, music battling for dominance with the groan of the old motor and the whine of the transmission. As they pulled onto the narrow two-lane strip of blacktop, they saw a police car a hundred yards ahead, parked on the shoulder. Matt ducked below the dash and pulled Hannah lower so only Armando's head was visible from ground level, the truck riding high. One of the two portly officers waved at Armando and walked out to meet him as he slowed to a stop.

The cop stood a few feet from the driver's side window, looking up at Armando. Matt and Hannah remained out of sight – unless he looked inside. Armando wiped sweat from his forehead with the back of his hand and coughed.

"*Hola*, my friend. How are you today?" the cop asked.

"Sick. I've got the flu. Half of Santuario is down with it. Don't get too close unless you want to spend the next week in misery."

Armando coughed again and gave the officer a suffering look. It had the desired effect. The cop took a step backward. Armando cleared his throat. "What are you guys doing out here?"

"Oh, we have to go find some gringo in Antonio Salguero. We're waiting for backup to arrive."

"A gringo? There?"

The cop shrugged. "I know. Not exactly what you'd expect, eh?" He eyed the chicken coops stacked high, strapped to eyelets along the edge of the flatbed. "How's the chicken business?"

"Long hours for low pay."

The cop laughed. "Isn't that always the way?"

Armando coughed again, and the officer waved him on. Armando pushed the transmission into gear and pulled away, unhurried, as the police cruiser disappeared in his rearview mirror. "You can sit up now," he said, and then squinted at the road ahead and stiffened. "Maybe not yet. Stay down."

"What is it?" Matt asked.

"Two black SUVs barreling down on us fast. That's weird. The police don't use those."

A pair of Suburbans flew by at high speed. Matt waited until Armando gave him the all clear signal and sat up, helping Hannah do the same.

"Usually a lot of traffic on this strip?" Matt asked.

"There's nothing out here except God's country and cocaine-processing plants and a few small towns along the rivers. If this road sees ten cars a day, I'd be surprised."

"Wonder where the SUVs were going?"

Armando shrugged. "Best not to wonder too much. They looked like narco traffickers to me. The cartels tend to favor those cars and ignore most traffic laws. Goes with being rich and all-powerful."

"I thought Colombia had cleaned out the cartels."

"The big ones, sure. But nature hates a vacuum. There will always be regional warlords." He eyed the dusty rearview mirror. "That's just the way it is around here. They leave me alone; I do the same with them. It's the best way to assure a long life in Colombia."

Matt had no argument with that and settled into an uncomfortable silence as he kept his eyes on the side mirror, a part of him dreading the reappearance of the SUVs. After a few miles he glanced over at Armando. "Do you have a cell phone I can borrow?"

Armando slipped a little black Nokia from his shirt pocket and handed it to Matt. Matt dialed Jet's cell from memory, but it went to voice mail, saying she was out of the service area. "Change of plans. We're headed for a town called Santuario. I'll see if I can buy a phone and call you once we get there. Should be a couple, three hours. Hope everything's okay on your end."

He terminated the call and handed the phone back to Armando.

"Thanks," Matt said, and eyed the speedometer. The truck was barely doing thirty miles per hour. "Does this thing go any faster? Don't take it the wrong way, but the sooner we're off this road, the better I'll feel."

Armando gave the big truck gas. "Sorry. I'm used to taking my time in order to conserve fuel. But if you'll throw a few dollars at the tank, I'll open it up – give the chickens the ride of their lives."

Matt smiled at the young man's entrepreneurial enthusiasm.

"It's a deal."

CHAPTER 30

Colón, Panama

Igor was finishing a late lunch of spicy fish at one of a half-dozen questionable seafood restaurants on the waterfront when his sat phone warbled at him. He set his fork down and thumbed the line into life.

"Hello."

"Igor, it's me. We're about to head into the town where the man and the little girl were last seen."

"That's great, Fernanda! Congratulations." He paused. "I don't need to remind you to take them alive."

"Of course. I've already advised the local police to stand down once we have them in sight."

"It's always nice to have the cooperation of the authorities."

Fernanda stole a glance at Jaime, his engraved Colt 1911 .45 pistol on the seat beside him. "I'm hopeful we'll get this put to bed in the next few minutes. Any progress on the woman?"

"No. The bar they met her at doesn't open until evening."

"What are you going to do?"

"I'll go in and see if anyone recognizes her. It's a long shot, but you never know. I've also called our Panamanian contact and asked him to put out the word to the lowlifes in the area that there's a big reward waiting for anyone who's approached to smuggle someone across the border. Money tends to talk with that group..."

"You might want to get to the bar a little before it opens so you can have a discussion with the bartenders before it's filled with customers. They usually have good memories if you wave some cash under their noses."

"Way ahead of you. The place opens at eight, so I'm planning to stop in around seven thirty or so. Can't hurt."

"Have you gone to see the other guy she beat up?"

"Not yet. I'm debating the wisdom of having both meet with unfortunate accidents on the same day. I was quite thorough with the one I interrogated. I don't think I'll learn anything new by taking the other one apart. Although if I don't make progress and the local smugglers don't cough up any leads, I'm open to suggestions."

"I'll call you as soon as I have the gringo and the girl. Then we can figure out how to lure our mystery woman into a trap. Or if we're lucky, he'll tell us where they're supposed to meet and we can arrange an unpleasant surprise."

"I'll keep my phone on."

Igor hung up and returned to picking at his plate of fish. The spicy red sauce it was slathered with set his lips on fire. He took a final heaping mouthful and pushed the plate away, chewing thoughtfully as he gazed through the restaurant picture window at the waterfront, where massive shapes of tankers in the distance were transiting the canal, and smiled to himself. It wouldn't be long now.

~ ~ ~

The Suburbans bounced along the rutted road to Antonio Salguero, tires throwing up muddy spray from the recent shower's rainwater that had accumulated in the depressions. The squad car in front crawled through the muck in low gear, as the police were uninterested in blowing out their suspension on the treacherous trail.

The vehicles labored around a bend and entered the town, little more than a line of clapboard buildings, each more unappealing than the last. Fernanda eyed the residents lounging in the slim shade provided by the roof overhangs, passing bottles and well-used stories back and forth as they watched the new arrivals roll down the main drag. She noted that even the young women had a beaten look to them, old before their time, the result of a harsh life and no expectation that anything would ever change for the better.

Jaime pulled to a stop outside a meager dwelling at the end of a small lane as the police officers climbed from their car and moved to the front door. Fernanda tensed as they knocked, and whispered to Jaime.

"We move in the second they give us the signal. No shooting. Please. Your men understand, right?"

"Of course. This is your show. We'll do it your way."

A wiry, dark-skinned man opened the door and looked from one officer to the other, and Fernanda saw him shake his head. The tension that had been building in her stomach changed to a sinking feeling that was by now a familiar norm on this assignment. The cops went inside and were back after five minutes, dour expressions on their faces. One of them approached the lead Suburban and Jaime rolled down his window.

"They're not there. The fisherman says they left last night after the fight – that the man was afraid of retribution once daylight came. He also says he'll swear that our victim was actually the instigator and pulled a knife on them. The fisherman wants to press charges against him for attempted murder."

Jaime looked at Fernanda, who shook her head. "Damn. Did he say how they left?"

"An old bicycle was missing this morning when he woke up."

"How far could they have gotten on a bicycle?"

"In…twelve hours? Far enough. There'd be any number of connecting roads once they made it to the main artery."

Fernanda's eyes narrowed. "I want to talk to him." She eyeballed the officer. "Tell them I'm a special investigator."

The cop fought to keep his composure. "A special investigator on a case involving a broken wrist in a swampy backwater?"

Jaime fixed him with a glare. "Just do it."

The unhappy cop returned to the front door and knocked again as Fernanda and Jaime got out of the car. Jaime turned to the second SUV and signaled to his men to remain inside. The fisherman opened the door again and the policeman gestured to Fernanda.

"This is the detective in charge of the case. She has a few questions."

Fernanda nodded. "Yes. Luis, right?"

"That's right," Luis said, his tone puzzled.

"I'm investigating this because I believe the man who was staying at your house may be someone we're looking for."

"Looking for?"

"Yes. Without going into too much detail, he's responsible for some very serious crimes involving a cargo ship. We believe that among other things, he stole a lifeboat and escaped to Colombia." She paused, gauging how thick to lay it on. "He's a very dangerous man, if he's our perpetrator."

"I don't know anything about that."

"How did you meet him, Luis?" She glanced up at the clouds, the sun burning through the overcast, and waved away a mosquito. "Do you mind if we come inside for this?"

"Oh. Um…it's not a good idea. I have two dogs. They don't like strangers. I'm sorry."

Fernanda's tone hardened. "Perhaps we'll take you to the station, then, to get your statement."

Luis shrugged. "I don't have anything else to do today. Do those trucks have air-conditioning?"

That hadn't gone as she'd hoped, so she changed back to the gentle approach.

"Hopefully that won't be necessary. How did you meet this man? Actually, let's start with his name."

Luis laughed nervously. "His name was Tom."

"And you met him…?"

"He was camped out in the jungle on a trail we use to get to the beach. Him and his daughter. Are you sure we're talking about the same man? He didn't seem very dangerous to me."

"He is. Look what he did to your friend."

"My friend? You mean Pedro? That drunk fool pulled a knife on us and tried to stab him."

"Then you've seen him in action – what he can do."

"All he did was knock the knife out of the idiot's hand with his cast. I don't think he was trying to break his wrist. Although it serves him right."

"Cast?" Fernanda asked in surprise, but recovered quickly. One of the first rules of questioning was to never admit to the subject you're interrogating that you don't know at least as much as he does.

"Didn't Pedro tell you?" The fisherman shook his head, an expression of disgust twisting his lips into a sneer. "That figures. He left out that he was not only trying to stab a man with a broken hand, but that he got his ass kicked by him." Luis looked at the officer. "I'm serious. I want to press charges against Pedro — I'm willing to go fill out the paperwork right now. He tried to kill me. Us."

"Let's get back to the man. You say he was camping in the jungle? Didn't that strike you as unusual?"

Luis shrugged. "Gringos do all kinds of crazy things, I hear."

"How did he wind up staying with you?"

"He said he wanted to have a genuine Colombian experience, and asked if he could stay one night. He offered money and seemed like a nice enough guy, so I agreed. Why not? Everyone can use a little extra cash these days."

"And you believed that?"

"Not really. I thought he may have misjudged how hard the jungle could be to camp in, and just wanted to get out of the rain and take a shower."

Fernanda switched gears. "Tell me about the little girl."

"What's to tell? Or is she also a suspect in your cargo ship case?"

"How old is she?"

"Maybe two or three? I didn't pay much attention."

This was going nowhere. "You say they left after the fight?"

"I warned him that Pedro was a liar and a cheat, and he'd probably try to hurt him if he stayed around. He decided that it would be safest to move on."

"Did he give you any idea where they were going?"

"No. It was late, and…I was tired. I'd had a few beers."

"You didn't ask him?"

"Why? I was beat. Why would I care where some gringo went? I had his money."

Back in the SUV, Fernanda glared at Luis through the windshield as he shut the front door of his house. She turned to Jaime, who'd stood silently by as she asked her questions, and frowned. "What do you think?"

"Oh, he might have been lying. But it's hard to tell. Lying's the national sport in these towns – it's a way to entertain yourself in a place where nothing happens." He tilted his head and regarded her. "You want me to have him taken? Put your questions to him more forcefully? We can come back tonight. We can't do it now – too many witnesses saw us come in, and when he disappears they'll raise a stink."

She sighed. "Let me think about it."

"No problem." Jaime paused. "Sorry your man wasn't here. But we still have the word out, and now we know where he was until last night, so we can narrow the search. He can't have gotten that far on a bike with a broken hand and a little girl."

"I don't believe for a minute he left on a bicycle."

"Which brings us back to taking the fisherman for his last ride tonight." He grinned. "No extra charge for the disposal of his body."

CHAPTER 31

Colón, Panama

Igor hung up after Fernanda finished telling him that the man and his daughter had escaped and remained at large. The call only soured his already bad mood further. He sat in his rental car down the street from the bar the woman had been trolling, and watched the staff arrive. An older, heavyset man with the physique of a gone-to-fat boxer trundled up the sidewalk and gave a high five to one of two younger men, both with the muscular bulk of bouncers, and then unlocked the front door and entered.

Igor gave them five minutes to get settled and then followed them in. At least twenty minutes remained before the shabby watering hole officially opened. The older man was behind the bar counting change, and looked up when the door creaked on its hinges.

"We don't open till eight," he called to Igor, who smiled disarmingly.

"I couldn't wait."

"Right, but we're not open for business yet, so you'll have to."

Igor held up a fifty-dollar bill. "I have some questions."

"That's nice. Come back in twenty minutes."

Igor shook his head. "They'll take no time to answer."

The bartender sighed and stopped what he was doing. "Look, mister, I'll be happy to serve you once we're open, but we're not yet, and I have shit to do. So scram and come back later."

One of the meatheads moved toward Igor from where he had been sitting in the shadows, and came up on him from behind. "Is there a problem, buddy?"

163

Igor smiled at the cloudy mirror over the bartender's shoulder and turned to face the man. "Not at all. Which do you want broken, nose or jaw?"

The muscle man looked confused, but Igor was already in motion, his blow to the bouncer's face so fast it was blinding. A sound like a tomato hitting the pavement split the air, and the big man went down holding his brutalized nose.

The second bouncer came in low, a wrestling or ultimate fighting move, but far too slow to be effective against a professional. Igor stepped back, seemingly unhurriedly, and kneed him in the face, snapping his head back. He finished the maneuver by slamming the bouncer between the shoulder blades with both fists clutched together as the man fell to the floor, knocking him senseless.

Igor regarded the pair of downed toughs, out of commission for the moment, and then faced the bartender again. He pulled his pistol from the small of his back and trained it on the man's forehead. "Will you answer my questions now, or do I break you into pieces for practice? Your girlfriends there aren't going to help you, so it's choice time. You either make fifty bucks, or leave here in a body bag. What's it going to be?"

The bartender swallowed hard at the pistol pointed at his face. "Just take it easy…"

"I couldn't be more relaxed."

"What do you want to know?"

"There was a woman in here last night with two creeps."

The bartender's eyes darted to the left for a split second, and Igor knew the next words he'd hear would be a lie.

"There are lots of women in here any night with creeps. Look around you. This isn't Las Vegas."

Igor thumbed the hammer back on his gun. "I'll start with your knees. Tell me about the woman, or there will be no more warnings."

"I…I think I know who you're talking about. Good-looking. Drank beer."

Igor smiled encouragement. "I already know she was looking for someone to help her get out of town. When I'm looking for that kind

164

of thing, I usually ask the locals. Bartenders usually know who's up to what in shitholes like this. And here you are – a bartender."

"I only told her to watch out for the two scumbags. I swear."

Igor shook his head sadly and leaned forward as the older man backed away from him, his hands up in a defensive stance. The shot sounded like a cannon in the enclosed space. The bartender howled as he fell to the floor, his knee shattered.

Two minutes later Igor left the bar and trotted to his car, wary of any police that would be attracted by the gunfire. It didn't fit his schedule to have to explain a recently deceased bartender and two dead sidekicks to the local flatfoots.

And besides. He needed to find his way to Portobelo as quickly as he could.

Because he now knew where the woman was, or where she would be soon enough.

~ ~ ~

Portobelo, Panama

Jet moved soundlessly down the cobblestone street, angry that she'd missed Matt's call while she was dozing. But he sounded strong, if a little harried, and hadn't used any of the code words they'd agreed upon if one of them was in trouble. She adjusted her bag and picked up her pace as she checked the time – Juan Diego had said nine, but she planned on being there at seven so she could reconnoiter the area and confirm she wasn't walking into a trap. She didn't think that the old smuggler would try to rob her, but after her prior adventure with the two lowlifes, she wasn't taking any chances.

The fort was quiet at sunset, and beams of gold glinted off the surface of the calm harbor water. The surrounding trees swayed from a mild trade wind blowing from the northeast, carrying with it the fresh scent of open sea. Young lovers ambled in pairs along the waterfront, the rusting cannons thrusting from the fort walls long an empty threat to the vessels moored offshore. Jet slowly walked around the outer perimeter of the crumbling battlements, noting areas that would have been ideal if she were a sniper or was laying an ambush, all of them devoid of threats.

The dock was several hundred yards away, empty. As the last of the crimson sunset faded into the hills behind the fort, Jet eyed the trees and the strolling couples, searching for anything out of place. Nothing triggered her internal alarms, but she still stuck to her disciplined scan, leaving nothing to chance, constantly moving, now nearly invisible as the shadows came to stay.

She sat beneath one of the trees, invisible in the darkness, watching the area. After an hour went by, out on the water the throaty rumble of a moving vessel drifted across the harbor. Faint red and green running lights signaled the boat's location. The clank of an anchor rode lowering into the water echoed off the fort's walls, and soon afterward the distinctive whine of a small outboard approached.

A tiny hard-bottom skiff materialized out of the darkness at the dock two minutes later, and Juan Diego's distinctive profile glowed in the dim light of the dock lamp. Jet took a final glance around to confirm she was unobserved, and then made her way to the dock, moving along the waterfront at a rapid clip.

When she reached the dock, the old smuggler looked up at her from his position in the rear of the tender, a scowl pulling at the corners of his mouth.

"You bring the money?" he demanded.

"Of course."

"Where's your friend?"

"Change of plans. It's just me."

Juan Diego's eyebrows rose, but he didn't say anything, only nodded. Jet moved to the boat and tossed him her bag, and then climbed aboard and sat in the front. He backed away from the dock, swung the stern around, and pointed the bow at the dark shape of a fishing vessel a hundred yards from shore.

"Gonna be a long trip. Hope you don't get seasick," Juan Diego said.

"How long?"

"It's about three hundred kilometers, so probably twenty, twenty-two hours or so, assuming nothing unforeseen."

She calculated quickly. "Then we'll arrive tomorrow around twilight?"

"*Mas o menos* – more or less."

"How fast does the boat run?"

"Eight knots, but it's not all in a straight course. There's some strategy to avoiding the patrols on the Panamanian side."

"And the Colombians?"

Juan Diego laughed harshly. "Little lady, not too many are trying to sneak into Colombia. The traffic's in the opposite direction. Let me worry about the Colombians – I haven't seen a navy boat in their border waters in three years."

They approached the vessel, a steel-hulled craft seventy feet in length, much of that devoted to rear deck and booms supporting nets and floats. She could barely make out the name of the boat in the darkness – *Providencia*.

Juan Diego pulled to the stern, and Jet and he disembarked as a wiry crewman tied the skiff's bow line to a rear stanchion. Juan Diego led Jet to the pilothouse, which stank of nicotine and alcohol, and after glancing at the instruments, waved at a crewman on the bow, who engaged the electric windlass and raised the rusty anchor.

Igor arrived at the fort as the dark shape of the skiff pulled away from the dock. He parked at the edge of the lot and ran the length of the waterfront as the tender made its way to the fishing boat, cursing under his breath when he reached the empty dock. He stood at the water's edge and watched impotently as the distant figures of a woman and man climbed aboard an old fishing vessel, barely visible in the night. He knew his pistol was useless at that range, and fought to contain his rage at being so close to his quarry but unable to stop her from escaping.

The fishing boat pulled away as he searched the waterfront for any craft he could steal that would get him close enough to board the departing vessel. Finding nothing, he squinted in the gloom and just made out the boat name in white lettering on the dark blue stern.

Igor repeated the name to himself as he withdrew his phone from his pocket and placed a call to his Panamanian contact. The man might be able to have the boat intercepted by a cooperative customs vessel.

Igor waited the usual few minutes while the man's underlings went in search of him, but when he came on the line and Igor explained the problem, he wasn't encouraging.

"I'll see who we have working the border, but it's been difficult for the last six months. There was a big shake-up, and now all the patrols have multiple agencies on them to reduce the chances of them taking bribes to let shipments get through."

"The woman's wanted for murder," Igor reminded him.

"Yes, but it's a big ocean, and without something more to go on than our say-so, I'm afraid the odds of convincing the Panamanian navy to intercept them aren't good."

"What about a fast boat? Something that can overtake it? I can get anywhere you need me to be within minutes."

"That's more likely. Let me make a few calls and see what I can do. I'll be back to you shortly."

Igor hung up with a curse, furious that the woman had managed to slip away yet again. In all his years in the business, he'd never seen anything like it. No matter what he did, they were always one step behind; but now that she was on a slow boat to nowhere, he would even the odds, one way or another.

~ ~ ~

The final fifty miles to Santuario seemed to drag on forever. The hills proved practically too much for the old Dodge, which slowed to barely twenty miles per hour. Matt's jaw was sore from gritting his teeth and willing the conveyance faster as each curve posed a laborious challenge, chicken coops tipping dangerously and bald tires struggling for grip.

Armando became more talkative as the hours passed, and eventually got around to asking what Matt intended to do once they got to Santuario.

"That's a good question. I'd hoped it would still be light out, so we could check out the town, maybe find someplace discreet to spend a few days."

Armando didn't say anything for several beats, and when he did, his tone was serious. "Do you have any idea who the goons in the black SUVs back there were?"

Matt answered honestly. "No."

A big part of his problem was that he had absolutely no idea. If he did, then he could at least try to come up with an offensive plan, rather than running away as he was being forced to do.

Armando drove in silence for a minute before glancing over at Matt. "Is someone looking for you, other than the police for breaking that guy's hand?"

"It's possible. But the truth is, I don't know who, and I don't know why."

"How did you wind up staying with Carlita and her family? It's not exactly a tourist destination."

"Yeah, I got that. It's a long story. Our boat sank on the coast and we were in real trouble. Luis offered us some hospitality. It seemed like a good idea."

"Which doesn't explain the two SUVs."

"I know. Believe me, it's a mystery to me too. But I have to assume whoever it is means us harm." Matt debated how to frame his next statement. "I've made a fair number of enemies in my life."

"And you think one of them may be after you here?"

"After the last couple of days, anything's possible. I think my boat was sabotaged. If that's the case, it could be that whoever did it is trying to finish the job."

"Sabotaged?" Armando asked, surprised.

"I believe so. We were lucky to make it to shore."

Armando absorbed that. "Is it likely that whoever it is could be working with one of the cartels?"

"I'd say that's possible, based on the two black SUVs, if you're right about them being *narcotrafficantes.*"

"Then you're really screwed. They're like cockroaches – their men are everywhere. You won't be safe in Santuario. Someone will see you, and they'll make a call, and before you know it a gunman will be emptying an AK into your room."

Matt shrugged. "What's my alternative? Is there a bus from Santuario to someplace safer?"

"That's the point. If you've got a cartel after you, no place is safer."

Matt gave him a sidelong glance. "You're not doing anything to improve my outlook, Armando."

"Sorry." Armando lapsed back into silence, concentrating on the road for five minutes before clearing his throat. "I may be able to help."

"How? And why?"

"My brother is a monk at a monastery just outside of town. There are only a few other monks, and there are several unused buildings that have been sitting empty forever – apparently the monk business isn't as popular as it was a hundred years ago. Maybe he could get you into one of them? Nobody would see you there, and even if the cartel had people asking questions in the towns along the road, they'd come up empty."

Matt considered the suggestion. "How about the why?"

Armando glanced at Hannah dozing on the seat next to him. "If you have a cartel after you, they won't spare your little girl. They're animals. Human life means nothing to them." He hesitated. "And of course, there's always money."

"How much are you thinking?"

He shrugged. "Whatever's fair. I don't know your financial circumstances."

They went back and forth and arrived at a compromise, and Armando called his brother, Franco, and explained the situation. After a heated discussion, Franco agreed to help, and Armando terminated the call with a nod to Matt.

"I'll drop you at the bottom of the mountain – you have to take an aerial tram to get up to the monastery. It'll be dark by the time we arrive, so nobody will see you go up. Franco will meet you at the top. It doesn't get much more remote, so you'll have complete privacy."

Matt eyed the landscape and turned to Armando. "I appreciate all the help, Armando. It could well make a difference in whether we make it or not."

Armando looked at Hannah again. "Let's just hope that it's enough."

CHAPTER 32

Juan Diego showed Jet to the bunk area in the bowels of the *Providencia* as one of his crew piloted the vessel, its single diesel engine wheezing beneath their feet. As far as she could tell, the old barge was heading east at about the same speed Jet could run.

The boat was in questionable condition – rust showed along the edges of every surface, the hull was badly in need of paint, and the companionways were worn. Below deck was a galley with a fixed table, a small refrigerator, and an electric stove. Aft of the common area was an equipment and engine room, and forward two cabins – one the captain's quarters with a single berth and a desk, and the other the crew stateroom, which consisted of four metal bunks and a locker. Each had an en-suite head whose smell announced its location.

"Make yourself at home. You can stow your bag below that bottom bunk. Now, let's get the money out of the way before we go any further."

Jet nodded and retrieved a thin wad of hundred-dollar bills from her back pocket and handed it to Juan Diego. "Five grand, as agreed."

He made a show out of counting the money, pausing to examine bills at random, holding them up to the light to verify they had the magnetic security strip. When he was satisfied that Jet wasn't passing off counterfeits, he grunted and slipped the cash into his pocket. The flesh of his face hung off his skull like a basset hound, and his bloodshot eyes betrayed the hangover that was probably pulsing in his head from the prior night's overindulgence.

He grunted and tilted his head at the galley. "Pleasure doing business with you," he said. "We've got beer, soda, and water in the refrigerator, and a decent provision of groceries for the trip. Help yourself, but don't use the knives – have one of the crew do it for you. Last thing I need is for you to slice yourself open a hundred miles from nothing."

Jet smiled and didn't bother to assure him that she could handle cutlery as well as anyone. She patted the switchblade in her pocket, her face a blank. "Thanks. I think I'll try to get some sleep once we're clear of the mainland. How far off the coast will we be running?"

"We'll pass about seven miles off Isla Grande and then veer southeast. Most of the trip we'll be four or five miles offshore, but we'll head further out as we pass the point at Cabo Tiburón so we don't arouse the interest of the Panamanian officials at the border – not that they particularly care about fishing boats, but why risk it?"

"What's our destination in Colombia?"

"Acandí. It's about twenty miles south of the border. There's no access to it except from the sea or the airstrip, so no border patrol or immigrations snoops will be nosing around. From there you can make your way across the gulf to Necoclí, which is a decent-sized town at the end of a main road."

"Make my way how?"

"I'd wait until morning and pay a fisherman to take you across. It's forty kilometers, so a two-hour boat ride in a panga. From Necoclí you can take a bus."

"Why can't you drop me off there?"

"I could, but then you'd have to deal with a whole lot of questions about why a young woman is getting off a Panamanian fishing boat at a Colombian port. I sort of intuited that you wanted to avoid that formality."

"Good guess. They won't stop the smaller boat?"

"No reason to. It's Colombian."

"Ah."

Juan Diego looked around the grim room and grunted again. "All right. That was the guided tour. From here on out, you're on your own. The less the crew knows about you, the better. I'd stick below decks as much as possible on the off chance a plane buzzes us. It's doubtful, but it's been known to happen – the Panamanians have a couple of single-engine prop planes they sometimes use, and a helicopter that patrols the border – when it's running, which hasn't been recently. But like I said, they're mainly concerned with boats moving north. All their good hardware is devoted to that."

"Thanks. I'll try to get some rest." She glanced around at the bunks and gave Juan Diego a neutral stare. "Tell your crew that if either one of them touches me, it'll be the last thing they ever try." She smiled. "Not that I expect anyone to behave like anything but a perfect gentleman."

"I'll have them sleep on deck. That work for you?"

"Of course."

He appraised her calm demeanor in light of the matter-of-fact way she'd warned him and offered a pained grin. "See you in the morning."

"Right. I presume you have coffee."

"You'll smell it all night."

~ ~ ~

Antonio Salguero, Colombia

Fernanda crept toward Luis' home, with Jaime at her side and flanked by two of his gunmen. They'd left the Suburbans behind a grove of trees on the outskirts of town and walked in, waiting until everyone had retired for the night, skirting the bars that remained open until late. Nobody had seen them, and with any luck they'd make their way back undetected.

The house was dark, and the partial overcast blocked most of the light from the full moon as they neared it. Jaime pointed to the back, and his men crept around as Fernanda knelt in front of the door and worked a set of picks in the simple lock. Twenty seconds later she rose, pocketed the picks, and quietly twisted the knob, a sound-suppressed .22 long rifle pistol Jaime had provided her gripped tightly in her right hand.

The interior was pitch black. She waited for her eyes to adjust as Jaime joined her, his shoes making a faint scrape on the hardwood floor. A whine sounded from the bedroom door, followed by barking. Fernanda froze as a male voice called to the dogs, and then the bedroom door opened and Oscar and Sammy came charging at her.

The pop of the silenced rounds sounded like firecrackers in the small space, and the two dogs cried out in pain. Neither of them made it to Fernanda, but she was already in motion as the fisherman backed away, the horrified expression on his face still visible in the darkness.

"Stop right there or I shoot," she said, weapon trained on him as she neared.

"Honey? Luis?" a female voice called from behind him in the bedroom.

"Stay in there," Luis said.

Fernanda shook her head. "No. I want everyone where I can see them. Tell her to come out. With empty hands, or you're both dead."

"Carlita, did you hear that? Come out into the living room. Now."

"Why? What's going on?" Carlita protested, her voice worried.

"Just do it. The police are here."

"Police?" Fernanda heard the bed squeak and bare feet pad on the wooden floor.

"That's right. Come on out. You too, Luis," Fernanda said, motioning with the gun.

They did as she instructed, and Jaime hit the light switch. A single lamp illuminated the room, and Carlita cried out when she saw the dead forms of her two dogs bleeding on the living room floor. Fernanda pointed her weapon at Carlita. "Shut up. Now, or I'll pop you to keep you quiet."

Carlita clenched her hand over her mouth as she cried over her beloved pets senselessly slain before her. Luis glared with hate at Fernanda. "You aren't police."

"Good guess, genius. Now both of you sit down on that sofa."

"What do you want?"

A child began crying from the bedroom. Jaime walked to the door and, after glancing inside, pulled it shut. Fernanda held her pistol with casual ease as the fisherman and his wife took seats.

When she spoke, her voice was flat and her eyes dead. "What I want are answers. Not the lies you told this afternoon. And I'll warn you – if you don't answer honestly, your children will grow up without parents. Assuming I decide to let them live." She allowed that to sink in before continuing. "These are very high stakes, so don't blow it. Tell me the truth, and you'll survive the night. Lie to me, even once, and I kill your wife. Lie to me again, I'll kill one of your children. Lie to me a third time, I'll kill the other one, like I did your dogs. Do you understand?"

"What kind of monster are you?" Carlita whispered, tears in her eyes.

"I'll take that as a yes. Now, Luis, first question. Don't make me do something I don't want to do. Where did the gringo and the little girl go when they left here?"

A frightened look crossed the fisherman's face. "I...I don't know," he stammered, fear in his eyes. Fernanda decided that might be true – he obviously believed that she would kill his wife if he lied. She reframed her demand.

"Tell me everything you know about them. How they left. Leave anything out, and you know what happens," Fernanda said, her voice menacing.

Carlita spoke before Luis could. "They got a ride with the man who buys chickens from us."

Fernanda smiled humorlessly. "Very good. Where were they going?"

"We really don't know. I don't think the man had any firm destination in mind. He just wanted to get out of here," Carlita said.

"Why?"

"To avoid the police. He said he didn't enter the country legally, and he was afraid he'd get into trouble."

Fernanda questioned them for another five minutes but learned nothing more. When she'd exhausted her questions, she paced slowly in front of them, pistol held by her side. If she killed them, there would be an investigation, and even if Jaime ran interference for her and it ultimately went nowhere, it would no doubt cost more to do so and might cause further problems. She stopped in front of Carlita, sensing that she was the backbone of the little family, and pointed the pistol at the center of her forehead.

"Do you love your babies?" she asked softly.

Carlita's eyes widened and she gasped. "Of course," she whispered.

"If either of you ever talk about tonight, I'll return and kill you without hesitation. I'll kill you" – she glared at Carlita, then moved the pistol to Luis – "and you, and then I'll take your children and sell them in Bogotá. They'll live their short lives as sex toys for AIDS-infected perverts. Do you want that for them?" she asked, conversationally.

They both shook their heads in terror.

"Do I need to kill him to prove I'm serious?" Fernanda asked, gun still on Luis.

Carlita wiped tears from her face. "No. Please. I believe you. We'll never say anything."

A thought occurred to Fernanda. She gave Luis a hard stare. "Do you have a cell phone?"

He swallowed hard. "Yes."

"Did the man use it?"

Luis glanced at the table. "Yes."

"Where is it?"

"Charging in the bedroom."

Her eyes narrowed. "What about a weapon? Do you have one in the house? A machete? A gun?"

His face twitched. "A shotgun. In the bedroom."

"Then you probably don't want to go near it. Let's go get your phone."

Luis stood and Fernanda followed him into the bedroom. The two infants were both mewling, obviously frightened by the strange people in the house in the middle of the night. Luis went to a dresser and slowly lifted the phone so Fernanda could see he wasn't trying anything funny, and then returned to the living room, giving her a wide berth.

He sat next to Carlita and handed Fernanda the phone. She took it and scrolled through the log. "Did you phone anyone after he made his call?"

"No. He made two. They should be the newest on the list."

"Good. I'm taking your phone. I trust that won't be a problem." Fernanda regarded the dead dogs lying in a coagulating pool of blood. "You should clean that up before your kids see it," she said, motioning with the gun again. "Remember what I said. You tell anyone about tonight, ever, and I'll kill you both. Don't be stupid."

Jaime spoke for the first time. "I'd shoot them anyway. Just to be safe."

Fernanda considered it and then locked eyes with Carlita. "No, I don't think that will be necessary. She knows I'm serious. Don't you?"

Carlita nodded, her lower lip trembling, tears streaming down her face.

Satisfied that the fisherman and his wife would stay mute about their visit, Fernanda pressed redial and held the phone to her ear, unable to control the impulse while understanding its futility. The call went to voice mail and she hung up. She'd give her Panamanian contact the information and see if he could triangulate the phone – but she understood that wouldn't work if there were no cell towers around. Still, she figured it was worth a shot, and she slipped the phone into her pocket.

Fernanda exchanged a glance with Jaime and moved to the front door. Jaime trailed her and they stepped over the threshold and into the faint moonlight. His two gunmen joined them when they heard the front door close, and together they moved back down the road, leaving the sad hovel behind them with a crying woman trying to get bloodstains off the wood in between vomiting sour bile into the toilet as her husband sat, numb, staring at nothing, deaf to their children's wails.

CHAPTER 33

Jet rocked on the bunk. The swell size had increased as the night passed, and she'd slept fitfully between bouts of restlessness as the engine droned its monotone lullaby. After four hours of uneasy slumber, she rose and climbed the ladder to the pilothouse, where Juan Diego was at the wheel, a pint bottle of seco at his side, still half full. She glanced back at the deck and spotted the two crewmen lying on blankets in the warm air, no worse for sleeping outdoors.

Juan Diego caught her eyeing the bottle and frowned. "Don't worry. That's just to take the edge off. I'm sober as a judge."

"As long as you don't hit anything and get me to Colombia, you're an adult and I'm not your mom."

"A most sensible attitude," he said, and took a short swig to acknowledge her wisdom.

She watched the radar for a few minutes, noting a stippling of glowing blips on the screen. "Fishing boats?" she asked.

"Mostly. But that big one? That's navy."

The distant roar of motors reached their ears across the black water, the sound like a Formula One race. She eyed the screen but saw nothing moving fast enough to be the vessel causing the sound. "And that?"

"Drug runner. Low to the water, probably doing a hundred forty or so kilometers per hour, built out of fiberglass, with nothing that would be radar reflective, so it won't show up on the screen. You'll hear them all night long."

"Where are they running to?"

"Either the outer islands in Honduras for refueling or the Yucatán. If they leave Colombia at six in the evening, they can make it to Mexico by dawn on a calm run." He shook his head. "That's a young man's game. Daredevils. When you're going that fast, you're asking to be picked up. But you'd be surprised how few are stopped. The numbers justify the tactic – they'll lose maybe one in ten. If each is carrying a million bucks U.S. wholesale of coke…figure it probably cost a hundred grand or less in Colombia. For the Mexican cartels, that nine hundred thousand is pure profit. So if they lose one, they've lost the cost of the boat, which is maybe a hundred, and the product, another hundred. But nine make it through and they've earned eight million, subtracting the two for the boats and product. They just ditch the boats off the coast of Mexico once they're done, or scuttle them – they don't really care. It's a great business. They just build it into the model."

"I didn't realize the margin was so big."

"Oh, well, I'm actually underestimating how much they make per shipment. Could be more like one and a half or two. Doesn't matter. You run, what, twenty boats a night, it's a nice business. Of course, you're also running submarines up the Pacific coast, and landing some in Panama and Costa Rica for truck shipment north, as well as cargo ships and airplanes…It's a full-time industry for much of Colombia."

They listened to the engines fade in the night as the invisible boat continued on its way north. Jet glanced to starboard, where flashes of lightning over the Panamanian jungle were lighting up the cloud cover. The celestial pyrotechnics were a near constant in the tropics, illuminating the strip of coast before the rainforest-covered hills retreated into the darkness.

"Are you going to turn around once you drop me off, or stay in Colombian waters?"

A sly expression flashed across Juan Diego's face. "Our business is done once you're off the boat. I won't ask you what you're doing from there, and you shouldn't worry about what I'm up to."

The old smuggler had probably arranged to bring a load of something north, and viewed taking her south as paid stowage for a part of the run that would have normally been unpaid. Taking her five grand the easiest money he'd probably ever made. Which Jet didn't begrudge him. She'd long ago learned that what others had to do to make their living was none of her concern. With what she'd seen and been ordered to do while in her country's service, she had no room to judge.

They stood together for half an hour, the predictable swells on the port side creating the slight roll she'd felt in the bunk, and then after yawning several times, she gave Juan Diego another neutral stare. "Are you piloting all night?"

He shook his head. "No, just a little while longer, and then my mate will take over for six hours. The good news is that moving at this speed, not much happens you don't have time to correct for."

"That's reassuring."

She stepped down the ladder and returned to her bunk, and fell into a light slumber, the rocking now so familiar that it no longer troubled her.

When she started awake, bright sunlight was streaming through the porthole, and she was sweating. She pushed herself up to a sitting position on the edge of the bunk and stretched, then resignedly used the toilet, which failed to meet even her lowest expectations. After a brief sink bath with a hand towel, she emerged into the galley, where one of the crew was playing a video game on a phone, a steaming cup of coffee in front of him.

He didn't say good morning and she didn't either, instead opting to pour herself half a mug and climb the ladder with it. The other crewman was at the wheel, looking punchy. The sea stretched endlessly to port, transitioning from deep azure to light turquoise as it neared land. A series of islands dotted the surface in the near distance, jutting palm trees shimmering in the offshore wind. Jet shielded her eyes from the sun and gazed at them before turning to the mate.

"They're beautiful," she said.

"San Blas Islands," he said, pointing. "That one there's Guna Yala, and that one's called BBQ Island by the gringos." He caught himself and fixed his eyes on the radar. "No offense."

"None taken."

She sipped her coffee and watched a few sea birds cross the vessel's path, including several hopeful pelicans far above off the stern, hoping for some easy pickings off the back of the boat. Eventually they tired of their vigil and wheeled south toward the islands, leaving Jet and the *Providencia* to their destiny.

The day wore on and the heat increased, the sea breeze providing scant relief. Juan Diego appeared an hour and a half later and took the wheel. His coffee was pungent with the smell of alcohol. They passed the time watching the waves roll by and studying the depth sounder and the radar, nothing else to do to avert the tedium. Flying fish shot from the waves, their flight exuberant as their blue and green flanks sparkled in the sun, and for a moment the world seemed benign and good. Hope for the future felt like a reasonable possibility for Jet until the memory of the toys she'd abandoned while running for her life dashed her optimism.

Forces she didn't understand were pursuing them for unknown reasons. There was little doubt in her mind that revenge was the motivation, but for what transgression, she had no idea. Not that it mattered much. At this point all she could do was react, and when she learned more, take action to eliminate the threat at the source, as she had with the Russian lawyer.

For now her priority was to get back to her daughter and to Matt, and she'd deal with the rest once they were safe. The prospect was depressing, but she knew better than most that an adversary was dangerous until you cut its head off, and running wasn't a long-term solution. If her last year had proved anything, it was that the world was smaller than she'd hoped, and her myriad enemies more resourceful than she'd given them credit for.

A mistake she couldn't afford to make ever again.

~ ~ ~

Santuario, Colombia

Hannah sat on the edge of a cot humming to herself as Matt stared at the valley below through a window set deep in the monastery's stone walls. He'd always thought of Colombia as jungle, and was somewhat surprised by the soaring mountains and rolling valleys surrounding their refuge. The monastery was nestled in verdant green, the only approach via a tram suspended by cables over the foliage. The four towers supporting the conveyance on the way up the steep slope were the only structures he could see between the compound and the road far below.

Franco had met them when they'd arrived at dusk and led them to an outlying dormitory that he said had been unoccupied for several decades. He'd handed them a fifteen-liter bottle of water and a loaf of crusty peasant bread for their evening feast, promising to bring something more satisfying the following day as he took his leave. Matt and Hannah had relished the bread after a long day of munching on dry rations from the survival kit; their breakfast of chewy breakfast bars washed down with tepid water had left much to be desired.

Hannah was being a trooper, accepting her strange new reality without complaint, and Matt again remarked to himself what an exceptional child she was. At times she would gaze at him with huge eyes and his heart would melt. That she'd been subjected to so much in her few years and had persevered, emerging relatively unscathed if not stronger, was a small miracle for which he was thankful.

The door creaked open on rusted hinges, and a small cloud of dust rose from the stone floor. Franco entered, adorned in the long robe he'd met them in the prior evening, a black plastic bag in one large hand and a bottle of orange juice clutched in the other. Hannah's eyes lit up when she saw the juice, and he smiled as she toddled over to him, a smile of welcome on her face.

"Good morning. Sorry it took me a while. I needed to attend to my duties before I could go into town and get some provisions," Franco explained. He set the bag down and handed Matt the bottle of juice. "These pastries are fresh baked. They're a guilty pleasure of mine, so my buying them won't raise any eyebrows."

A heavenly aroma wafted from the bag, and Hannah's nose twitched like a rabbit's. Matt smiled at the kindly monk's generosity.

"Thanks. Judging by the size, that should do us for a while."

Franco reached beneath his robe and Matt froze, and then relaxed when the monk's hand emerged holding a roll of toilet paper. "I thought this might come in handy."

Matt laughed. "I was afraid I might be reduced to using my socks."

"Fortunately not." Franco looked around the bare room. "Sorry it's not more comfortable."

"Are you kidding? There are no gunmen, and we even get a little breeze. We'll live." He paused. "Any luck on the cell phone?"

Franco closed his eyes for a moment and sighed. "Sorry. I almost forgot. Here," he said, and pulled a small Nokia box from somewhere in the depths of his robe. "I have change for you, but figured you'd want me to put it toward more food later." He glanced around the stone chamber and gave Hannah another warm smile. "I wish I could stay and share some breakfast with you, but it would be better if I went about my business as customary. We don't want any of the others getting curious, do we?"

"I understand. Thanks again for everything."

Franco departed on sandaled feet, pulling the heavy plank door closed behind him. Matt opened the phone box, removed the charger, and plugged in the phone. Hannah was waiting patiently by the bag, clearly anxious for Matt to dole out the delectables. He hefted it as though considering the contents and then smiled at her.

"Seems about two pounds, maybe more. Wonder what's in it?" he said, and waggled his eyebrows. Hannah giggled and then composed herself, her typically somber expression returning. Matt opened the bag and gazed inside, and then removed a fistful of napkins and several breakfast pastries. Their sugary glaze gleamed in the sunlight, coating layers of thin dough with pastry cream between them and topped with caramel. "What do you say? Do we try one?"

Hannah nodded. "Yeth."

They both bit into their treats. Hannah looked like she was in heaven as she chewed. Matt smiled at the caramel smudged around her mouth and decided to let her make a mess of it before cleaning it up. What was the point of being a kid if you couldn't get your food smeared all over your face while eating?

He eyed the cable car at the bottom of the slope as he munched. It hadn't moved since Franco had sent it back down the hill, a courtesy for the other monks who were in town running errands. The monastery was a veritable fortress; the tram was an effective way of limiting who could enter the grounds, which were remote enough that he hadn't seen another living soul besides Franco and a few distant pedestrians far below on the winding street.

When they were done with their snack, Matt helped Hannah clean up and then cautioned her to stay put until he got back. After donning a robe Franco had left for him, he checked the new cell phone to ensure it had sufficient charge and took the cable car down to the bottom of the hill, where there was cell coverage – there was none in the monastery due to the location of the only tower in the area.

He dialed Jet's phone from memory and it went to voice mail – not unexpected if she was in the wilds, on her way from Panama. He left a short message reassuring her that they were safe and read off the new cell number, and then explained that he'd try to call later because there was no coverage in the monastery.

When he hung up he felt unaccountably deflated, and even the breathtaking view as the cable car ascended the mountain failed to raise his spirits. When he came back into the little room, Hannah was humming to herself on her cot, watching a squabble of sparrows fight over a few bits of pastry she'd set on the windowsill. The angle of her face reminded him of her mother, and for a moment he felt a pang of loneliness so intense it almost took his breath away. After living so long as a loner, first in the concrete jungle of Bangkok and later in the very real ones of Laos, he'd let Jet and her daughter into his life, and now he was paying the price.

~ ~ ~

Fernanda and Jaime sat at a breakfast restaurant in Apía, three miles north of Santuario, enjoying the idyllic setting on the veranda where they were the only diners. They sipped coffee and wordlessly nibbled at their eggs, lost in their thoughts. Fernanda tried Igor's sat phone again, having been unable to reach him that morning, and he picked up on the third ring.

"Hello," he said curtly, the rumble of motors in the background so loud she could barely make out his words.

"Good morning."

"It is, isn't it? What's happening on your end?"

"We have a line on the man and the girl. We're tracking down the truck driver they got a ride with. Hopefully we'll find him today," she reported.

"That's good. But it may all be for nothing. I'm about to leave Colón in a fast cigarette boat our friend arranged for. It'll make short work of the seas, so I should be able to overtake the fishing boat before it gets to Colombian waters. When I do, she's as good as dead."

"Well, she's proved resilient, so I'll keep working the truck-driver lead. This woman seems to have nine lives. We've underestimated her resourcefulness before. I don't want to again." She stopped, thinking. "Why don't you fly into Colombia and take a boat north instead of trying to get her in Panamanian water?"

"We don't know their end destination, so there's no guarantee we would spot her. Besides, this boat is equipped with good radar and a seasoned captain. I have no idea what condition the Colombian boats might be in, but from everything I've heard they're likely to be primitive around that area. Our best bet is to follow them, not try to head them off."

"I understand. I spoke with Jaime, but he doesn't have any contacts with the Colombian navy in that part of the country. His power is concentrated on the Pacific side." They were speaking

Portuguese, so she had no worry about Jaime overhearing and taking offense. "At any rate, I'll keep after the man and the girl. Good luck catching up with them."

"At worst you'll have wasted a little time. And it will give you something to do with yourself while you wait – I know how you get with idle hands." She could hear the smile in his voice. "And thanks for the good wishes, but luck will have nothing to do with it."

"I'm sure it won't. Enjoy your boat ride."

She signed off and turned to Jaime, who was texting on his phone. He glanced up at her and pursed his lips. "We found the driver's distribution center in Viterbo, but he's already left on his route. The girl didn't know where he was going today, so we're watching the roads."

"Where's Viterbo?"

"It's a larger town about nine kilometers from here. We'll head over after breakfast."

"What about his cell phone? Can't we track it?"

"Yes and no. Many areas in these hills don't have coverage, so it's hit or miss. And there's still some latency between when I get someone at the phone company to run a trace and when it gets done. I've already asked for it, but there are no guarantees." He smiled. "Nothing happens fast in Colombia, so relax, enjoy the view, and be patient."

She returned the smile. "I'm not good at being patient, or passive."

He held her stare. "I'll have to remember that."

CHAPTER 34

Santiago, Chile

Drago shifted from foot to foot as the phone rang. His agent was taking longer than usual to pick up. When the man's distinctive voice came on the line, he sounded cautious.

"Yes?"

"It's me."

Silence. When the agent spoke, his tone was typically flat, devoid of inflection. "Been a while since you checked in. Our client is...unhappy."

"Something came up." Drago told him about the river, the hospital, and his scrabble over the last days to accumulate sufficient cash through muggings to have some reasonable options.

"I see. That's quite a tale," the agent said neutrally.

"I need some help. I want the word put out about our boy. He had help. A woman. Professional. He couldn't have gotten that help without a local contact. That spells either an intelligence agency or organized crime."

"I have some contacts with the Chilean government."

"Good. Nose around and see what you can learn about their clandestine group. Do you have sufficient pull to confirm whether they're helping the target?"

"I should be able to," the agent said dryly.

"Fine. As to the local mafia, find out who the groups are that run Chile and put out feelers to them. Someone will know something."

The agent cleared his throat. "We have an issue with the client. He's not happy about your going dark."

"He can feel free to pull the contract, and I'll gladly go home."

The agent was silent for several moments. "I need to discuss this latest development with him. Where can I reach you?"

"I can call you back in an hour. Will that be enough time?"

"I should think so. Are you…fit, after your hospital stay?"

"A little worse for wear, but I'm fine."

"No concerns about your ability to conclude the assignment?"

"None, unless you don't do as I've asked – in which case we're wasting each other's time. So make your call and I'll touch base shortly." He hung up before the agent could argue.

He expected the man had taken some flak for his being out of touch for so long, but he was well paid and could deal with a few ruffled feathers – the client would understand, given the situation, and it wasn't like Drago had been off on a binge. The real question was whether the client would still want to move forward with Drago, or whether he had contacted someone else to replace him.

Drago was sitting in the shade of a tree near one of the city's wide boulevards, the snowcapped Andes in the distance. It had been an unpleasant few days, having to assault pedestrians to build up a bankroll, stealing everything he needed – shoes, money, a watch, a heavier jacket. But after four muggings in four different neighborhoods, he had the equivalent of five hundred dollars, shoes that fit, a decent shirt, and the newly purchased burner cell phone he planned to toss as soon as he completed his next call to the agent.

An hour passed as he watched pretty girls stroll down the sidewalk toward the university, and he thought to himself that Chile might not be a terrible place to go to ground after this episode was over – good food, passable wine, friendly locals, acceptable weather. It definitely warranted looking into; he understood that Colombia would be too hot for him after this contract was finished, regardless of how it turned out.

His agent sounded slightly more relaxed when Drago called him back.

"The client has expressed his desire for the contract to proceed as agreed, and he reiterated his sense of urgency."

"Very well. I need some money and a passport. Can you get a package to Santiago, Chile, within twenty-four hours?"

The agent hesitated. "That's tight."

"I didn't ask whether it would be difficult, I asked whether you can make it happen."

"I'll see what I can do. How much do you see yourself needing?"

"Figure ten grand cash, a credit card I can use for flights and cars, and a full set of papers. You still have my photos, correct?"

"Of course. I'll have my technician get to work. But getting it to you in that time frame might prove to be more complicated than you imagine."

"Ship it via LAN airlines to be picked up at the Santiago airport – that will be faster than sending it DHL or FedEx. Use the name Guillermo Cribi." One of the men Drago had relieved of his wallet bore a decent resemblance to him, and he'd kept his identification for just this reason.

"Right. I'll see if he can turn this in time to get it out by this evening or, worst case, first thing tomorrow. If he can, figure tomorrow afternoon at the latest."

"Fine. In the meantime, put out the word. Someone will know something."

The agent hesitated. "You're absolutely sure you're up to this?"

"Oh, never more so. I'm not going to say that this is personal now, but let's just assume I have a burning interest in seeing the contract satisfied sooner rather than later."

"Very well. I'll get to work."

"Good. Send the details to my email. I'll check it tonight."

~ ~ ~

NE of Acandí, Colombia

The lights of Colombia glimmered in the distance as the *Providencia* crossed the invisible line that marked the end of Panama and the beginning of Colombian water. The trip had taken longer than Juan

Diego had expected, due to a headwind strong enough to rob them of several hours, and he was now estimating that they'd be off Acandí in another forty minutes, or about twenty-five hours after Jet had set foot on the fishing boat's deck.

She'd spent most of the trip below. The vessel's movements were conducive to dozing, abetted by the hypnotic drone of the motor. Once it had gotten dark, she returned to the pilothouse with her bag in tow and watched the black coastline slip by, occasionally studying the glowing screen of the radar and the few blips at the far edge of its range.

"That's strange," Juan Diego said, following her gaze and eyeing the radar. His ever-present bottle of seco was wedged among the instruments, and the smell of alcohol seeped from his pores whenever Jet got close to him.

"What?"

He tapped the screen with a gnarled finger. "That. It's moving pretty fast. Probably forty knots. You don't see that kind of boat down here unless it's headed north."

"How far away is it?"

"Maybe thirty kilometers."

"Navy?" Jet asked, watching the glowing dot inch a little closer to the center of the screen with each sweep.

"Way too small. That looks like maybe forty, forty-five feet."

Jet stepped away from Juan Diego. "How much longer till you drop me off?"

"Figure half an hour, tops. I'll have one of the crew take you to the beach in the tender."

"I don't suppose you know of any hotels in Acandí…"

"Never had the pleasure, but if there are any, I can't imagine you'll have any trouble getting a room. Acandí's not exactly a high-traffic destination."

"I'm surprised there's anything there, based on your description."

"A lot of Colombians go to these border beach areas for vacation, to get away from the crowded towns." He unscrewed the cap on his seco, drained the last of it, and studied the empty bottle with a sad expression. "Takes all kinds."

Half an hour later Juan Diego backed off the throttles as Acandí's waterfront main street glowed along the dark stretch of coastline to starboard. He turned from the wheel and called to the crewman who was using the head in the cabin below. "Gerardo. Get up here. Time to take our guest to shore."

A few moments later Gerardo arrived, with the distinctive smell of cannabis on his clothes and a faraway look in his eyes. Juan Diego either didn't notice or didn't care, and pointed at the tender that was trailing the boat, twenty feet off the stern. "Reel her in and let's get this over with." The old smuggler looked at Jet. "Nice having you aboard, and good luck with whatever. Safe travels, and all that. Watch your back – Colombia can be a dangerous place."

"Thanks."

Gerardo had the skiff ready in thirty seconds, and Jet stepped aboard as Juan Diego put the larger vessel's transmission in neutral. The little outboard whined like a jilted bride, and then they cut across the water to Acandí, no more than a quarter mile away. Jet turned to watch the approaching outline of thatched roofs and a few buildings with lights on. The beach was deserted, most of the dwellings already dark.

The roar of high-performance motors reached her from across the water, and she glanced back at the *Providencia*. A low-slung cigarette boat was bearing down on it from behind, seemingly on a collision course.

"Hang on," Gerardo said.

The skiff bounced through the mild surf as it neared the beach, and then the bow bumped softly against the sand. "Watch your step," Gerardo warned. Jet waved over her shoulder as she climbed over the bow and leapt onto the beach. He gunned the outboard in reverse and the tender slid off the sand, lifted by an incoming roller, and then he was gone, invisible in the darkness, the skiff's dark hull blending with the surface of the sea.

A tickle of apprehension stirred in her stomach as she watched the speedboat pull alongside the *Providencia*. A fast-moving vessel coming from Panama and beelining directly to the fishing boat might have been any of several innocent things, but that wasn't how her luck had been running. A man boarded Juan Diego's craft in the dim light, and she didn't wait to see the outcome. Instead she bolted across the sand to the relative safety of the small town.

On the *Providencia*, Juan Diego saw the approaching boat and moved below with surprising agility, returning with his flare gun just in time to see the other craft bump against his vessel's hull and a man leap aboard. He squinted against the glare of a spotlight that blinked on, temporarily blinding him, and was struggling to see when a presence materialized next to him and twisted the weapon from his hand.

"You're not going to need that," Igor said, tossing the gun on the deck and pointing his own pistol at Juan Diego's head. "Where is she?" he demanded, then turned and slammed the butt into the second crewman's head as he tried to tackle him. The man went down in a heap, knocked senseless, and Igor turned back to the old smuggler.

"Tie him up."

Juan Diego shook his head. "You're insane."

"You either tie him up or I shoot him. Your choice."

Juan Diego frowned and moved to the cabinet below the helm.

"Easy – I better not see anything but rope in your hand, or you're a dead man," Igor warned.

Juan Diego grunted as he knelt and opened the storage area, pulled a length of cord from inside it, and secured the crewman's wrists before standing and facing Igor.

"We don't have any money onboard, so you're wasting your energy," Juan Diego said.

"Don't play dumb. Where is she?"

"What do you want?" Juan Diego demanded.

"You heard me. I know you took on a passenger. Is she below?"

"There's nobody below."

Igor cocked the hammer. "Show me."

Juan Diego eased down the ladder, his movements stiff, hoping to trick the newcomer into letting down his guard – he was, after all, an old man. Igor followed him down using one hand, the pistol in the other, and then motioned with the gun. "Sit down at the table and keep your hands where I can see them," Igor said.

Any hopes Juan Diego had of being able to take the gunman evaporated – the man was obviously a seasoned pro.

Igor's eyes traveled to the front of the boat. "Those are the staterooms?"

Juan Diego nodded. Igor eyed him as he moved to the first door. "Move and I shoot you."

"There's nobody there."

"So you say." Igor's hand slid onto the lever handle, and with a twist he pushed the door open and swept the tiny room with his gun. Finding no one, he repeated the move on Juan Diego's cabin and finished with the two heads. When he got back to where Juan Diego was sitting, his face was dark. "What else is down here?"

"Machine room. Engines. Fish hold accessible through the deck."

Igor did a perfunctory search and returned to Juan Diego. "No more screwing around. Tell me where she is, or I start shooting off body parts."

"I really don't know what you're talking about. You've got the wrong boat."

Igor considered shooting him in the stomach, but decided to give it one more try. "I watched her get on in Portobelo, you turd," he hissed, venom dripping from every syllable. "Do you want to die tonight, or live to smuggle more dope north? I really don't care which, but you might. And I'll find her anyway."

The blood drained from Juan Diego's face at the mention of Portobelo, and he realized the man was serious about killing him – he knew enough stone-cold murderers to recognize he was dealing with one.

"We dropped her onshore."

"Where?"

"Capurganá," Juan Diego lied, naming a town further north just below the Panamanian border.

Igor saw the lie in his eyes and raised the gun. "I told you, you lie to me, you die. I guess you didn't believe me."

Juan Diego instantly recognized his mistake – his poker face might have been good enough to fool some half-wit customs officials, but not a professional.

"No. Wait. All right. We just dropped her off in Acandí, the town off our starboard side. My crewman gave her a lift in the dinghy. Please. I don't know anything about her other than that she wanted a ride south. That's it. This isn't my fight. You should be able to find her there – there's no road out, so she'll be looking for a boat to take her to a larger town."

Igor studied Juan Diego's red eyes and twitching face, and then raised his pistol and shot him between the eyes. The back of the old man's head blew off as the slug expanded and took a baseball-size chunk of skull with it, and he collapsed forward on the table.

"You know what? I believe you," Igor said, unable to help his involuntary smile.

Back on deck, the bound crewman was still out cold. Rather than waste a bullet, Igor slipped the pistol into his belt, grabbed the unconscious man's head with both hands, and snapped his neck with a powerful twist. He was just rising when he heard the skiff pull to the stern of the fishing boat. Gerardo was staring with wide eyes at the cigarette boat alongside it.

Igor moved toward the skiff and drew his pistol. "Where did you drop her off?"

Gerardo stammered his answer. "On the beach."

Their eyes locked, and Gerardo saw something in the gunman's that sent him flying over the side of the boat, diving deep into the water before the shooter could kill him. Igor swore and weighed firing at the man, but opted for stealth. The shot inside the boat would have been barely audible in the small town, but a shot out in the open would have half the population reaching for its guns, which he had no doubt a remote Colombian border town would have plenty of.

Igor watched the surface for the man's head, and when it didn't appear after twenty seconds, he leapt across to the cigarette boat and pointed to the dark town. "Can you get this thing onto the beach?"

"If there's no reef, I should be able to," said the captain, a twenty-something man with slicked-back hair and a scar running down his face. Igor guessed that he was a veteran of the runs from Colombia to Panama that brought much of the locally distributed cocaine into the country. He looked like the stereotypical fast-money player who'd never live to see thirty.

"Then put us there. We're right behind her and she's got nowhere to go."

Igor called Fernanda on his sat phone on the way into the beach and gave her a short report. When he was done, she was equally terse.

"Call once you get her."

"Absolutely. This will be over within the hour."

Fernanda hesitated. "Be careful."

"Always."

CHAPTER 35

Acandí, Colombia

Jet heard the muffled pop from the *Providencia* and stopped, instantly recognizing the sound of a handgun inside the boat. She squinted at the pair of vessels in the darkness, but after a few seconds forced her attention back to making her escape. She had to assume that Juan Diego and the crew had told her pursuers where she'd gone, which meant that the relative comfort and safety of a hotel was out of the question. It would be just a matter of time until they came for her, and in a town with no way out but the sea, she didn't have many options.

She gazed down the sand at the beached pangas tied to coconut palms, their long multicolored hulls gleaming in the moonlight, and debated liberating one, but dismissed the thought when the cigarette boat's engines revved and its bow light blinked to life. She'd never be able to outrun a vessel like that in one of the pangas, and it had radar, so she'd be a sitting duck. Her only choices were to hide or to lure her pursuers into a trap and ambush them.

Time was working against her, and by morning her pursuers would have been able to call in reinforcements if they hadn't found her. She had no idea what kinds of connections they had in Colombia, or even who they were, but judging by their ability to mobilize the Panamanian police, she had to assume the worst.

The boat picked up speed. At the rate it was cutting through the waves, it would be on the beach in a couple of minutes. She eyed her footprints in the sand and cursed that she didn't have time to brush them away with a palm frond or to wait for the surf to mask them – they would lead directly to her.

Jet couldn't do much about that, so she ran to the dirt road that fronted the beach and searched for a good location from where she could watch who disembarked from the boat so she would know how many were after her. She settled for the shelter of a darkened wooden building on the corner of a mud intersection. Once she was out of sight, she peeked around the side and watched as the cigarette boat neared the beach, its approach as subtle as a panzer division charging up the boulevard.

The vessel's long snout slid onto the sand, and the captain killed the engines. The area plunged into silence, although a few lights flicked on in some of the waterfront dwellings at the unexpected sound of a large go-fast boat beaching itself in the middle of the town.

A man jumped from the bow onto the sand, followed by a second. After a brief conversation, the second man leaned against the boat hull and lit a cigarette as the first made his way up the beach to the road, following her footsteps, the distinctive outline of a gun in his hand obvious to Jet.

So it was only one.

Her spirits rose, although she was a little surprised. Whoever this was had no idea who he was dealing with.

Or he was exceptionally skilled and didn't think he needed backup.

She watched him lope up the strand, no wasted movement, every step efficient, and her relief evaporated. Overconfidence had killed more adversaries than her bullets, and she wasn't about to fall prey to that trap.

The challenge was how to dispatch a lone pursuer who was armed and probably more than competent.

Jet decided to draw him off the beach into the snarl of small homes and directionless dirt paths that served as streets. She weighed simply shooting him as he passed her hidden position, but that would wake the entire town. Better to see if she could wound him without firing a shot, and learn who he was and why he was after her.

The gunman looked to be at least six feet tall and athletic. So his physical strength in a direct confrontation would overwhelm her, even if she was adept at a multitude of martial arts. That left the element of surprise and outsmarting him.

Or completely avoiding him and tackling the second man watching the boat.

She froze when the gunman looked directly at her position and began sprinting toward her as though he had laser vision. After a moment's hesitation she bolted up the muddy street, away from the waterfront, aware that she was leaving footprints that would be easily followed. If she wanted to draw him in, she didn't have to work too hard.

The dark street lit up like it was daylight for a brief second, and then an earth-shattering explosion rocked her surroundings – lightning and thunder, moving northwest from the mainland. A moment later another flash illuminated the line of shabby buildings, and a massive detonation reverberated off the sea, and then sheets of rain blew across her path as the skies let loose.

That hadn't been part of the plan, but she was flexible enough to incorporate it. Visibility had just dropped to twenty feet, which would more than work in her favor.

She chanced a look over her shoulder and couldn't make out the building she'd hidden behind. That would slow the gunman. Or maybe it wouldn't. She paused and glanced around at her surroundings, and then overhead to the second-story balcony of the half-completed structure she was standing in front of.

A construction area was perfect for her purposes. Jet ducked inside and made her cautious way around a primitive collection of tools before working her way upstairs, snagging a hammer and a length of two-by-four as she went. The outline of a strategy began to form as heavy rain peppered the corrugated metal roof, and by the time her pursuer pounded up the lane, she'd made her decision.

Jet waited until she heard the man's footsteps splashing in the water outside and tossed the hammer downstairs. It landed with a thump on the hardwood floor. She listened, the sound of rain leaking in streams through the roof the only disturbance in the quiet interior, and then she spotted the gunman creeping back toward the building, stepping carefully, his pistol at the ready.

She clambered up a beam, leaving her bag at the base of a wall, and pulled herself up into the snarl of pipes running across the ceiling. Her abdominal muscles were rigid as she hooked her legs over a beam and pulled herself up, clutching one of the pipes with one hand and the plank in the other. A scrape sounded from the base of the stairway, and then a creak as the gunman ascended the steps, his footfalls silent as he neared where she was waiting, suspended over the doorway. Jet held her breath as she sensed him near. Her perception narrowed to the familiar tunnel vision that always preceded action.

The gunman stepped into the room, leading with his weapon, and she waited, completely still. A tarp protecting some cabinets near the terrace flapped in the wind, drawing his attention. He flinched and took a step toward it, his gun trained on the undulating fabric.

Thunder boomed and the room lit up in a flash as Jet swung down, hanging upside down by her knees, and slammed the wooden beam into the gunman's skull as hard as she could. He grunted, and his pistol clattered across the floor as his knees buckled. Jet dropped the plank and swung down, landing in a crouch as her assailant pitched face forward onto the hardwood floor.

Another flash of lightning preceded a rumbling explosion of thunder. The man's head was bleeding where the wood had struck his skull. She gripped his shoulder and flipped him over. She could barely make out his face in the gloom, but noted the right side was covered with wet blood.

His eyes flittered open a few moments later, and he found himself staring down the barrel of Jet's Glock. He appeared dazed, and she waited until he seemed able to focus before she spoke.

"Who are you, and why are you after me?" she asked in Spanish. Her voice was calm, her tone even.

No answer.

She reached down and picked up the plank. "One final time and then I start breaking bones. Who are you, and why are you after me?"

The man glared at her but didn't say anything.

His tibia cracked like a matchstick when she swung the edge of the two-by-four against his shin, and he cried out in agony. He gasped for breath and she gave him time to recover, and then asked her question again. "Who are you?"

The man gritted his teeth and wheezed a response, forcing her closer to hear him. As she neared she caught the movement of his left hand just in time to avoid the slash of a razor-sharp stiletto blade. Jet slammed the plank against his head with a wet thud and he shuddered, spasming for ten seconds before falling still. The groaning rattle of his last breath was unmistakable in its finality. The blade dropped from his still fingers, and she kicked it to the side, and then felt his carotid artery for a pulse.

Nothing.

Jet swore to herself for reacting instinctively with a death blow instead of breaking his arms. Now she knew nothing more than when he'd entered the building. She glanced at her watch – only a few minutes had passed since he'd followed her from the main street, but time wasn't her friend with an accomplice waiting for him at the boat. She searched the man's pockets and retrieved a fat wad of hundred-dollar bills and a satellite phone. No identification. He'd obviously been a pro. But not quite good enough, she thought, as she retrieved his gun.

Jet carried the phone and money to her bag and stashed the bundle in a side pocket with her own cash. She checked the pistol magazine, confirmed that it was loaded with 9mm cartridges, and emptied it, stuffing the bullets into her pocket for future use. She eyed the phone and thumbed the screen to life, then recorded the numbers in the call log into her phone.

Jet collected her bag and returned to the rainy street. The cloudburst ended as abruptly as it had begun, leaving only mud and small streams coursing down the lane on either side. At the waterfront road she peered around the corner of the building and confirmed that the captain was in the boat, taking shelter from the storm. She remained motionless as he emerged from the cabin and looked around, then hopped off the bow onto the beach and lit another cigarette.

Watching the smoking captain, she pressed redial on the dead man's phone and listened as it rang. A woman's voice answered.

"Well, is it over?" the voice asked.

Jet didn't recognize the language. Portuguese? She listened, saying nothing, and then a peal of thunder roared overhead. The voice spoke again. "Igor?"

Jet hung up. A woman, speaking a foreign tongue that sounded like a romance language but wasn't Italian or Spanish, had called the dead man Igor. Jet searched her memory for any Mossad assignment that had involved Portugal or Brazil, but there were none.

The sat phone vibrated as a call came in. Jet debated answering, but decided that there was nothing more to learn. If the woman was also a professional, Jet would be giving her information by saying anything. She let the call go to voice mail.

The captain walked a few feet from the boat on the wet sand, blowing a puff of cancer at the clouds, and Jet began her approach down the dark street, running in a crouch, her Glock out. She made it past the side of the boat where the smoking man was standing and crept along the water's edge, intending to surprise him. As she neared the hull, she heard the clear sounds of a struggle and then a loud splash as a body dropped into the sea.

She rounded the bow with her pistol clutched in both hands and came face to face with Gerardo, dripping wet, standing over the boat captain's inert form floating in the surf. His gaze locked with hers and she lowered the weapon.

"He dead?" Jet asked.

"Yes. Nose cartilage through the brain. My days as a marine weren't completely a waste."

"What about Juan Diego and your friend?"

Gerardo shook his head.

Jet glanced at the boat. "You want a ride?"

"Where?"

"Other side of the gulf. From there, anywhere you want to go with your new boat."

His grin was luminescent in the faint light. "Why not?"

She looked at the dead man's sat phone, which was vibrating again in her hand. With another glance at Gerardo, she pitched it as far as she could into the sea and gestured to him.

"Let's see what this thing can do."

CHAPTER 36

Viterbo, Colombia

Fernanda paced in front of the hotel suite window, pushing the redial button on her cell reflexively, Igor's phone now saying it was out of service. The call she'd received had thrown her. Igor never did that – called, then didn't say anything. A sinking feeling in her stomach was spreading to her back, and a headache was building.

She didn't want to consider the possibility of anything happening to him. He was as good as they got. An experienced player who knew the ropes. And the only man she'd ever had real feelings for.

He couldn't be dead. It was impossible.

Meeting his fate in some Colombian border town? Where was it he'd said they'd tracked the woman to?

Acandí.

She opened her web browser and searched for it. A fishing hamlet. A dung hole. Literally nothing there.

How could she find out what had happened? Maybe he was injured. They'd both been wounded before during an operation, nothing catastrophic; but in the middle of nowhere, it could be disastrous, especially without backup.

A knock at her door jarred her from her thoughts. She collected herself, took a deep breath, and opened it. Jaime was there, looking dapper and rich.

"Can I interest you in some dinner?"

"I...I don't have an appetite."

"What's wrong?"

She told him about the call and about Igor's closing in on their target. He listened, his face impassive, and then nodded. "I have a helicopter at my compound on the outskirts of Medellín. I can send a couple of men in to check on the town, if you like. It's a few hundred kilometers from my place. Let me know if you'd like me to do so."

Fernanda wanted to fly there herself, but that was impractical, a panic move. If there was a problem in Acandí, a pair of Jaime's best could learn what it was better than she could, and far sooner. Besides, she was already here and close to finding the man and his daughter.

"Would you do that?" she asked, turning on the charm.

He grinned. "For you? Of course. I'll put it on your tab. Assuming you join me for dinner, that is."

"I may not be good company."

"I suspect the worst dinner with you would be better than the best with anyone else."

"Please have the helicopter go to Acandí, and I'll get ready to join you," she said.

Jaime beamed at her and pulled his cell phone from his pocket. He barked orders as Fernanda slipped into the bathroom and rinsed her face with cool water, taking a moment to study her reflection and regain her composure. When she returned, she had a smile on her face that was completely artificial. Jaime hung up and regarded her with a serious expression.

"My men will be in Acandí in a few hours at most. They'll call when they have something to report."

"Thank you, Jaime. Maybe I'll be able to work up an appetite after all. Where are we going?" she asked, doing her best to put a brave face on the anxiety that was gnawing at her.

"There's an excellent restaurant a few blocks from here. Famous for miles around. Good Colombian country cooking."

"That sounds great." She hesitated. "I almost forgot. What happened with the chicken truck driver?"

"No sign of him. But his secretary said that he often does two-day runs – he covers a lot of territory. Worst case, I would expect him to show up tomorrow by close of business. I have a man watching the building in case he arrives earlier. Don't worry. We'll find him."

"This has been very frustrating. Even now they could be escaping," she complained.

"Well, we aren't in a huge hurry. We know the woman was in Acandí as recently as an hour ago, right? That's a long way from here – the other side of the country."

"So it will take her some time to reach us, if…if my associate failed to terminate her."

"Exactly."

A thought occurred to her. "What if she somehow finds a plane to fly her here?"

Jaime laughed. "Not likely. Private planes are rare in Colombia, especially outside of the major metropolitan areas. And if I recall, the airstrip at Acandí is gravel, with no facilities like fuel or hangars. Nobody who could afford a plane would want to live anyplace like Acandí, much less keep their aircraft there. But let's not get ahead of ourselves. It sounds like your associate can take care of himself. It could be that his phone got wet, or died, or broke, or fell overboard. I wouldn't assume the worst just yet. There's likely a reasonable explanation."

She took Jaime's arm and allowed him to lead her to the lobby, ignoring the ugly feeling in her stomach. There was no reasonable explanation, she already knew, in spite of Jaime's assurances. Igor was either wounded or dead. She didn't know how she knew, but she was sure.

That intuition had rarely failed her throughout her career, and while she would do anything to be wrong this time, she wasn't banking on it.

If she was right, she'd mourn Igor in her own way, in her own time. For now the only thing she would focus on would be finding the woman and extracting a terrible vengeance. Whereas the contract only required them to execute her, if she'd killed Igor, Fernanda would use every bit of her considerable knowledge of torture to ensure that the woman's last hours on the planet were the most agonizing possible.

~ ~ ~

SE of Acandí, Colombia

After stopping at the *Providencia* to open the sea cocks, so the fishing boat would sink to the bottom with Juan Diego and the dead crewman, Gerardo retrieved the five grand Jet had paid for her safe passage and pocketed it. He returned to the cigarette boat and secured the tender to the stern as Jet maneuvered the sleek vessel away from the sinking ship, which was already low in the water.

Jet eased the throttles forward and the boat surged ahead as though eager to run wide open. "Are you sure the dinghy's secure?" she asked, glancing over her shoulder to where the skiff's bow line was tied to a cleat.

"Yes. Just don't try to break any speed records."

Jet punched up their position on the GPS and zoomed in on the Gulf of Urabá coastline, and studied the two towns that were obvious possible destinations. Turbo was closer to Medellín than Necoclí, but she remembered Juan Diego's warning about Colombian customs boats at the larger port and the increased risk of scrutiny she'd run.

"I'm going to make for Necoclí. Have you ever been there?" she asked Gerardo.

"Yes. Not much to speak of. There's no port. Ugly beaches."

"So no patrols?"

He laughed. "Not likely. Everyone in a town like Necoclí's trying to get out, not the other way around."

Jet punched coordinates into the autopilot. The bow swung several degrees to starboard and then steadied. She turned to Gerardo.

"If I leave this boat in your hands, you think you can find a home for it in Colombia so there's no fallout for you, and no trace of it ever being found?"

Gerardo nodded, his eyes hooded. "Probably. There's always a demand for fast boats at the right price."

"Then consider this your retirement fund. I'll take the dinghy, and you disappear. Deal?"

He smirked. "That would work." He eyed the GPS. "Forty-five kilometers. We could easily do that in an hour."

"You're reading my mind." Jet didn't want to be on the boat one second longer than absolutely necessary. She adjusted the trim tabs and goosed the throttles a little more, and then eyed the fuel gauges and did a quick calculation. "You should have another hundred kilometers of range after you drop me off."

"More than I'll use. I have a few ideas of where I can find a new home for this thing."

She appraised him. "I suspected you might."

They settled in at a thirty-knot cruise, barely testing the big motors. The seas were relatively calm, fortunately, with a swell two to three feet and a mild headwind. Gerardo busied himself below, rummaging through the cabin in search of valuables. Jet watched the radar for any signs of other vessels, but the screen was clear. She closed her eyes as the breeze blew through her hair and drew deep breaths, the salt air fresh in the warm night.

When she opened her eyes, she moved back to the GPS and pulled up the roads around Necoclí so she would know where she was headed when she made landfall. There was a main road marked as a highway that led south from town, through Turbo all the way to Medellín. It looked like no more than two-hundred fifty miles to Santuario from Necoclí, but she had no idea what the road conditions would be like or how fast or often the buses ran. Her instinct was to expect the worst, in which case it could easily take twelve or more hours, which would put her in Santuario by late morning, presuming any buses operated at night. Jet knew that in many rural areas of Venezuela, Colombia, and Brazil, they didn't, the danger from bandits being far too great.

Gerardo headed back to the helm and watched the bow make short work of the waves. The drone of the motors drowned out the beeping of the radar and whining adjustments of the autopilot. Before long they were nearing Necoclí, the GPS blinking their proximity as they approached. Jet pointed to a number of large blips on the radar.

"Should I be concerned?" she asked.

"No. Those are navy ships and cargo boats moored for the night. Just give them a wide berth, go dark and slow, and we should be fine."

She switched off the running lights and backed off the throttles. The cigarette boat glided between the large ships like a ghost, its underwater exhausts a muted burble at barely idle speed. The glow of the town lights appeared out of a fine mist dead ahead, and she handed the wheel over to Gerardo.

"Get me within a few hundred meters and then take off," she said as she hoisted her bag.

"You got it."

As they approached the coastline, Gerardo shifted the transmissions into neutral, and the boat slowly drifted to a stop. Jet climbed into the dinghy and started the outboard, and then gave Gerardo a thumbs-up. He untied the skiff's bow line, rolled it into a bundle, tossed it into the tender, and then Jet was pulling away into the night, the only evidence of her passage the hum of the small motor as she made for shore.

Jet beached the boat a few minutes later on a dark stretch of gray sand. She removed her bag and hopped onto the beach. After placing it safely away from the water, she returned to the dinghy and unscrewed the drain plug in the bottom, and then pushed it out into the mild surf as it began to fill with water. She watched as the waves pulled the hardy little boat out to sea, and turned as it drifted out of sight, already half full of water and not long for this world.

Jet made for what appeared to be a path through the jungle dead ahead. When she arrived at the opening, she saw that it led toward a row of houses down the beach, but looked like it let out beyond them. She worked her way along, staying low and avoiding making any noise. The clamor of radios playing and car motors revving from town gave the only evidence of civilization in the dense underbrush.

The trail connected to a road. She followed it past a cluster of houses that framed it, most dark now at ten p.m. She spotted a bicycle leaning up against the porch of a small house next to a postage-stamp-sized church. After glancing around to confirm she was alone, she darted over and wheeled it away.

A minute later she was pedaling easily toward the highway she knew lay on the other side of the hospital that lit up the night ahead of her. When she arrived at the parking lot, she asked a teenage security guard whether there were any buses running to Medellín at that hour.

He shook his head. "No. At night they stop at Turbo and don't come this far. I think the last one to Medellín leaves there in about an hour, then nothing until morning."

Jet frowned. "How far is Turbo?"

"Maybe thirty kilometers."

She quickly did the math. If she could average a little more than a half kilometer per minute on the tired bike, she could just make it.

"Where do the buses stop?"

"There's a place next to a market on the main road. You can't miss it. It's the only thing open after dark near the highway. That's its last stop on the way out of town." He looked at Jet. "It can be dangerous on the bus at night. You might want to wait until morning."

"Thanks. I'll do that," she said, and then rode off into the night, forcing her legs to pump as fast as they would go and hoping that the bus would, like most things in Latin America, run late rather than early.

CHAPTER 37

Santiago, Chile

Alejandro yawned, another long day of stress finally at an end. Now that he was the head of the family business, he was working twelve to fourteen hours a day trying to integrate the Verdugo family's infrastructure into the Soto's, and it was wearing at him. He'd always had tremendous respect for his father's stamina and vision in creating the criminal organization that now controlled all of Chile, but now that he was walking in his father's shoes, he had even more.

The afternoon had been spent negotiating with elements of the military that were responsible for security at the ports – Valparaíso and San Antonio – to ensure that their shipments of cocaine to North America weren't discovered by prying eyes, and that their containers of cash and gold made it through without inspection. Of course, everybody wanted to test the new boss' authority, grind him for more, try to carve out a bigger piece of the same pie. It was perennial, and he didn't take it personally, although he'd singled out two especially avaricious officers who would meet with ugly accidents over the next week. Their untimely demises would send a necessary message to the others, and he suspected that within a day of the discovery of their mangled bodies the others would see the wisdom of settling for what he'd proposed, rather than lacing their demands with veiled threats.

He'd finished up his day by meeting with the organization's bookkeepers and their financial advisor, who had the bulk of their nonworking income invested in financial products he didn't understand – derivatives that tracked the price of gold and silver, ETFs that were plays in the global petroleum markets, and a short position on the Japanese yen that was up twenty-five percent for the year, a handsome profit for money that was really just being laundered as it passed from broker to hedge fund to exchange and back again.

Alejandro yawned as he strode to his new AMG gullwing Mercedes coupe, a congratulatory gift from his father before he'd gotten on the private jet that winged him to Spain for a comfortable retirement at his multimillion dollar seaside villa, his neighbors Russian oligarchs and Saudi princes, the yachts moored in front of their ostentatious homes vying for most obscene display of wealth in the area.

His bodyguards nodded to him as he made his way to the car. The underground garage was his exclusive domain, housing Porsches, Ferraris, a Maserati, two more Benzes, and his BMW. Responsibility came with its perks, and he remembered his father's parting advice: "Work hard, but play hard too, because it'll be over before you know it, and the play is what makes the work worth it."

Wise words from a man who'd fought for every peso and emerged from the struggle a force of nature.

Alejandro thumbed the remote and the car chirped at him, blinking its lights in welcome. He climbed into the low-slung vehicle, started the engine, and the twin exhaust burbled with barely constrained power. Two minutes later he was accelerating like the devil was chasing him, enjoying the release of acceleration, pure adrenaline his reward as he stomped on the gas without concern for speed limits or fuel consumption.

He pulled up to a club that the organization owned and tossed the valet his keys. The heavyset bouncers were expecting him, the bulges in their jackets silent warning that there were better places to start trouble. The manager led him wordlessly to a reserved table where a twenty-something starlet waited with a pout. The three-hundred-dollar-a-bottle champagne had done little to improve her mood at being kept waiting.

Alejandro kissed her cheek and she sighed. "You're late," she complained, eyeing the platinum Rolex President with a tanzanite dial he'd gifted her the prior week. He took in her flawless profile and breathtaking beauty and offered a conciliatory look.

"I know, *mi amor*, and I'm sorry. I had a meeting run late. But I'll do whatever you want to make it up to you, Aurelia. I promise."

She took a sip of champagne and her eyes danced in the colored lights. "That sounds interesting. Be careful what you promise."

"I am your slave. Just say it and I'll make it so."

Aurelia smiled impishly and leaned into him, her hand dropping casually into his lap as she whispered her demand in his ear. His eyes widened just a hair and a smile of his own curved the corners of his lips, and he turned and brushed her lips with his.

"Sounds…dangerous."

"You know me too well already," she purred.

They finished the bottle in record time and he slid out of the booth, adjusting his slacks so his interest in his young friend wasn't obvious. "See you at your place?" he said, and Aurelia nodded. She had an apartment only a few minutes away in one of the most exclusive buildings in Santiago.

The manager saw him rise and murmured into his headset, warning the valet to have the car ready by the time he made it to the club's entrance. Alejandro took his time, pausing to shake hands with a group of dark-haired men at a private booth, business associates of his out on the town. Their night was just getting started, to judge by the bottles of expensive scotch and vodka on their table and the professional smiles of their companions.

When he reached Aurelia's building, he parked in the subterranean garage in the vacant space next to her customary slot. He was easing himself out of the car when a blinding pain shot through his head and he dropped to the polished concrete floor, barely registering the legs of his assailant before losing consciousness.

Alejandro came to with a pounding headache and immediately realized he was naked, bound to a chair. He glanced around but didn't recognize anything – bare brick walls, dirt everywhere, a single overhead bulb lighting the area.

A man stepped from the shadows. Alejandro stared at him, memorizing the face, but didn't recognize him. The man's face crinkled as he offered Alejandro a sad smile, as if apologizing for the impolite treatment he'd received.

"What do you want?" Alejandro asked. His tongue felt thick and clumsy, the words slurred in spite of his best effort.

"Information. I want information, nothing more." The man's voice was as cold as an open grave, and Alejandro shivered involuntarily.

"Where are my clothes? Why are you doing this?"

"Because I'm afraid you might not take me seriously if I didn't impress upon you how completely helpless you are, how dependent on my graciousness you are for every breath you take."

"What information do you want? Shipments? Bank accounts? Because I don't have them memorized. I couldn't tell you any of it even if I wanted to."

The man grunted in agreement. "Oh, I'm quite sure that's true. No, nothing so mundane as the details of your enterprise, which are your concern. What I need to know is more…specialized."

Alejandro's eyes shifted behind the man, where he could make out another form tied to a chair. He squinted to chase away the double vision and gasped when he saw who it was. Aurelia's sightless eyes stared at him from the gloom, the gash across her throat staining her naked flesh with drying crimson. The man followed Alejandro's gaze and grunted again. "Ah. Yes. I'm afraid your young friend came across me as I was loading you into the car. A shame, really. Although she went out with a bang – quite a remarkable body, I'll give you that. You're a lucky man," he leered.

Alejandro strained at the bindings and could feel his pulse thudding in his ears. "You sick bastard. I'll skin you alive. You'll beg for death before I'm done with you."

The man ignored his outburst and moved behind him, then reappeared with a butane welding torch and a lighter. "I trust I have your full attention now?" He flicked the lighter absentmindedly as he spoke, almost a nervous tic.

"What do you want?"

"You arranged for a man and a little girl to travel on a container ship that was later found with its crew murdered off the coast of Nicaragua. I need to know everything you do about them. Who they are, what they were doing, where they were going." The lighter flared and the man twisted a valve as he held the torch. Blue flame shot from the nozzle as he inspected it like he'd never seen the torch before.

Alejandro's heart skipped several beats as his eyes met the man's — he saw nothing but death.

Fifteen minutes later, Drago stepped back from Alejandro's inert form, the room sour with the acrid stink of seared flesh and bodily fluids. He carefully wiped down the welding torch and moved to the door of the abandoned industrial building, taking care to use the rag from his back pocket when handling the knob. He stopped in the doorway and took a final look at the corpses. His face was expressionless, the skin slack, like putty on a mannequin. Then he switched off the light and pulled the door closed behind him.

CHAPTER 38

Viterbo, Colombia

Jaime toasted Fernanda with his brandy snifter. Dinner had been marvelously relaxed, and the food had lived up to the restaurant's reputation, as had the slavish service from a staff that seemed to recognize Jaime. He clinked his glass against hers, their Dictador 20-year Añejo rum fragrant in the evening's warmth.

"To beauty and courage," Jaime said, eyeing her over the rim of his glass as he took an appreciative sip and sighed in satisfaction.

She forced herself to take a small mouthful and swallow it with a rapturous expression that was as fake as the enthusiasm she'd shown for her dinner, every bite tasting like wood to her as her mind ran into the redline with thoughts of Igor. But she needed to ensure Jaime's continued cooperation, especially if she would be tackling the mystery woman on her own, so she was playing the drug lord like a Stradivarius, using every ounce of her considerable charm and skill to make him feel fascinating and powerful.

Fernanda had long ago learned the right words to use, the subtle signals to send, the questions to ask so that men believed she was captivated by them. She was so good at it she barely needed to think about what came next. Men were simple creatures, easily twisted to do her bidding, whether a brutal cartel boss or a target, and she found Jaime to be no exception.

The quiet was broken by the chirp of Jaime's cell phone, and Fernanda had to keep from jumping up and snatching it out of his hand as he answered. He listened for several long beats, asked a series of short questions, and then hung up. He took another long draught of his rum and set the snifter down with a sad shake of his head.

"A body had already washed up on the beach in Acandí by the time my men made it there. They're sending me a photograph for you to identify."

"A body," she repeated woodenly.

His phone pinged and he checked the screen, waited a moment, and then handed her the phone. She took it from him with surprisingly steady hands and regarded the snapshot without reacting. When she handed it back to him, her face was expressionless. "I don't know who that is."

"Ah. Then that's good news. Bodies have been known to wash up on that shore – it's not that unusual an occurrence."

"What are your men doing now?"

"They've enlisted the help of the local constable, who's showing them through the town in case there's any sign of a fight."

"No reports of gunshots?"

"None."

Fernanda felt a momentary glimmer of hope, but forced it away. Hope was a luxury she couldn't afford. But she allowed herself to try Igor's phone one more time, only to get the same out-of-service message she'd gotten earlier.

She set the phone down and took a larger swallow of the rum. The silky spirit burned as it went down, spreading a flush of warmth through her stomach seconds later. She wasn't much for alcohol, but tonight she wished she could dive into the bottle and drown in it, welcoming the oblivion it promised so she wouldn't have to think.

They nursed their drinks in solitude, the other patrons having left long ago. The waiter stood patiently by the kitchen, averting his eyes so they had complete privacy while he could still respond to their every wish. Jaime was finishing his glass and signaling for another when his phone went off again. He sat back and listened, then hung up after a grunted sentence. "They found another body in a construction site. I'll have a photo in a moment." He paused and lowered his voice. "But I must warn you – they said that the man's face was...he'd suffered considerable trauma. Perhaps you might want to wait to look at it."

She shook her head and downed the rest of her drink. "No. I need to know."

They sat in silence, the cool mountain air crisp on her skin, the thick candles dotting the restaurant flickering with each gentle gust. When Jaime's cell beeped again, he seemed reluctant to check it, and only did so once his second glass of rum had arrived.

He studied the image and closed his eyes for a second, then handed her the phone. She glanced at the image and nodded as she returned it to him. "That's him. How did he die?"

"Best they can tell, he was beaten to death with a piece of wood. A plank."

"Killed with a plank?" she said disbelievingly. *One of the most adept assassins in the world sent to the afterlife with a two-by-four?* She couldn't help herself and barked a hoarse laugh. It was absurd. There must be some mistake. That couldn't happen.

Jaime looked at her strangely, and she struggled to maintain her composure, stress cracks appearing at the brittle edges that she hoped were only obvious to her. He motioned to the waiter and pointed to his glass, and the man rushed to get another snifter for Fernanda. He was back in moments and whisked away her empty glass before vanishing into the back of the restaurant. She lifted the rum to her lips and drained the snifter in two swallows, then set it back on the table with a trembling hand.

Jaime knew enough to stay silent; the pain and rage in Fernanda's eyes were obvious. She sat staring a thousand miles into space as he took his time with his drink, and by the time he was finished, she'd regained control.

"Do you want to talk about it?" he asked softly as he slipped a sheaf of bills onto the tray holding the check.

She shook her head. "There's nothing to say. She killed him. He must have missed something, made a critical mistake, and it cost him his life."

Fernanda pushed back from the table and stood. Her face betrayed nothing, the veneer back in place after an uncharacteristic slip. Jaime rose, and the waiter moved to the door to hold it open for them, having locked it to keep any unwanted late night patrons from intruding on their intimate evening.

They walked slowly back to the hotel in silence, the only sound other than traffic on the distant highway the thudding of their footsteps on the cobblestones, the bright moonlight illuminating their way.

When they reached the hotel, Jaime saw her to her room and, at the threshold, took her hand in his and spoke softly. "I'm sorry for your loss. I'll do everything I can to help you. You can count on me."

Fernanda nodded at the words, barely hearing them. "Thank you." She pulled away and turned to go inside, and Jaime tried one more time.

"Good night, Fernanda. Knock on my door if you need anything. Even if it's just to talk."

She swallowed a sour spurt of bile that threatened to choke her and gave him a small smile. "That's very kind of you, Jaime. I'll see you in the morning."

He watched her enter the room and push the door shut behind her, and then walked slowly to his room. Inside hers, Fernanda glanced around with tear-blurred eyes and threw herself down on the bed, stifling a tortured scream with her pillow before dry-heaving as she sobbed, gasping for ragged breath in between her cries. The only man she'd ever felt anything but contempt for was gone forever.

CHAPTER 39

Turbo, Colombia

Jet mounted the rusty stairs of the retired school bus that was her overnight passage to Medellín and paid the driver in dollars, which he stared at as though he didn't recognize the currency before nonetheless pocketing the money. She eyed the half-full interior, taking in the ragged seats, some with the stuffing torn out and others patched, a smell of onions and sweat permeating the fabric, and moved to the rear of the compartment. She sat across from a woman with the stony countenance of a carved statue, years of hardship etched into her mahogany-colored face, whose luggage appeared to consist entirely of black garbage bags spread out on the seat and floor beside her.

The bus lurched into motion, the transmission protesting as it accelerated to no more than twenty miles per hour, the chassis shaking like a satellite on reentry. Jet tried to ignore the sweat running down her spine and the sheen on her face from the mad dash on the bicycle, with no success. After a few minutes, she half-stood and heaved on the window until she forced it open, the ventilation barely sufficient to dry her over the course of an hour.

She removed her phone from her pocket and powered it on – she was trying to conserve the battery, having been unable to charge it since Portobelo – and the voice mail indicator blinked at her along with the low-battery warning. Jet checked her messages and listened to the one from Matt assuring her that he and Hannah were fine at the monastery, but that there was no cell service there. Frustrated at not being able to communicate with him, she dialed the new number he'd left and it went to voice mail. She left him a short message confirming she was on her way, and then signed off, the phone beeping its warning in her ear.

Jet switched off the phone and stared through the dirty lower portion of her window. The film of road dust rendered everything a hazy brown. She'd be reunited with Hannah and Matt by tomorrow afternoon, worst case, and then they'd have to make some tough decisions about where they would go. In a perfect world, she would have been able to extract details from the assassin she'd killed in Acandí and have been able to formulate a better plan than to stay on the run. But Jet had long ago given up on the hope that the world would be anything close to fair, so she focused on what she could control rather than what she couldn't.

Her fingers moved to the leather lanyard around her neck and the little satchel containing her emergency stash of diamonds. They had their passports and, thankfully, plenty of money. Armed with that, they should be able to disappear. Matt and Hannah weren't on any immigration radar in Colombia and neither was Jet, so anyone trying to follow them would be out of luck. In that respect, they were fortunate – it would make it easier to disappear for good, since they'd already effectively done exactly that.

Their biggest problem was that they couldn't go north – she was wanted in Panama, so traveling through Central America and perhaps settling somewhere in Costa Rica or Mexico wasn't an option. Maybe Medellín or Cali? She'd heard good things about them – that the cartel violence that had marred both for a decade was long over, and the cities were relatively safe, with good infrastructure. Nobody knew they were in Colombia, and the country was in the same state of perpetual civil war that it had been for fifty years, so the computer systems that would have made them easily tracked in more developed regions simply didn't exist. It was one of the beauties of developing countries – they were easy to move around in without triggering any alarms.

Two hours after the bus picked her up, after a series of stops to let passengers off and take a few on, the antique conveyance rolled to a stop in the jungle town of Chigorodó. Several young soldiers with machine guns climbed aboard and took the first row of seats, their serious faces telling Jet that they weren't there for show. They seemed to know the driver and held a quiet conversation with him as he continued south, the headlights of the old bus the only ones on the road.

The suspension managed to make a lousy trip into a truly terrible one, as each pothole and rut delivered a jarring blow to her sacroiliac. Jet tried to get comfortable on the stiff seat, the stink of partially combusted fuel, exhaust, and questionable hygiene an added bonus, but it was no good. Even with all that, though, she was still feeling more upbeat than she had been for days, knowing that soon she'd have her daughter in her arms.

Eventually she drifted off, the creaky old school bus bouncing along and the stops few and far between, and she managed to get a few hours of fitful sleep before the first orange rays of dawn painted the morning sky as the bus rolled into the central terminal in Medellín, already jammed with travelers making their way out of the city.

Jet disembarked and studied a route schedule, and then purchased a ticket for the next bus headed to Santuario, departing in an hour and twenty minutes. Pocketing her change, she followed her nose to a café outside the station that was serving breakfast fare with cups of strong black coffee. Taking a table near the back of the small dining area, she studied the menu for a moment and then ordered the special. She eyed her fellow travelers as she waited for her food – a motley crew of the impoverished and the desperate, mostly laborers, with a few obviously foreign backpackers thrown in for seasoning, their dreadlocks and tattoos and sunburned pale skin displayed like badges of honor.

The food was delicious, and she was able to charge her phone, which brightened her mood somewhat. She tried Matt's cell again, but not unexpectedly he didn't answer, and she didn't leave a message.

If Jet had thought the night bus from Turbo was bad, it was a first-class ticket on a 747 compared to the dilapidated rust bucket that creaked into the depot to ferry her to Santuario. She surveyed the bus, wheezing like an asthmatic, and shook her head as the driver took her ticket. At this rate it looked doubtful that she'd make it by nightfall. More likely was that they'd wind up stranded by the side of the road while the hapless driver scratched his head under the open hood.

She thought the bus wasn't going to make it on the uphill climb to the town of Santa Barbara, as gears ground and the engine strained; it would have been faster to jog alongside than sit on the wood slab that served as a bench. By the time they were on the downward slope, it had taken three hours to travel just under forty kilometers. The exhausted bus shivered like a malarial victim, making her estimation of her arrival time at the monastery look wildly optimistic.

When her cell warbled at her, she practically jumped out of her seat. She fumbled the phone from her pocket and answered on the fourth ring.

"Hello?"

"Hey. You here yet?" Matt asked, as though he'd seen her only a few hours earlier.

"I'm working on it. I'm on the bus ride from hell. Probably be late afternoon, best case."

"The monastery is at the top of a mountain on the north end of town. The only way up is the cable car, so when you arrive, that's what you need to take. The monk who's helping us will leave it at the bottom for you."

"How's Hannah holding up?"

"Oh, fine. She's a trooper. A perfect angel...like her mom."

"Now I know you're blowing smoke." She paused. "I was followed from Panama." She told him about the cigarette boat and the two men aboard. "Do you have any idea who these guys are?"

"Nope. Could be some of Tara's crew? You took care of all the Russians, right?"

"Correct. Although you never know. There could have been more lurking in the background. But I nipped that one at the source, so I seriously doubt it's them. As far as Tara's group, you'd know more about what they're capable of than I would."

"The answer is anything. They have the reach and the scale to do anything," he said softly. "Including following you to get to me."

"But the diamonds are gone. They know that."

"Which is why I thought we'd be in the clear." He hesitated. "I hope that wasn't wishful thinking. Looks like it might have been."

"Well, it doesn't matter at this point. We're clean. So start thinking about where you want to settle down. Because I don't know about you, but I'm tired of living out of a suitcase and looking over my shoulder."

"Let's talk about it when you get here. Meanwhile, I'll put on my thinking cap."

"Me too."

When Jet disconnected, she checked her watch and exhaled in exasperation. The schedule had promised that the bus would arrive in Santuario by three, but there was no way that was going to happen. It was nearly three now, and by her calculations they still had at least four more hours to go. Obviously the Colombian idea of promptness was fluid. One of the aspects of Latin American society that taught patience, she told herself, shifting on the plank in a futile attempt to get comfortable.

She watched the little town of Riosucio drift by in slow motion and closed her eyes, willing herself to a calm place where the irritation she was feeling could melt away, leaving her focused, relaxed, and above all, vigilant.

CHAPTER 40

Santuario, Colombia

Matt turned to the door as Franco entered with more bags of food, a bottle of milk, and two fresh towels. He set them on the table and smiled warmly at Hannah before clearing his throat and addressing Matt.

"I'm glad to hear your stay is coming to an end. You must be relieved."

"Yes. I want to thank you for your hospitality. It's been a lifesaver. Literally."

"I'm in that business. Although I don't draw the line at soul saving, either."

Both men smiled, and then Matt grew serious. "I hope you don't take this the wrong way, but I've been thinking. Those who are looking for me are dangerous. I'd hate for anything to happen to Hannah. So...do you have any weapons in the monastery?"

Franco's eyes narrowed as he considered the question. "We have an old shotgun for hunting, but I'd have to look around for shells that aren't older than I am. It's been years since anyone hunted." He stopped, thinking, and then snapped his fingers. "But there is a weapon one of our brethren used to use for boar hunting when he was younger. I have to warn you, though, it's ancient and bulky. Not exactly the kind of thing you could carry around and not attract attention, if you take my meaning."

"Really? What is it?"

"A crossbow. They say it's at least two hundred years old, and the last time it was fired was probably decades ago. But it might still be serviceable. I'm afraid I wouldn't know – that's not my strong suit, as you might have guessed."

"A crossbow? Hmm. In a pinch it would be better than nothing, I suppose. Could I trouble you to get it for me so I can see if it's in working order?"

Franco glanced at Hannah and frowned. "Do you really think you need a weapon here, in God's house? You're quite safe, I assure you."

"I'm sure we are. But I'd rather be safe than sorry. It's always possible that the girl's mother is followed, and if that's the case, I'd rather be as prepared as I can be, instead of…trusting fate."

Franco nodded. "The Lord does help those who help themselves. Your point is taken. I'll see if I can sneak away with the crossbow without anyone noticing. All I ask is that when you leave, it stays with the monastery. It's part of our history…"

"Of course."

"No guarantees it even works. Like I said, not my specialty."

"I can usually make anything work in a pinch."

"A resourceful man. An admirable quality in uncertain times."

Franco moved to Hannah, patted her head, and then walked to the door. "I'll return when I have the item, and I'll root around for some shells for the shotgun." He smiled. "I trust you're comfortable enough?"

"It's exactly what we needed, Franco," Matt assured the kindly monk. The truth was their chamber was drafty at night and hot during the day, there were mice that had the run of the place after dark, and the water pressure was slightly worse than nothing. But it was safe, which made it a kind of paradise.

When Franco left, Matt sat with Hannah and distributed food from the bag: a selection of rolls, pastries, fruit, and cheeses that were mouthwatering, if not the healthiest selection. They were just finishing up when Franco returned carrying a burlap sack with the distinctive outline of a crossbow inside.

"I tried to blow most of the dust off of it, but perhaps you can clean it more thoroughly," he said. "And there's a case with six arrows in it – I think that's what they call them, right?"

"Or quarrels. Thank you, Franco. I'll get to work on it. It'll give me something to do while I wait for Hannah's mother to arrive. She's on a bus."

Franco looked heavenward. "Ah, well, then it's in His hands when she'll get here. The buses in Colombia are notoriously unreliable."

The monk took his leave, and Matt removed the crossbow from the sack and examined it. The wooden stock was scarred – a working man's hunting bow, not a museum piece. The bow string was in good shape, and thankfully didn't snap when Matt strapped on the accompanying belt, bent his knees, and slipped the attached hook on the string, and then drew it by straightening his legs. A primitive but effective accessory, far more practical than the rack and pinion or lever systems he'd seen in museums.

When he was confident the medieval-looking device was stable, he took a quarrel from the leather quiver and eyed it. Wood, with a sharp steel tip, it would be lethal at whatever the bow's range was – likely at least fifty yards, possibly considerably more. The prod appeared to be in perfect shape and fit snugly. He sighted on one of the heavy wooden beams that supported the bed and cautioned Hannah to take cover behind him and, when she was out of harm's way, fired at the wood column.

The bow snapped with a loud crack and the quarrel plunged through the beam, embedding itself three inches. Matt eyed the damage with satisfaction. Anyone on the receiving end of that would be stopped as surely as being hit with a fifty-caliber round at close range.

He set the bow down and moved to the bed, and spent the next ten minutes working the quarrel out using the bread knife Franco had brought to cut the loaves with. When it was free, he slipped it back into the quiver and selected another, and after repeating the cocking procedure, set the crossbow out of Hannah's reach in the tall wardrobe on the far wall.

Matt returned to where Hannah was watching him with wide eyes and sat in front of her.

"You know who's coming to see you today?" he asked, his tone playful.

She shook her head solemnly. "No."

"Mommy!"

Her face radiated joy and she squealed with glee and squirmed. "Mama! Mama come!"

"Yes, sweetheart. She'll be here soon, and then we'll find someplace quiet so we can all be together again. Would you like that?"

"Mama! Mama!" Hannah cried, her big eyes moistening at the thought.

"So we need to give you a bath and get you cleaned up so you're not dirty, kid, and maybe brush your hair, and then it'll be my turn. Then we'll pick out some clean clothes for you, so we can surprise her with how nice you look."

Hannah leapt to her feet and ran to the bathroom door, and Matt's throat tightened at how eager she was to get cleaned up to impress her mother. She'd had such a rough time of it with everything that had happened, yet her capacity for happiness seemed undiminished, and she wanted nothing more than to see her mom again.

Matt glanced at his watch and caught a glimpse of himself in the wall mirror. He rubbed his good hand over the stubble that covered his jaw, acknowledging that Hannah wasn't the only one who needed some attention. There had been little time recently for niceties like grooming, but with Jet on her way, he'd make the effort to shave and shower so he didn't look like a jungle fighter coming out of the brush after a two-week campaign. He moved to their bags and extracted his hygiene kit, and then smiled at Hannah. "It won't be long now."

"Mama!"

CHAPTER 41

Armando finished unloading the last chicken coop, its feathered occupant glaring fearfully at him as he set it next to the others, and straightened, one hand on his back, which ached from the effort. His helper was nowhere to be found, which didn't surprise him – lunch usually took two hours, from two to four o'clock – and upon his arrival back at the depot there had been nobody there, his secretary also gone, the doors locked.

He walked stiffly over to a steel sink and scrubbed his arms and hands with soap, then did the same with his face. The two-day trips were the worst, he thought. The lack of air-conditioning in the ancient truck coupled with the dust from the dirt roads left him with grit in every nook and cranny. He studied his nails and shook his head, and then moved to the office, where a pile of invoices awaited his attention.

Once inside, Armando approached a half-height refrigerator and withdrew an icy cold bottle of Cerveza San Tomás: Dubbel beer. He palmed a bottle opener from a nearby shelf and popped the cap as he carried it to his desk. He'd earned it. His business, his father's before he took it over, wasn't going to ever make him rich, but it was a good living, hard but honest work. He took a long pull of beer as he flipped on the ceiling fan and then sat in his swivel chair. Propping his feet up on the desk, he leaned back and closed his eyes, trying to ease the tension in his neck, which was stiff from the hours on the harsh roads.

His eyes popped open and he frowned when a creak from the depot gate echoed through the compound over the squawking of hundreds of chickens. Nobody ever visited his business – he was a delivery wholesaler, supplying chickens to the slaughterhouses that catered to the neighboring restaurants.

Three men entered his office, all hard-looking, and the middle one, dressed in expensive linen trousers and a spotless silk shirt, snapped his fingers. Armando stiffened as the two larger men grabbed him unceremoniously, holding him in the chair, immobilizing his arms as the third one neared.

"Armando. We've been waiting for you for some time. Nice to see you made it back safely – you had us worried," Jaime said.

"I…who are you? What is this?"

"Who I am isn't important, it's the problem I have that is. Listen carefully. You picked up a man and a girl from Antonio Salguero and gave them a ride. I want to know where you took them. It's a simple thing I ask, no?"

"Why? What do you want them for?"

"That's none of your business. What you should be concerned with right now is telling me where you left them. Be honest, and everything will be fine."

"I…I dropped them off at the bus stop. They were headed for Cali."

Jaime shook his head. "You know, I play poker when I have the time. High stakes. I've made a hobby out of reading people." He sat down and inspected the crease of his trousers. After a few moments he picked a piece of lint from his right leg, inspected it, and flicked it away. "You wouldn't last one hand. You're a terrible liar." He fixed Armando with a cold stare, his obsidian eyes flat as a shark's. "You don't even know me, and you're lying to me. How am I supposed to take that?"

Armando didn't say anything. Jaime sighed. One of the toughs squeezed a pressure point on his arm and it went numb. Jaime rose and pulled a knife from his back pocket. The snick of the blade snapping into place froze Armando's blood, and he shook his head as Jaime approached.

"I'll start with your ears. Then I'll begin cutting off other appendages. Every time you lie to me, you'll lose something vital. Do you understand? So again. The man and the little girl. Where did you take them?"

Armando's screams rang through the chicken yard, causing the birds to squawk even more, as though accompanying his agonized melody with impromptu harmonies. Jaime exited the office five minutes later, a look of distaste on his face at the odor of chicken excrement that rose from the coop area, his men trailing him as he spoke softly on his phone.

"That's right. A monastery. No, I have no idea, but he was quite convincing in his belief that they're still there. Fine. I'll be back in ten minutes. No, I'll tell her."

He hung up and got into the passenger seat of the black Suburban. The driver started the engine as his two enforcers climbed into the rear seat and they roared away, finally with a destination in sight after an interminably long wait. Jaime looked at his men in the rearview mirror and spoke softly. "Jorge, you have blood on your chin." He tapped his own chin with his finger, and the larger of the two men wiped his face with the back of his arm.

When the big SUV arrived at the hotel, Jaime made his way to Fernanda's room while the rest of the men gathered by the trucks. He'd called for additional muscle the prior day, and another vehicle with three more toughs had joined the three he'd traveled from Frontino with, bringing his group to a total of nine, including Fernanda. More than ample for the task at hand, he thought as he knocked on the door.

Fernanda opened it, and he was struck again by her odd combination of exotic beauty and deadly intensity – a mixture that he found more than intriguing and hopefully would get the opportunity to explore once their little errand had been attended to. She eyed him expectantly, and he offered a satisfied grin.

"We found them."

CHAPTER 42

Santuario, Colombia

The high whitewashed walls surrounding the hilltop complex of buildings glowed in the late afternoon sun. Jaime shifted in his seat as Fernanda studied the monastery through a pair of binoculars. He cleared his throat and eyed her.

"Why don't we leave one of my men to watch the area, and he'll call us whenever they come down or your woman shows up? There's no reason for us to stake the place out and wait in miserable conditions. Come, we can get a coffee," he suggested, tired of the game after an hour of sitting and doing nothing.

"You can leave if you like. She's on her way here. That's why she came to Colombia. I can feel it. I'm not going to trust this to one of your goons – she's as good as they get, and they'll tip her off," Fernanda said. She'd already had Jaime pull his men well back, not wanting a repeat performance of the debacle at the Vacamonte harbor. This was her chance to extract her revenge, and she wasn't going to allow anyone to blow it for her.

"But there's only one way up or down. She has to show herself, and when she does, she's a sitting duck." He studied Fernanda's profile. "If they come down to her, same thing. They have to be on the cable car. It's a simple surveillance job that's beneath your skills." What he meant was, beneath his station – but he didn't say it, preferring to flatter than to complain.

Fernanda twisted and glanced at the AK-47 in the backseat, its curved banana magazine as distinctive as its wooden stock. She checked her watch. "How long do you think it would take to get from up by Acandí to the monastery? Is it possible she's already come and gone?"

He shrugged. "Anything's possible, but it's unlikely. My money says they're still up there. But if you like, I can take some men and go get them – that might give you more leverage than lying in wait. Depends on how patient you are."

When she spoke, her voice was barely a whisper. "I'm as patient as I need to be."

Jaime sighed. "I'm sure that's true, but I'm afraid I don't have endless amounts of time to wait. No offense, Fernanda, but I have other demands. If this woman doesn't show herself by dusk, let me go get the girl and the gringo. Otherwise, I'm afraid I'll have to leave you with a couple of my men while I return to Frontino. We have a small crisis there I'm needed to handle."

She weighed the wisdom of allowing Jaime to go charging into the monastery versus taking a stealth approach. If she was simply taking forever to arrive, the woman would have no way of knowing that they had been captured, so she'd still have to make a play for the cable car. The trail that had at one point run alongside had long ago been closed as too dangerous after a local child had broken his spine in a fall, and the entry point had been walled off at the base near the docking station.

Fernanda looked at Jaime and reminded herself that she still needed his cooperation; this wasn't over yet. Now that they'd located their quarry, he was tiring of the hunt, and he obviously wasn't prepared to play a game of cat and mouse for hours or days. While she was laser-focused on taking the woman down, she also wanted to remain in Jaime's good graces, and he was becoming petulant as they sat in the SUV, three hundred meters from the cable car, hidden in the shade of a massive oak on a small opposing hill.

She'd picked the spot because the woman would no doubt reconnoiter the area, which ruled out any of the closer surrounding buildings. Fernanda had slowly walked by the cable car station doing exactly that, and had picked out all of the natural surveillance spots a pro would monitor. It was a difficult location, but nothing was impossible, and even at that distance, with the assault rifle she would be able to pick the woman off when she appeared.

What Fernanda really wanted to do was stick an ice pick into her eye after skinning her alive and boiling her appendages, but that wasn't practical, given the layout she had to work with.

"Look, taking them is a good idea," Jaime pressed. "They may have talked already and have made plans to meet the woman somewhere else, in which case we'd be at a disadvantage because she would be staking that spot out just as we are this one. Our edge is that we know they're up there. But we have no guarantee she'll show, and if we have to follow them, we run the risk of losing them or that she'll be tipped off."

Fernanda realized he was probably right. She was sure that the woman would show up, but that was a gut feeling, not a certainty. Even now the gringo might be preparing to rendezvous with the woman miles from this spot, somewhere secluded where getting a clean shot might be impossible. *Was her rage over Igor's death clouding her judgment?* The smart play was to have Jaime's men capture the pair in the monastery and see what they knew, while Fernanda lay in wait near the cable car.

She nodded and forced a wan smile. "You're right. It'll be dark in an hour. If she hasn't shown herself by then, go up and bring them down. I'll stay here watching for her."

He studied her profile. "You don't want to come with us?" He sounded surprised.

"No. Your men are more than capable of handling a simple snatch, aren't they?"

"Of course," he said, in an offended tone. "I'll go up myself to ensure it is dealt with effectively."

"I can't ask you to do that, Jaime. Your time's too valuable to bother with something minor like this," she said, pouring on the flattery, just the right amount of respect and awe in her voice. Jaime sat up straighter and moved his hand to hers, patting it like a doting parent.

"We've come this far together. Might as well see it through."

The minutes ticked by, with no sign of life on the street other than a skinny stray dog loping down the sidewalk, followed by an old woman shuffling along with a shopping bag, a scarf over her head. Jaime held a muted conversation on his cell phone as they waited, issuing instructions to his group in preparation for their ascent. When the shadows lengthened and the sky faded to gray, Jaime looked to her.

"It will be dark soon. Time to do this."

"All right. Remember, I want them alive. They're of no use to me as bargaining chips if they're dead, and I can't interrogate a corpse."

"I promise I won't harm a hair on their heads," Jaime said with a malevolent grin.

"Send the cable car back down once you're up there, so everything looks normal while you're looking for them. It's a big place."

"Of course."

Jaime started the SUV, and Fernanda stepped out clutching the assault rifle, nearly invisible in the approaching gloom beneath the tree. She took up position with her binoculars and continued to scan the area as the Suburban's brake lights faded down the hill and disappeared into the tangle of buildings near the base of the mountain.

Minutes later, Jaime jogged to the cable car followed by five of his men, their rifles left in the trucks in favor of more discreet handguns. She watched as they slid open the cable car door and trooped inside, and then the tram began its crawl up the hill to the monastery four hundred meters above.

It passed the towers that supported the steel cables that led to the monastery docking area, and then Jaime was leading his men to the main building as the car headed back to the base, silhouetted against the steep slope in dusk's dim glow.

CHAPTER 43

Matt pounded on Franco's door, the nearest to the side entry of the main building. "Franco, hurry up. This is an emergency."

The monk arrived and pulled the door open, robes flapping around him like some kind of ungainly bird. "What is it?"

"A group of men are coming up in the cable car. The motor noise gave them away. I don't know how, but they must be onto us."

Franco glanced around. "Are you sure?"

"Do you routinely have a half-dozen armed men visit the monastery after hours?"

The monk's eyes widened. "What do you want me to do?"

"We need to hide Hannah somewhere safe. They'll be here in seconds."

"Come," Franco said, looking over Matt's shoulder at the upper docking area. Matt hefted their bags, and Franco picked Hannah up after closing and bolting the door, and carried her into a long hallway with tall rustic doors lining each side. He moved to the last one and unlocked it with a key hanging around his neck, and pushed past some dusty crates and a few casks to an old bookshelf, its volumes covered with a patina of filth and cobwebs. After nodding to Matt, he reached up to the top shelf, gripped a thick book, and tilted it forward. A click sounded from behind the bookshelf and he pushed against it. The base screeched like a wounded bird, and the entire bookshelf swung aside, revealing a passageway carved into the mountain rock.

A draft blew from the dark tunnel, carrying the dank smell of wet earth and decay. Franco put Hannah down and turned to Matt. "This leads down the back side of the mountain, where there's a small river.

It was used over a century ago to hide rebel forces and, later, to smuggle enemies of the cartels out of danger."

Matt held his stare. "Franco, stay here with Hannah. Her mother is on her way. If these goons know we're here, then they probably suspect she's coming and laid a trap for her. I won't let that happen."

Franco shook his head. "I can't. The others know nothing of what I've brought into this holy place. I must warn them."

"Who else knows about this passageway?" Matt murmured.

"Only the abbot and I. And the abbot is nearly beyond his earthly concerns. He's been unwell for years." Franco hesitated. "Dementia. Half the time he doesn't know where he is, so the secret is safe."

Matt knelt down and gazed into Hannah's eyes, and then groped around in the survival bag and found the small flashlight. He handed it to her and twisted it on, showing her how to work it, and then switched it off. "Honey? I need you to be very, very brave and wait for me here. If you get scared, you can't make any noise, but you can turn the light on and it will be just like Momma and I are with you, okay? I need to go take care of some stuff, but I'll be right back. Do you understand?"

The fear in Hannah's eyes was palpable. "Yeth," she whispered.

"But no noise. Not even if you hear things that are scary, all right? Because there are some bad men who are looking for us, and I don't want them to find you. So be extra quiet for me and Mommy."

Another doubtful nod from Hannah. Matt rose and withdrew the crossbow from the burlap sack, strapped on the special belt, and cocked and loaded it. A pounding sounded from down the hall; the intruders were at the door. Matt quickly placed their bags in the passageway, patted Hannah on the head and held his finger to his lips, and then Franco pulled the bookshelf back into position.

Matt shouldered the crossbow and rooted in the bag for the quiver. He pulled the strap over his head and nodded at Franco as more pounding emanated from the front door.

"How do I get up there?" Matt whispered, pointing to the second-floor balcony that overlooked the main courtyard.

"Stairs at the end of the hall." Franco pulled the heavy chamber door shut and locked it, then removed the key from around his neck and handed it to Matt. "Keep this. I don't know what will become of me, but it's up to you to lead the child to safety."

Matt pocketed the key. "Don't open the front door. Let them stew outside."

"No. They'll terrorize the other monks. I must—"

Matt cut him off. "You must save yourself, Franco. How can I get into the main monastery from here?"

"Through the kitchen area."

"Then go warn your brothers. But don't say a word about us. They can't reveal what they don't know." A thought occurred to him. "Where did you say they kept the shotgun?"

"Over in the main hall, mounted over the fireplace. From here you won't be able to get to it easily."

"Then I'll have to make good with this," he said, patting the bow. "I've got six quarrels. I like my odds."

Franco shook his head. "Go with God, my son."

"If not him, with the devil. But I'll try to take a rain check today, if that's okay with you," Matt said, and then dashed down the hall toward the stairs. Franco's gaze followed him to the end of the gloomy corridor, and then he turned to where the pounding on the front door was increasing in urgency. He crossed himself and hurried in the opposite direction, to where the few other monks in residence were no doubt wondering what the commotion was all about.

~ ~ ~

Jet's pass in front of the monastery had detected nothing out of place – the area was empty, any likely hiding places devoid of threat. She'd purchased the second-hand clothes and donned them in town, disguising herself as an ancient woman trudging along with her shopping as she reconnoitered the area. A friendly hound had decided to escort her, lending further credibility to her act, and she'd just about decided that the coast was clear when she heard the rev of

238

a big motor, and a black SUV had rounded a corner behind her and parked a hundred meters from the cable car entrance.

She'd continued on without breaking her stride, pausing to inspect the odd trash can, calling the dog in her best imitation of an aged voice, and when she was out of sight, peeked around a building corner to see six thugs moving toward the cable car with pistols in their hands.

Her heart rate accelerated at the realization that somehow Matt's whereabouts had been discovered, but she willed it back to normal as the glacial operational calm that was second nature to her seeped through her and she calculated the best next step. The faint whir of the distant cable car climbing the hill forced her into action – her baby was up there, and if she didn't stop the gunmen, anything could happen.

Jet shrugged out of the disguise and rolled her long black cargo pants back down before slipping on her bag, the Glock stashed in her waistband where she could quickly access it. The only surprise as she bolted from doorway to doorway was that the cable car was returning, empty, to the ground level. That gave her pause. Perhaps it was an automatic return? That was probably it, but if not...it meant that there could be more gunmen waiting for her to show up.

Jet looked up at the sky. It would be dark in a few more minutes. An eerie quiet hung in the air, and she forced herself to wait until darkness arrived, and with it, increased odds of making it out of the situation alive.

The only positive was that there were no streetlights on the empty stretch of road that ran in front of the docking station. The buildings where she was hiding were quiet, the businesses closed, any inhabitants thankfully not at home. When the cable car arrived at the street level, she surveyed the area, her senses quivering, hypersensitive to any movement or sound that might reveal a threat.

She heard a distant pounding, like a drum, from the monastery. After a few seconds she recognized the sound: the gunmen were banging on the doors. That could work in her favor. It meant they were certain they weren't facing any opposition. Certitude had cost many of her adversaries their lives; this time would hopefully prove no different.

Night arrived with a whisper of breeze, and suddenly it was dark enough that she could make it to the docking station if she stuck to the far side of the street, where untrimmed bushes provided welcome concealment.

She checked her bag to ensure the strap was tight across her chest, leaving both arms free for uninhibited movement, and after taking a deep breath and exhaling it slowly, she sprinted across the road and blended into the far shadows.

CHAPTER 44

Fernanda scanned the street with the binoculars, but as the light faded so did their usefulness. She cursed her lack of night vision equipment, especially a scope – what had made perfect sense during daylight was now a dicey proposition. Making a shot at three hundred meters in daylight without a scope would have been child's play for her, but now the darkness would make everything far less certain.

She mulled over her options and decided that she needed to move closer to the docking station. If the woman appeared, Fernanda would pick her off without hesitation, but the only way to guarantee a clean kill was to close the distance. The question was how near she could get without giving herself away. There was no perfect solution, but she'd spotted one other place by an abandoned shack that would be a marked improvement over her current position.

Fernanda stood, the assault rifle in her hands, and trotted down the hill, avoiding open areas, favoring the brick wall that ran along one side of the mountain road, whose dark color blended with her muted clothes to better conceal her presence. Her black running shoes were soundless on the cobblestones as she ran toward the shack in her fluid stride, breathing evenly.

She was halfway there when the unmistakable pop of a pistol shot rang out ahead. She froze as three more shots followed in close succession, and then all hell broke loose as the night sky erupted with orange flashes from the monastery high above.

~ ~ ~

Matt sighted the crossbow on the nearest gunman below him, no more than twenty meters away, and squeezed the rusty trigger of the ancient weapon. The quarrel hurtled at blinding speed straight for the man's torso. The thwack of the bow string was answered a split second later by a scream as the gunman went down, impaled by the hunting bolt that had driven three-quarters of the way through his chest.

The other gunmen took several seconds to react to the silent killer in their midst, twisting with their pistols pointed at ground level. Matt stepped back from the high window and recocked the bow, carefully fitting another quarrel into place before peering out into the gloom at the exposed men. One spotted him and got off a shot just as Matt fired the bow again, and this time the bolt tore through the throat of the man behind his target – an unintended fortuitous shot, but one that brought a volley of rounds that peppered the stone around him, sending chips flying as he repeated the exercise with the bow. He locked the bow string and seated another quarrel, and then ran the length of the second floor to take up another position on the far side, where if he was lucky, he could get off a third kill before the gunmen wised up.

Luck wasn't on his side. More pistol fire anticipated his move, and then the gunmen were dispersing into the dark, running for the other building entrances, now moving targets he had no hope of hitting.

He'd trimmed the size of the attacking force from six to four in a matter of moments, and even if he'd lost the element of surprise, his adversaries were now forced to scramble to find him, a moving target himself, rather than taking prisoners they'd assumed would be unarmed and docile.

A door below him crashed open as one of the gunmen kicked it in, and he slowly backed away from the window. The fight had moved from an outdoor shooting gallery where he had the high ground to a fight in a building where he was toting around a single-shot antiquity while his enemies had semiautomatic pistols.

~ ~ ~

Jet had nearly reached the cable car when the gunfire exploded above her. She didn't wait to evaluate what had happened, but instead leapt into motion and streaked to the cable car, caution discarded at the sound of a pitched battle from the monastery, which could only mean one thing: Matt had seen the gunmen and engaged. But six against one, and Matt with a broken hand, weren't odds she liked, and she felt an overwhelming pressure to get to him at all costs.

She slid the car door open, crouched low, and cursed the strip of rope lighting that illuminated the interior from the door frame – a thoughtful touch for nocturnal visitors, but not for someone trying to sneak into the car without being seen. Now committed and having no way out but forward, Jet stepped aboard and punched the button that activated the tram motor. The car lurched from the platform, and then she was climbing, suspended above the sheer side of the dark mountain five meters below, an ocean of brambles and brush.

~ ~ ~

Fernanda saw the light flicker to life in the cable car as she arrived at the shack. Someone had opened the door. She raised the binoculars and spotted the top of the woman's head, just the forehead, hair, and eyes. She dropped the glasses and brought the rifle to bear, but the car was now moving, swinging on the cable, a trickier shot even at the closer distance.

She tracked the tram's ascent and smiled when the woman stood, illuminated by the faint lamp, her profile clear. Fernanda hesitated for a fraction of a second – the woman looked enough like her to be her sister. She quickly recovered from her surprise, lined the sights up on the woman's chest, and squeezed the trigger. The rifle kicked against her shoulder, and she fired again for good measure and then peered through the binoculars and eyed her handiwork.

~ ~ ~

A shower of glass blew from the window opposite Jet and an exit hole punched through the far wall, and then a second shot followed it as she dropped to the floor of the cable car. Her intuition that a shooter had been watching the street was correct. But the shots had missed, instead hitting the window where the sniper must have fired at Jet's reflection, leaving her with a tough choice – wait for the gunman to realize she wasn't hit, or drop into the unknown below the tram and hope for the best.

She decided to punt and began rocking back and forth, moving the cable car ever so slightly as it continued its climb, adding to the level of difficulty of the shooter getting a decent shot. Every meter of distance increase her survival odds, and a moving target was always trickier than a stationary one.

A chatter of rifle fire shredded through the thin metal walls of the car, forcing her hand. She rolled to the open doorway as bullets punched holes by her head and threw herself through the gap at the scrub a story and a half below.

~ ~ ~

Fernanda flipped the fire selector switch to full auto and sprayed the car with rounds, reasoning that nobody could survive twenty-eight shots concentrated in that small a space. Her ears rang from the deafening noise of the rifle, and then she blinked in surprise when she saw the unmistakable form of the woman plunging through space toward the side of the mountain. She ejected the magazine and slapped the spare Jaime had given her in place, and fired half of it at the brush where the woman had landed.

~ ~ ~

Rounds whistled above Jet as she tucked and rolled when she landed, sliding twenty feet, out of control, before she was able to stop her drop. She held completely still in the undergrowth, and then cautiously tested her arms and legs to ensure she was unhurt.

Satisfied she was in one piece, she rose to a crouch, concealed by the underbrush, and looked around.

To her right was a game trail, barely discernible in the dim starlight, that appeared to lead straight up the steep face of the mountain. She waited for more shots, but none came. The shooter had lost sight of her and likely wouldn't spot her now that she was on the ground, surrounded by bushes.

Jet made her way to the trail, her boots slipping on loose gravel before finding purchase on the track, and drove herself upward. She felt for her Glock and her hand came away empty – it had dropped from her waistband somewhere in the tumble. Jet cursed under her breath and continued her climb. The muscles in her legs burned from exertion, her calves on fire, and determination etched furrows in her brow as she summoned every ounce of strength to get to the monastery before it was too late.

CHAPTER 45

Jaime pointed to the main hallway in the monastery and his men moved into it, weapons held in front of them in two-handed grips. He grabbed the arm of the nearest one and pulled him close. "Go watch the cable car platform in case they somehow get around us."

The gunman retraced his steps to the main door, then raced across the courtyard, zigging and zagging past the bodies of his dead companions in the event the archer was still watching the exterior.

Jaime took silent steps toward the first door as one of the gunmen waited on the other side of it, hand on the lever. Jaime gripped his pistol two-handed, and the gunman twisted the lever and threw the door open. Jaime ducked into the doorway, weapon sweeping the room, and stopped when he came to an ancient monk looking up at him in surprise.

"What is the meaning of this?" the monk demanded, his voice like an old woman's, high-pitched and seasoned by time.

"Where are the man and the girl?" Jaime snarled, moving toward the man.

"Who?" the monk asked, genuinely puzzled.

Jaime smashed the butt of his pistol against the monk's cheek, splitting his skin like parchment and knocking him back into his chair.

"Don't play games with me. Where are they?"

"You…I have no idea what you're talking about," the monk whispered, his hand on his face trying to stem the bleeding.

Jaime took two steps forward and pressed the gun barrel against the priest's forehead. "Last time, then you're meeting your maker."

The monk's agitation seemed to drain from him and he closed his eyes. "I cannot tell you what I do not know."

246

Jaime eyed the holy man with disgust and clubbed him with his gun again, knocking him unconscious before turning to the waiting gunman. "Come on."

He led him further down the hall, where the other shooter was training his weapon on a room with a half-dozen monks in it, fear etched on their faces at the apparition of murderous armed men invading their abode. Jaime stepped into the chamber and pointed his gun at the nearest monk.

"The little girl. Where is she?"

"Little girl? This is a monastery. A holy place. There are no girls here," the monk stammered, eyeing the gun.

Jaime's eyes locked with the monk's and he saw the complete absence of guile in them, along with shock and surprise. Much as he hated to consider it, the man didn't know what Jaime was asking, and was confused as the other monk had been.

"If you don't give me answers, I'm shooting you one by one," Jaime snarled.

"Please. You speak in riddles. We don't have any girls," another monk said. "There's been some mistake."

Jaime thumbed back the pistol's hammer and switched his aim to the new speaker. "Tell that to two of my men who are lying dead outside. You'll be joining them if you don't tell me what I want to know."

A loud clang sounded in the hall, metal on stone, and then the lights went out in both the corridor and the room, plunging it into darkness. Jaime cursed and whispered to his men, "The doorway. Find the doorway."

The gunman who had followed Jaime into the room groped for the door jamb, and then he called out, "Over here. Follow my voice. I'm in the hall—"

His words were cut short by the roar of a shotgun in the corridor. He flew backward into the room with a strangled cry. Jaime froze, as did his remaining gunman, their weapons pointed to where their companion was lying on the stone floor, his breath gurgling from his chest, bloody froth bubbling from his mouth as he tried to form words.

Hearing nothing from the hall, Jaime felt his way toward the other gunman and whispered to him, "On my count, you roll into the hall and I'll duck around and cover you. Sounds like he's gone, which only leaves one direction for him to go." He paused. "Are you ready? One, two…three!"

The shooter rolled across the threshold and Jaime peered around the doorway, his gun pointed down the corridor. After holding their position for a few seconds, Jaime stepped further into the dark hall. "This way."

~ ~ ~

Matt heard the shotgun blast right after the lights went out. He closed his eyes, waiting for them to adjust, the only light the faint early starlight seeping through the high chapel windows of the chamber he'd entered.

Franco must have gotten to the shotgun.

Matt hoped the monk would find someplace safe to hide after firing the shot, because the men he was up against were killers. He opened his eyes and could make out the faint outline of the chapel's pews – and the heavy wooden door he'd been moving toward when the lights had died.

Judging from the sound of the shot, the action was out that door and to the left, in the main area of the monastery, which made sense based on the direction the gunmen had been headed. Matt offered a word of silent thanks to the cross at the far end of the chapel that Hannah was safe in the other end of the building, but his thoughts were interrupted by the sound of footsteps in the hall outside.

He took cover behind one of the pews and leveled the loaded crossbow at the door, taking deep breaths, attention riveted to the doorway. He listened, ears straining for any hint of movement, and heard a whispered instruction outside before the knob rattled and the heavy door flew open.

~ ~ ~

Jet paused at the docking platform at the top of the tramway and eyed the iron pegs that served as a primitive service ladder to access the machinery in the room beneath it. A detonation sounded from within the monastery – the deep roar of a big gun, possibly a shotgun – and she pulled herself up the rungs, thankful that the area was exposed variegated brick so her black clothes didn't stand out against the pale perimeter wall.

Her head rose over the platform floor and she spotted a man with a gun, turned toward the monastery, obviously surprised by the sound of the shotgun. Jet didn't hesitate and climbed the rest of the rungs and charged at him before he could bring his pistol to bear on her. She slammed into his chest, knocking the wind out of him, and the gun flew from his hand and landed near the courtyard.

He hit the ground hard and she heard ribs break from her weight on top of him, her elbow serving as an effective wedge to compound the damage. He tried to punch her in the head, but the blow glanced off the side of her skull. Aware that his far greater weight and size would make up for any advantage in skill she might have, she released him and brought both her hands down on his ears in a hard clap, instantly rupturing his eardrums and earning a howl of pain. She rolled off him and moved to the pistol as the man rolled on the ground, clutching his head in agony.

She scooped it up and checked to ensure a round was chambered and, with another glance at the downed man, raced across the courtyard, foregoing the final blow that would end his life in favor of speed – seconds could count in a battle of many against one. She registered the bodies lying at the far end of the monastery as she neared the main door, which yawned open like the mouth of a cave, and did a mental count. Three out of the fight. The odds were suddenly better for Matt.

Inside, the darkness was total, and she had to feel her way through the entry to the main room, which was empty. Voices reached her from what sounded like a hall, and she followed the sound until she was in a long corridor. Muted light from a series of high windows provided just enough visibility for her to make it to where the voices were murmuring.

She swung in a crouch and found herself facing an inky blackness. A wet sucking sound came from the floor by her feet, and she instantly recognized the distinctive wheeze of a terminal pulmonary wound. A tremulous male voice whispered from a far corner, "Who's there?"

Jet ignored the question and moved further down the hall. If anyone asking questions was a black hat, they would have shot first, making the likeliest explanation that the speaker was one of the monks.

She was taking hesitant steps toward the end of the hall, which she could see terminated in a right-hand junction, when the crash of a door swinging wide and slamming into a wall sounded from her right.

~ ~ ~

Matt waited a split second after the door opened and fired blind into the opening, hoping to hit whoever was coming for him. He heard the bolt strike the stone wall beyond the doorway and dived over the first pew, dropping the now useless crossbow as he went. His only hope was to use the darkness to somehow slip away. The gunmen would be equally blind, so even if it was a long shot, it wasn't impossible.

A voice called out from the doorway, "Hold it. I see you in the pews. Come out with your hands up or I'll shoot."

Matt squinted and realized too late that the light from the high windows was brightening as the night progressed, making him just visible in the chapel – an error on his part that might now prove fatal.

A second voice, deeper and authoritative, spoke. "We *will* shoot you, you know. I suggest you do as instructed, because I'm running low on patience."

The dark shape of a man entered the chapel, and Matt could just make out that he had a pistol in his hand. Matt waited until the gunman closed the distance and then slowly stood. The shooter didn't see the flare gun from the survival kit in his hand until it was too late. Matt fired, and the white-hot missile streaked toward him, blinding everyone, before searing into the torso of the gunman, who shrieked and fell to the ground, where he curled into a fetal ball as the incendiary continued to burn through him.

Matt had played his last hand, and now he stood defenseless. The second gunman stepped into the room, which was now flickering with light from the flare's grisly glow, and pointed his gun at Matt. The gunman skirted the room until he was standing at the side of the pew, where he could confirm that Matt was weaponless.

"So. The game is over. Where is the girl?" Jaime demanded.

"I don't know what you're talking about," Matt said.

"I promised not to kill you, but I didn't say anything about wounding you. Would you like that? To be shot in the leg? I understand that can be extremely painful."

Matt didn't say anything, but his brow furrowed when Jaime moved abruptly backward, next to a support column that held up the roof. Then he heard a rustle from the doorway, and Jaime spoke softly.

"Put down your weapon, or I'll shoot him. You have three seconds. One…two…"

Jet's pistol clattered against the flagstone tile and Jaime stepped toward her, his weapon now pointed at her chest. "Go stand next to him," he ordered.

"You're a dead man," she said matter-of-factly.

"We all are, in the end. Some sooner than others," Jaime said agreeably. The light in the room gradually dimmed as the flare burned out from the dead gunman's smoldering corpse. "Now move."

Jet walked slowly over to where Matt was and stood next to him. She understood why Jaime wanted her with him – two closely spaced targets instead of one. She also saw the change of expression on his face as she reached Matt.

"Who are you? Why are you doing this?" Jet asked.

Jaime shrugged. "On behalf of a friend. Who wants you dead. Which, come to think of it, I can easily take care of for her." He shifted the pistol and pointed it at Jet's head, no possibility of missing from less than five meters.

A scrape from the doorway drew his attention for a split second, his weapon instinctively shifting to the apparent new threat, giving Jet enough time to snap open the switchblade she'd taken from the Panamanian lowlife and hurl it at Jaime.

The knife buried itself to the hilt in the base of Jaime's neck. Jet was a blur of motion, throwing herself at him before he could react, her knowledge of knives such that she knew he would still be a danger even if mortally wounded. His finger squeezed the trigger of his pistol, but the shot went wide, and then she was on him, pummeling his face with strikes as he grappled with her. She delivered a brutal strike to the nerve meridian in his gun hand, causing him to release the pistol, and then pulled the knife free and drove it through his eye.

Jaime stiffened, his arms convulsing around her like a macabre lover in a dying embrace, and then he shuddered and lay still.

Jet looked up at where Franco stood with the shotgun, staring down at the smoking remains of the dead gunman killed by the flare. Matt moved around the pew to her. "Are you okay?" he asked softly.

"Just a little bruised. You?"

"A few scrapes."

"Where's Hannah?"

"Safe. We hid her in a tunnel that's the back way out of the monastery."

"We?"

"Oh. Sorry. That's Franco. He's the brother of the truck driver who gave us a lift."

Franco nodded at them, but even in the gloom she could see he looked drawn and sick.

"I count six down. That's all of them," Jet said.

"For now."

Jet took Matt's good hand and led him toward the monk. "Good point. We need to get out of here. It'll be just a matter of time until reinforcements arrive." She looked at Franco. "Can you turn the lights back on?"

"Of course."

Sixty seconds later Franco had flipped the breaker, and the building was flooded with light. Jet scooped up the pistols and handed one to Matt, and then retrieved a spare magazine from Jaime's trousers along with a slug of cash big enough to carpet a home.

"Let's find Hannah and make ourselves scarce," Matt said. He turned to Franco. "You should get the other monks out of here. They're not safe."

"I'll show them to the tunnel once you've had time to escape. How long do you think we have?" Franco asked.

"Can you turn off the power to the cable car? If so, it would take them at least half an hour to climb up here," Matt said.

"I'll go shut it down," Franco said. "And I'll call the police on our landline. For this, they will probably bother responding."

Matt held his stare. "Thank you for everything Franco. I hope Armando is okay."

Franco looked away, his face grim. "It's out of my hands. But I do too."

CHAPTER 46

Fernanda debated taking the tram up and joining the fray at the monastery, but her iron discipline forced her to stay put. There was only one way out, and she'd pick the woman off when she eventually emerged from the underbrush at the bottom of the hill. Assuming she had survived the fall, which Fernanda felt was a good bet given the distance from the car to the ground.

She settled in for a wait, reminding herself that nothing would be served by her getting involved in a firefight. If six cartel killers couldn't handle themselves well enough to prevail, that wasn't her problem – her only concern was the woman, who was somewhere on the side of the mountain, hopefully wounded and in agony. The thought of her gasping out her dying breaths, hit by some of Fernanda's rounds, made her smile, even if her instinct was that the woman wouldn't go down that easily.

Five minutes later, sirens wailed from down the road. Cursing, Fernanda stashed the rifle under some refuse and sprinted down the alley that paralleled the main road. When she arrived at an abandoned two-story home on the very edge of visibility from the cable car station, she forced the plywood blocking the entrance aside and mounted the crumbling stairs. From the upper floor vantage point she could see the entire lower platform and the plants around it. She sat well back of the gaping window opening and watched the area with the binoculars.

A part of her wanted to retrieve the rifle and try a long shot as soon as the woman showed herself, but she was now past the weapon's accuracy limit, making the odds of a kill slim. And if the police searched the surrounding buildings and she was discovered, right now she had no weapons and would be allowed to go without question, whereas with a rifle… She looked up just in time to see a dozen emergency vehicles roaring up the hill, followed by two pickup trucks spilling over with heavily armed soldiers.

Anyone else would have been long gone, but she had a personal stake in seeing the ordeal through. If the woman died on the mountain, once the police finished their investigation there would be a body bag to prove it. If she was somehow still alive, she'd emerge from the bottom of the trail…and Fernanda would be right behind her.

There would be ample opportunity to settle the score once they were well away from the police. That the woman would have assumed she'd gotten away clean would only make the moment she realized her fatal error that much sweeter. Fernanda imagined her face only inches from the woman's as the life seeped out of her eyes, and she smiled. Maybe she'd kill the little girl first, just to heighten the woman's agony. After all, she'd robbed Fernanda of Igor – it was the least she could do to return the favor, erasing the woman's hopes and dreams before ending her miserable existence in the most painful manner possible.

~ ~ ~

Matt opened the door with the key Franco had given him and left it in the lock. He moved into the room, trailed by Jet, and reached up to the book that opened the bookcase and pulled it forward. When he heard the click of the latch giving, he called out, "Hannah? Step away from the door. I'm coming in."

He put his shoulder into pushing the bookcase open, and Jet gasped when she saw Hannah sitting on the cold stone passageway floor, the flashlight almost dead, silent tears rolling down her face. Hannah leapt up when she saw her mother and flew to her with a soft cry. Jet knelt and hugged her, tears of her own streaming down her cheeks at the sight of her beautiful daughter, alive and well, but put through so much.

After a minute of hugging her close, Jet held her at arm's length and brushed her untamed hair out of her eyes. "It's okay, honey. Everything's going to be okay now. Momma's here."

Hannah closed her eyes and savored the moment before whispering, "Momma."

"That's right, sweetheart. I'm here, and you're safe."

Matt cleared his throat. "For now. Might be a good idea to move before the flashlight completely gives up the ghost."

Jet glanced at the little light on the ground where Hannah had dropped it. "You got it. Lead the way."

Matt pushed the bookcase back into place and the lock clicked shut. He hoisted the two bags, leaving the survival kit where it lay. "Won't be needing that anymore," he said, and scooped up the flashlight.

The passage narrowed after a hundred meters, the ceiling closing in to the point where Matt had to stoop to avoid hitting his head. After a lengthy trek, they came to a rusting iron grid surrounded by tall grass and vines, the metal so corroded it was all they could do to work the bolt free. The hinges were frozen shut, and it took both Matt and Jet's best effort to push the grid open, snapping the hinges off in the process. The heavy grate tumbled down the slope and came to rest near the bank of a small river.

Jet lowered herself to the ground first, and then Matt handed Hannah down, dropping the bags after her and squirming out of the opening himself. Once they were free of the tunnel, they took careful steps the remainder of the way to the river, the gravel river bank crunching underfoot. Matt paused and glanced back up at the monastery far above them, the mountainside a sheer cliff stretching into the night sky.

Jet called to him in a loud whisper from the water. "There are a bunch of boats downstream. Wooden skiffs."

He took a final look at the monastery and made his way to where Jet stood, her arm around Hannah, pointing down the riverbank at where a half-dozen small craft were beached. He leaned his head into her and gave her a deep kiss, and then nuzzled the side of her face, his lips grazing her skin.

"I missed you," he said quietly.

"Me too." She stood on her tiptoes and kissed him again, and then gazed downstream at the boats, their hulls glowing in the moonlight. "Nice night for a boat ride."

CHAPTER 47

Frontino, Colombia

Mosises scowled as he read the sheaf of documents before him. After scrutinizing for the tenth time the crime scene photograph of his beloved son, the abominations of his punctured eye and throat captured in high-definition detail by the camera, he sat back, his expression ugly.

"You say the woman who did this never returned to the monastery entrance?" he demanded, his voice thick.

Fernanda nodded. "Correct. I waited a full day and night. It looks like they escaped somehow." She gestured at the report. "It's all in there. The monks claim that they knew nothing about what happened. The working theory was that the killings were some sort of drug-related double cross. One faction luring another into a remote location and executing them."

"You're sure that she didn't somehow sneak past the police?"

"Impossible. They had the entire area sealed off, soldiers everywhere, spotlights, the whole works. And I watched as a team of climbers searched the area around the tramway. They found nothing."

Mosises' eyes narrowed as he read the final words of the report again. "Somebody must know something. Three people can't just disappear into thin air." His face changed as an idea occurred to him. "Is it possible that they're still somewhere in the monastery?"

She shook her head. "I doubt it. The report describes the police doing a room-by-room search, looking for anything that would offer a clue to why six men were killed."

Mosises held up a hand. "I convinced the authorities to allow our attorney to have access to the lone survivor. His ears are a mess and he's in extreme pain, but he managed to tell our man that he was attacked by a woman. So there's your explanation as to why she didn't come out of the brush. She made it all the way up to the monastery after jumping out of the cable car." He stopped, staring off into space. "Which is astounding."

Fernanda had to admit it was. "She's obviously got incredible skills."

Mosises grunted. "Yes, well, that won't help her. I want her head. Actually, I want all three of their heads."

"I do too."

"You'll handle it?" Mosises asked softly, glaring at the cigar smoldering in the clay ashtray as though it had bitten him.

"Yes. I'll need some logistical support, but I will. She won't get away."

He fixed her with a penetrating stare. "She did this time."

"With all due respect, Jaime told me to stay put at the base of the mountain while he went up. That wasn't my choice. He could be quite…forceful."

Mosises' attention seemed to drift, and he lowered his gaze. Fernanda could barely hear him when he spoke. "Yes, even as a little boy he had a stubborn streak. I…I loved him more than life itself." He wiped his eyes with a shaking hand and then stared at her with haunted eyes. "I want her, no matter what it takes."

Fernanda stood. "I'll hunt her down and kill her in the most painful manner imaginable. You have my word. I wanted to tell you that personally." She eyed her watch. "I need to get back to Santuario. Every hour that goes by, the trail grows colder. Can you have your helicopter fly me back?"

"Yes. Tell my man on the way out whatever else you need, and I'll see to it. Anything you want, it's yours."

She sighed her frustration into the breeze. "Jaime was an incredible man," she said, hinting at something more than the truth. The old man had no idea what had transpired over the days they were together, and she needed him firmly on her side. If he believed that she and Jaime had shared more than dinner, that could work to her benefit. She suspected she would need far more of his cooperation than he thought it would take, and it wouldn't hurt for him to think there was a deeper connection between Jaime and herself than they'd enjoyed – certainly not for want of his trying.

"Yes. Yes, he was." Mosises cleared his throat. "Find her. Kill her. Scorch the earth."

"That's my plan."

Mosises watched Fernanda head over to the French doors and enter the house. When she was out of earshot, he lifted a tiny micro-cell phone to his ear. When he spoke it was with quiet deliberation. "I want you to take a personal interest in this matter. Do not disappoint me. I'll have the report scanned and in your hand within the hour."

Mosises' assistant came out on the veranda as he was finishing the call. He studied the old drug lord without expression, and then spoke in a low voice. "I thought you were having the woman deal with this?"

Mosises flipped the phone onto the table. "She failed once, and now my son is dead. Think of it as insurance."

Awareness dawned on the assistant's face. "Of course. And the woman? She gave me a list of her requirements."

"Give her what she needs, and let's see if she can perform. If she can, then we'll cross that bridge once she's avenged Jaime."

"And if she can't?"

Mosises watched his prize mare canter around the clearing, unfettered by reins, savoring unimaginable freedom as she enjoyed what was left of the blustery day.

"Then she will pay the price for disappointing me."

The assistant nodded and returned to the house. Helicopter blades thumped from the front of the estate, increasing in tempo as the aircraft lifted into the sky. Mosises shielded his eyes and followed the helicopter's flight until it shrank into a tiny speck and disappeared behind the jungle hills.

ABOUT THE AUTHOR

A *Wall Street Journal* and *The Times* featured author, Russell Blake lives full time on the Pacific coast of Mexico. He is the acclaimed author of many thrillers, including the Assassin series, the JET series, and the BLACK series. He has also co-authored *The Eye of Heaven* and *The Solomon Curse* with Clive Cussler for Penguin Books.

"Capt." Russell enjoys writing, fishing, playing with his dogs, collecting and sampling tequila, and waging an ongoing battle against world domination by clowns.

Visit RussellBlake.com for updates
or subscribe to: RussellBlake.com/contact/mailing-list

Co-authored with Clive Cussler

THE EYE OF HEAVEN

THE SOLOMON CURSE

Thrillers by Russell Blake

FATAL EXCHANGE

THE GERONIMO BREACH

ZERO SUM

THE DELPHI CHRONICLE TRILOGY

THE VOYNICH CYPHER

SILVER JUSTICE

UPON A PALE HORSE

RAMSEY'S GOLD

The Assassin Series by Russell Blake

KING OF SWORDS

NIGHT OF THE ASSASSIN

RETURN OF THE ASSASSIN

REVENGE OF THE ASSASSIN

BLOOD OF THE ASSASSIN

REQUIEM FOR THE ASSASSIN

The JET Series by Russell Blake

JET

JET II – BETRAYAL

JET III – VENGEANCE

JET IV – RECKONING

JET V – LEGACY

JET VI – JUSTICE

JET VII – SANCTUARY

JET – OPS FILES (prequel)

JET – OPS FILES; TERROR ALERT

The BLACK Series by Russell Blake

BLACK

BLACK IS BACK

BLACK IS THE NEW BLACK

BLACK TO REALITY

Non Fiction by Russell Blake

AN ANGEL WITH FUR

HOW TO SELL A GAZILLION EBOOKS

(while drunk, high or incarcerated)

Made in the USA
Lexington, KY
02 June 2015